SHUNNED NO MORE

A LADY FORSAKEN (BOOK ONE)

Christina McKnight

La Loma Elite Publishing

Dedication
To Lauren Stewart
You kept my passion for writing alive, even when it was the last thing I wanted to do. Your friendship is truly one of a kind.

PROLOGUE

Hyde Park
April 1806

Viola clutched the handle of her pink parasol to her chest tightly in anticipation of the spectacle to come. Her gaze fixed on the two figures shrouded in the early morning fog of Hyde Park. The men, really only boys, began to count as they paced away from each other. Shiny, pearl-handled pistols positioned in their right hands were at the ready.

She clamped her lips tight to suppress the giggle that threatened to escape.

Who would have thought that she, Lady Viola Oberbrook, would have two men seeking her hand in marriage—and in the first week of her very first season, no less? That they were the twin sons of Lord Haversham was an even greater *coup de grace* for her. She'd be the envy of every debutante. The talk of the town. As well she should be! Her father was the Duke of Liperton, after all.

If only she'd found a way to get all of London here to witness the duel. She'd done what she could by leaving word with Mrs. Tenchard. The old gossipmonger was sure to spread the news more quickly than Vi could spend her monthly allowance at the milliner's shop.

And Vi prided herself on her ability to spend her father's money.

"Miss Viola, beg'n yer pardon, but it be wise to don ye wool kid gloves," her lady's maid, Sarah, whispered beside her.

"Shhhh," Vi hissed in return, raising her hand for Sarah to hold her tongue. She didn't want to miss a single moment of what was to come. She would remember this for the rest of her existence. The day two men of the *haute ton* battled in her honor. She sighed.

The twins—Cody, with his hair cut longer than the current fashion permitted, and sporting a determined glint in his eye, and Winston, with his smartly trimmed blond hair falling respectfully above his collar—reached the required twenty-pace distance and turned.

Their pistols fired in unison. Vi's heart soared. Her first duel . . . and certainly not her last, if she had anything to say in the matter.

The swift morning breeze pushed the smoke from the scene as both men dropped to the ground, soggy with morning dew. Shouts of urgency rang out in the air. Men rushed in to assist the twins.

A cold chill inched up her spine; her breath caught in her lungs.

Neither man moved.

A sharp inhale of breath sounded next to her, but

Vi was hesitant to remove her attention from the scene as the pungent smell of a spent firearm reached her.

"Call Doc Durpentire. Post haste!" bellowed Mr. Rodney Swiftenberg. As a distant relative of the Havershams, Swiftenberg stood as Cody's second during the duel. Others, vaguely familiar, knelt over both fallen men.

The gossip rags would have much to write about this day. Vi could hardly wait to see her name in print. Maybe her father would increase her dowry, seeing as she would be in high demand by the day's end.

"Miss," Sarah called. "I think it best we be head'n home. Ye Pa is going to be right mad when he finds you snuck out and now these poor men be lying dead at ye very feet."

"Surely you jest. They are simply play acting for dramatics—in my honor, I do suppose." Viola eyed the two groups of men where they stood, their heads shaking in turn. One took his coat off and laid it gently over Cody's still body. Vi's glare snapped to Winston, where another man shook out a horse blanket. The thick, coarse material drifted on the morning breeze and settled on the second body.

She studied the scene in front of her. It had the potential to be ever so romantic. A story she would regale her grandchildren with. It was a shame neither twin was the first born and, therefore, unworthy of her hand. But she'd seen no reason to inform them of this minor issue and spoil her fun. They'd find out soon enough.

Slowly, the eyes of every person present settled on her. She took a step back at the harshness of their stares. Her chilled hand rose to cover her mouth. She wanted to tell them to avert their eyes; she was the daughter of a Duke. They need show the respect due her. None of these men held a title higher than Baron. How dare they look at her thus?

A tall, slender man carrying a large cloth bag rushed to Winston. She assumed this was Doc Durpentire. He would have both men patched up in no time. But with both Cody and Winston taking a bullet, their feud would not be resolved. Viola imagined what the pair would think up next to prove one deserved her hand over the other. Perhaps a curricle race through Mayfair District. She knew she would be able to convince Cody to let her ride along on the adventure. She could practically feel the wind against her face as the carriage took the corners at a high speed, shifting across the seat so that her soft body might come to rest against Cody's hard one.

Imagine what the silly, empty-brained young females would think. They'd envy her further. An unbidden smile played across her lips.

The doctor drew the heavy blanket aside and his hands moved over Winston's body. Then, they stilled. His head dropped forward. He spoke to the men around him, but Vi was too far to hear their conversation.

Rodney, hands shoved deep in his pockets, moved in her direction.

"Whatever is the matter with them?" she asked when he was close enough to hear.

"I think you should go, Lady Viola. This is not a scene any innocent maiden should witness," Rodney replied. His blond hair was so much like Cody and Winston's, but his attitude had always struck her as arrogant for a man with no title or wealth to speak of.

4

"Who are you to order me about?" Viola closed her parasol with a swift click and handed it to Sarah, her hands coming to rest on her rounded hips.

"It is not the time for this. My cousins . . . they are both dead." Rodney paused. "I must alert my uncle to his misfortune."

"You are mistaken."

"I assure you, no mistakes have been made this day." He abruptly turned, stalking back to the crowd gathering between the fallen men.

He must be jesting, Viola thought. She looked between the fallen pair again, their motionless bodies so at odds with the twins she'd come to know in recent days. The heat of exhilaration drained from her as a hand settled at her elbow. Viola felt the calloused fingertips through her thin morning cloak.

"We should be going, Miss."

Vi shook Sarah's imploring touch from her arm and tried to focus her gaze on something—anything—other than the lifeless men on the ground.

"Well," Viola stated. "This was…" Dread clawed at her insides, and her spirit shattered as she stared at the two men lying prone and unmoving before her. "…unexpected." Her entire life had been leading up to this moment—a life of societal demands and the rigors one had to follow to be accepted. A life that had just stopped, as quickly as those of the two men who now lay dead. *Dead.* She had murdered these men—the realization came at her all at once, even as her mind rebelled. Cody and Winston, the silly twins who had entertained her so, were no more. Yet, she continued to breathe. With each breath, standing in the chill of early morning in Hyde Park, she felt the obligations of her station, its standards and protocols too powerful for a seventeen-year-old girl to overcome.

She glanced around her for help, for someone to tell her what to do, but all focus was on the boys on the ground. Years of being taught how to behave hadn't prepared her for anything like this.

"Miss, what should we do?"

"I suppose we should . . ." She cleared her throat. "I suppose it is time to start over." She sensed, somehow, that starting over might be impossible.

"Start over, Miss?" Her maid's dark brow pulled low over her eyes.

Viola straightened her already impeccably postured back and forced her prized smile before continuing. "To find another suitor, you silly girl! This time, I intend to set my sights a bit higher." She spun on her heels, determined not to stumble, to not falter before so many. She started back towards her carriage, moving through the men without meeting anyone's eye, feeling the weight of their stares as she passed. It didn't matter. She had the evening's entertainments to prepare for and an image to uphold—no matter the cost to her soul.

CHAPTER ONE

Winchester, Hampshire
July, 1815

Lady Viola Oberbrook tallied the list of figures on the page for the fifth time. "Impossible," she muttered. For the last eight years, she'd run Foldger's Foals at a tidy profit. But the tides had been changing over the last six months.

Setting her pencil aside, she surveyed the room, adorned in lavish blues and golds, paired with dark cherry wood. The surroundings were her home. Decorated soon after she'd fled London, the room exuded the expensive tastes of her youth. The dark wood of her desk passed smoothly under her fingertips. It would fetch a handsome price. She would have to sell more furnishings, since the foals weren't fetching a higher return.

How she'd changed, that she now valued simplicity over extravagance. A part of her would be glad to see it all vanish.

A soft tap at the door drew her from memories better left in the past. "Come in." Vi closed the ledger and stood, smoothing her gown with charcoal-smudged fingers.

The office door opened on rusted hinges to reveal Connor Cale, her assistant and stable master. As a middle-aged man of the *ton*, he'd been a savior when she had needed a friend all those years ago. Now, his salt-and-pepper hair, honest face, and connections in London society enabled her to complete her life's work while remaining in the background.

He strolled hesitantly into her office, stopping in front of her desk. "A new client has arrived to assess our available stock."

"We are not expecting anyone today." Vi opened her desk drawer and placed the ledger inside.

"I understand, but he has traveled all the way from Kent and wishes to meet with the owner." Connor's gaze flitted around the room, not focusing on any one thing.

"Then, by all means, show the man around." She always worried when allowing someone onto the property. One overly inquisitive client could disrupt her life—and the lives of all who depended on her— immensely. "Are you familiar with his family?"

"I do not *personally* know him. He is newly arrived in society."

"Newly arrived in society?" Vi relaxed into her seat, the cause for alarm passing. The threat of a prior acquaintance with the gentleman would be null and the added bonus of fresh coin to spend would be a boon.

"From his appearance, I am led to believe he has

returned from the Battle of Waterloo. While he was away, his father passed on." Connor's gaze finally met Vi's.

Odd, he was never one to shy from eye contact.

"I am confused as to why you are here. Show the man about, but impress upon him that our newest crop of foals will not be ready for another two weeks. That is non-negotiable."

Connor cleared his throat. "There is a problem," Connor paused. "He would like to speak with you."

"Whatever for? Most men are content to handle their business transactions with you." She looked about her desk to occupy herself. Beyond the obvious reason—her past—she truly couldn't spare the time to show the man around.

"While I agree with you, the man is very insistent. I do not think we can afford to send him away unhappy." Connor leaned against the desk, his hands placed firmly on the smooth surface.

"While I understand your concern, *we* also cannot afford him recognizing me." Vi leaned forward, mirroring his posture. She didn't care that her pose and tone appeared defensive, verging on hostile even.

"I agree and I will tell—"

A latch clicked and the door behind him swung inward. She'd have to install a bell—or better yet, a sturdy lock.

"I am sorry to interrupt, but I do not have the luxury of spending all day waiting. I have a long return trip to my estate," the intruder said, entering her office.

She looked from Connor to the intruder and back again. Her stable master had been correct, the man before her had earned his way in the military. Until very recently, she suspected. His skin was tan, his eyes intense and his hair dark brown, cut short on the sides and left longer on top. She could fairly picture a warm summer breeze ruffling its tawny locks.

The room turned overly warm, even for late August, as her mind wandered.

"Can I preview your stock today, or should I return at a later date?" Impatience infused his voice.

She'd been staring, with the great possibility of her mouth hanging open. She snapped her gaze away from his exquisitely sculpted male form, his alluring hair and brown eyes, and trained them on Connor instead. Sensible, practical Mr. Connor Cale.

"Mr. Cale will be more than happy to show you around the stables." She locked eyes with Connor, pleading for him to remove the man from her office. "We have excellent quality young, almost mature enough for purchase."

"Indeed, please allow me to—" Connor turned to the man with his arm wide to guide him back to the stables.

But the intruder held his ground. "Are you responsible for this business?"

"I am." Viola answered.

"But, you are a lady . . ."

"Thank you for noticing." Vi stood and smoothed her skirts, ready to escort him out of her office herself. "If you'll please—"

"Oh, yes, it certainly is a hard thing *not* to notice." He took in her body from head to toe and back again.

Vi stepped around the desk to confront him. It was times such as these she was glad she'd retired from society, and their notions of what a lady should and should not do with her time. While it was a forced retirement, she *had* retired all the same. "Mister—"

"Lord," he corrected.

She should have guessed he'd be a lord, and not just a younger son. His arrogance was evidence of his silver-spoon upbringing. "Well, lord . . . might I inquire as to your name?"

Vi continued past the irritatingly smug man and out the door into the stable yard, giving him no option but to follow her—which she prayed he wouldn't—or be left behind. If he answered her question, she didn't hear him.

"I have run Foldger's Foals for the past eight years. And very successfully, I might add," she called over her shoulder.

"Should I find that impressive?" He had indeed followed her out the door.

"Yes—"

"I have saved hundreds of men on the battlefield."

Vi stopped mere feet from the entrance to the stable. "Is it now my turn to be impressed?"

When she turned in his direction, they almost collided. Outrunning him didn't seem to be a viable option.

"I only state—"

"Since you seem determined to compare the size of our egos, would you also like to beat your chest and howl at the moon?" she demanded, her gaze now heated.

His hands flew up in defense, but she saw a glimmer of humor in his eyes. "We have started off on the wrong foot. Let us start anew. Apparently, I am the overgrown ape with the manners of a wild dog, who lacks all social grace." He bowed at the waist.

She laughed, hiding her enormous grin with her hand. "And I seem to be the woman determined to emasculate every half-ape, half-dog in my vicinity," Vi said, dropping in a curtsey.

"I am Lord Haversham. . ."

Haversham? The smile drained from her face and the laugh stuck in her throat, cutting off her air. Abruptly, she pushed past him once more and moved back toward the safety of her office. She hadn't heard that name in years. Her legs trembled with each step, much like that day long ago. Could it truly be? She searched the man's face, in her mind's eye, for any resemblance. But no, she saw nothing. While Winston and Cody had been fair-skinned and light-haired men of average height, the man before her stood over six feet and looked of French descent.

". . . and I did not mean to offend. I simply seek to understand the inner workings of a stable." He'd followed her back into the office.

Clearly, he hadn't recognized her either, but why ever would he? They'd never met. Brock Spencer, heir to the Earl of Haversham, had left years before in service to King George III. She needed to sit down before her knees buckled beneath her.

"Is something amiss, Lady—" Connor started.

"No, it is just warm and I have been working many hours," she said, cutting Connor off before the ignorant man used her given name. She moved behind her desk and regained her seat. She felt her confidence return as she laid her palms on the cool surface. "Starting over would be advantageous for this situation. My name is Lady Posey Hale. I have been the proprietor of

Foldger's Foals for many years. How can I help you today?"

She kept her eyes trained on Brock. If she looked in Connor's direction, she was sure to find the man staring at her, his face a mask of confusion. Had he not made the connection yet? It had been many years since she'd discussed her past—and her need to keep it hidden—with her stable master. He'd tried to soothe her anxiety, but she had spent many days in this very office, dreading the time when her identity would be revealed and her present life ruined.

It couldn't happen; she wouldn't allow it to. There were too many people who depended on her.

"I seek to build a stable at my country estate. I was told at Tattersalls that Foldger's Foals raises top-quality horses."

"You were informed correctly, my lord." If he noticed her discomfort, he didn't show it. "My man of business can show you the foals that have not been spoken for this season." She wanted him out of her office, off her property, and safely on his way back to wherever his estate lay.

"Right this way, my lord," Connor said, herding Lord Haversham toward the door.

He bowed in her direction. "It is a pleasure to meet you, Lady Hale. I look forward to meeting your husband when I return."

The nerve of the man! It may have been a natural presumption, but it made her want to scream nonetheless. Instead, she tamped down her anger and pasted a thin-lipped smile on her face. "You may call me Lady Posey or Lady Posey Hale, my lord."

His brow rose in surprise as his gaze traveled the

length of her body and back to her face. "My apologies again, Lady Posey. I hope we have cause to meet again soon."

"Yes, I will look forward to that." It would be a cold day in hell when they would meet again. She forced a smile to her lips, hoping it didn't appear as a grimace to the two men. "Do let me know if I can aid you with anything else. Have a pleasant day." Vi turned her attention to the papers littering her desk, effectively dismissing the pair.

The soft click of the door told her they'd departed. Only then did her body go limp in her chair. That had been a close call. This was the reason she had policies and procedures that she, Connor, and her other staff followed to the letter. Their livelihood depended on her ability to hide her identity.

She leaned forward and rested her cheek against the cold surface of her desk, her eyes closing. No one would purchase foals from the girl responsible for the death of two young men of the *ton*. It hadn't mattered that her father was a duke or that she'd spent the last eight years redefining her purpose in life. She'd been shunned by polite society and it was something she'd live with for the rest of her life.

"Viola?"

Damn, she really must look into installing a bell on that door. How long had she been sulking?

Lifting her head, Connor stood in the doorway.

"What is it?" she asked.

"Lord Haversham has selected eight foals."

"Eight?" She hadn't acquired this large an account in six months. It should thrill her to be able to make her self-imposed donation on time, without having to liquidate furniture from her office. Instead, she was unnerved.

"Yes, he will return in a few weeks to collect them."

Exactly what she'd been afraid of—his return to Foldger's Foals.

"Can you not deliver them to him?" she asked.

"You can discuss that with him. He will be back in the morning to negotiate the price for each foal."

Vi eyed him from behind her desk. Was he smirking? "You know who he is, do you not?"

Connor moved the rest of the way into the office and closed the door behind him. "I realized only after you fairly fainted in front of him."

"You do realize this is bad, correct? *Very* bad."

"He is only buying a few foals." Connor took the seat across from Vi and stretched his legs. "He will come tomorrow to negotiate the price, and then you will have no reason to see him again."

Vi appreciated Connor's straight approach to problems; he'd soothed her anxiety more times than she could count. "That sounds reasonable. I will handle him in the morning and never have cause to see him again. We will keep this short."

"Of course."

"I will draw up the paperwork now and have it ready for tomorrow." She had a sinking feeling things wouldn't quite transpire as she planned.

CHAPTER TWO

Brock Spencer, the Earl of Haversham, pulled the wooden, high-backed chair out and sat heavily. The room smelled of tobacco and sweat, even at this early hour. It was as if the scent of men had been absorbed into the very walls, like a woman's perfume on delicate skin. The men who lounged around the room, drinking ale and eating a stale breakfast, attested to the low standards of the establishment. He'd sought shelter here the previous night to await his meeting with Lady Posey. A smile spread across his face. The woman was a spitfire, and he looked forward to bantering and bickering over the price of her stock.

"Can I get ye sumthing, sir?"

When had the lady, and he used the term loosely, materialized before him? She leaned her hip against the round table in front of him and set down a grimy mug filled with what must be ale. Didn't she realize it was barely eight in the morning?

"I would enjoy whatever is the cook's specialty,"

Brock replied.

She jerked her thumb back toward the kitchen. "Me ma does the cook'n and she don't specialize in anything." With a heave of her ample bosom, she sighed. "I'll be bringing ye a plate of cheese and bread . . ." She paused for a moment, allowing her eyes to travel up and down Brock's lean form. "It be me favorite," she finished with an expectant look, as if she foresaw him asking her to join him for his meal.

"That will do." He only hoped the wheat wasn't infested with ergot. He'd seen many a comrade overtaken by hallucinations and racked with seizures, eventually succumbing to unconsciousness and death. It wasn't a pleasant way to perish.

"I be right back with yer meal." She straightened from her perch on the edge of his table and turned with a flip of her midnight-black hair. Her hips moved to a rhythm only she could hear as she sauntered back toward the bar.

Brock sat back, looking around the room. He hated to wait and waste time. His years serving the King had taught him idleness led to foolishness. A newspaper sat on the unoccupied table next to him. Taking a bit of the paper, he wiped the rim of his mug. Not that it would help, but at least his lips wouldn't slide from the glass when they came into contact with the greasy surface.

As he set the paper aside, a headline grabbed his attention. "Local Earl Dies at Dawn." A duel had claimed another life. "Ignorant men," he mumbled as he made to set aside the paper. Unfortunately, the name printed in the article again drew his attention. He read on:

The Earl of Davenderly was killed on Tuesday morning

after a duel in Hyde Park. This writer wonders if Lady Viola Oberbrook is currently in town. Has the Murderous Maiden struck again?

The article went on to discuss the legality of dueling at dawn and the consequences if caught by the magistrate. But none of that interested him. His mind fixated on the name he cursed almost daily since his return to England. No longer did he have the distraction of war, the peril and danger of it, to keep him otherwise engaged.

Brock threw the paper to the floor in disgust. How dare the article's author drag before society the tragedy of his past? Did they not have any courtesy for his grieving family? True, his brothers' deaths had occurred eight years before, but the pain still rocked him to his core. Having only recently returned to polite society and his ancestral family home, he finally had to deal with the loss, compounded by the unexpected death of his father while Brock had still been away. Coming home hoping to find the open arms of his father waiting, only to learn he'd passed had devastated him. Not a single person had sent word to him. It was a blow he had not expected, opening fresh the unhealed wound of the loss of his brothers.

"We don't be gett'n the press rags very often, so we handle 'em gentle like." The bar maid set his plate of cheese and bread before him and bent to retrieve the paper he'd thrown to the dirt-covered floor boards, her breasts almost tumbling from the top of her dress. "Enjoy yer meal, sir."

There was no reason to correct her inaccurate greeting. Though he was still getting used to being addressed by his father's title, it would only cause more attention to be focused in his direction. He lifted the hunk of stale bread to his mouth as she again sauntered away, her hips gyrating a bit more forcefully on the return trip. If she ever fancied leaving her family's business, she would surely be appreciated as a comfort woman behind his troop of men.

Correction: They were no longer 'his men.' And he was no longer fighting at the front line. Part of him couldn't help but wonder if society would prove more dangerous a life than his previous as a soldier.

He pushed the thought from his mind. He needed to get used to being back in society. He gathered his lump of moldy cheese and the remaining bread in his napkin, using his other hand to retrieve coins from his pocket. The chair scraped against the rough-worn wooden floor as he stood and made his way up to his room to gather his few belongings.

# # #

The ride to Foldger's Foals wasn't a long journey, but the road was rut-ridden due to frequent use. A peek through the window in his room revealed a bright morning with nary a cloud in the sky, although the weather could change suddenly and let loose a downpour within minutes. Weather in this part of the country was fickle, to say the least.

Brock stuffed his remaining personal effects into his saddle bag and headed back downstairs to retrieve his stallion, Sage. He quickly made his way through the common room, avoiding the penetrating gaze of the barkeep's wanton daughter. He had more pressing matters. He had a stable to establish, an estate to refurbish, a family name to polish, and a wife to find— not necessarily in that order.

Sage awaited him outside the inn's main door, hitched to a post. He hoped the stable hand had fed him substantially and brushed the sweat from his coat after their long journey the day before.

"Hello, boy," Brock greeted the only stable presence in his life. Sage had been by his side for more years than he could count. With the animal's muzzle in his palm, he scratched just the right spot. Sage swooshed his tail to and fro.

"He be watered and fed for ye, just as ye asked last evening."

Brock turned to face the stable lad behind him, a warm smile on his face. "Many thanks." He flipped the boy a shilling, loaded his knapsack with the few things he'd brought with him, and mounted the horse.

Sage made quick time of the trip to Foldger's Foals, and Brock was glad for it. As the stable came into view, he searched the open fields, the horse corral, and stable yard for any sight of Lady Posey. He told himself it was only to conduct their business as swiftly as possible and return back to his estate.

Is that really true? Whether it was or not didn't matter; he had responsibilities to attend to at Haversham House. At this moment, lumber should be arriving to repair the neglected carriage house and stable. His butler and housekeeper would be training a new household staff, and he hoped to bring home a wife soon.

Yes, Brock was tired of being alone, living the solitary life of a military man. He missed his mother's laughter, his father's barking, and the twins' hijinks.

Maneuvering Sage onto the lane leading up to the stable office, he spotted Lady Posey entering the yard through an ivy-covered gate before heading into the stables. *Was that a potato sack the woman was wearing?* Surely her maid should be relieved of her duties for allowing her mistress to leave her dressing chamber in such disarray.

Brock spurred Sage to a gallop and moved swiftly down the road, dust flying in his wake. He feared she'd disappear into the stables and not return for their meeting. He was stunned to realize he looked forward to bantering with her; she would drive a hard bargain, Brock was certain.

"Lady Posey!" He brought Sage to a stop feet from the entrance to her stables. "Good morning." He leapt from his horse and threw his reins to the lad who ran out.

Her dress was not exactly a sack, but the sturdiness of the brown material would most likely hold the weight of one hundred pounds of potatoes. Gone was the young maiden with the sensible-yet-fashionable gown he had met yesterday. In her place stood an old maid.

"And to you, my lord." Her gaze coyly directed at the ground as she sank into a curtsey the likes of which he hadn't seen in years, if ever. Rising, she continued. "I have drawn up the appropriate paperwork. Please accompany me to my office. Tuck, please find Mr. Cale and direct him to my office, as well." She addressed the lad leading Sage into the stables.

"Yes, miss."

"I had not expected you this early," she said as they walked the short distance to her office.

"I have long been an early riser. You've likewise

surprised me." Her coffee-colored dress, if that was indeed the exact shade, moved around her ankles as she walked two steps ahead of him.

"How so, my lord?" she asked over her shoulder. Stopping, she slipped a key into the lock of the door.

"It is my understanding that most maidens are wont to rise before the noon-day meal." From her stern look and the hardness in her eyes, he feared he'd insulted her again. Another thing he would be made to apologize for. "I meant no disrespect, Lady Posey, I only—"

She stepped into the room and turned to face him. "You will learn in short order that I am not your common society miss or debutante." She held her stance, blocking him entrance to the room.

Is she awaiting an apology? "Again, pardon my rudeness. I have only recently returned to polite society."

She continued to stare at him, and he at her. He didn't mind, as it gave him time to inspect her indigo eyes, clear as the channel he'd crossed between the continents.

"Lord Haversham," Mr. Cale called from behind him. "So lovely to see you back. Shall we finalize the sell? I am sure you are most eager to return home."

"As I was telling Lord Haversham, I have the necessary papers ready for signature," Lady Posey said, severing eye contact with him.

"That I am," Brock assured her. He moved to the side to allow her man of business to enter.

"Wonderful, wonderful. Lady V—Posey, I can handle this if you have other pressing matters to attend to." Mr. Cale crossed the room to stand next to Lady

Posey's desk, his body creating a virtual shield between Brock and the woman. "I know you have an important *meeting* to prepare for."

The pair held eye contact, and Brock felt as though he was intruding on a private moment. He grew uneasy. Though Lady Posey didn't appear to reciprocate the feeling, it was clear from his possessive posturing that Mr. Cale had more than a professional interest in his employer.

"That would be most helpful, Connor." Lady Posey slipped past the man and Brock. She didn't stop until her hand rested on the door handle, ready to pull the door shut after she departed. "The papers are drawn up according to our policies, and places marked for signatures. Lord Haversham, Connor can deliver the foals to your estate in two weeks' time, if that is agreeable?"

She didn't give him a chance to reply before she pulled the door shut behind her.

A part of him wanted to run after her. She intrigued him as no other had in a long time—possibly ever. That her looks were as appealing as her personality only further garnered his interest.

Instead, he turned to Mr. Cale while the man laid out the necessary paperwork.

# # #

The corridors of Foldger's Hall were deserted at this hour. It was too early for cleaning, too late for stoking the fires. Viola's luck couldn't have been better as she raced up the stairs and down various halls to the wing she shared with her nearest and dearest friend, Miss Ruby St. Augustin.

Vi rounded the last corner and continued past her door to the room next to her own. Sliding to a stop, her booted foot caught on the rug and she nearly knocked over a vase full of flowers on a hall table. She grasped the vase when it tilted precariously, water splashing over the thin, delicate rim, to steady it.

Damn boots! Why did she have to wear the ugly things? She'd spent the previous evening assembling a suitably appalling outfit so as not to draw undue attention to herself. These boots, belonging to one of the maids who delivered coal to her room, had been the final touch. Besides, Vi had sought a way to replace the girl's old, worn-out boots without wounding her pride. Countless times, the hardworking maid had declined Vi's gift of a new bonnet or warm woolen socks.

The door opened before she could knock.

"Viola! I expected you to already be at the stables. I was readying myself to depart in that direction." Ruby blocked Vi's entrance with her tall, regal frame.

Vi pushed past her, not giving the other woman a chance to leave. "I fear it is not safe for either of us to be there at the moment."

"Whatever are you talking about?" Ruby turned a suspicious eye to her. "You look piqued. Do sit down and tell me what is going on."

How much to tell her? Ruby had been her companion and dearest friend for going on seven years now. If there was anyone who knew all Vi's secrets, it was Ruby. Was it fair to burden her friend with her newest predicament, or would it only worry the girl needlessly? She perched on the edge of Ruby's bed, not wanting to mess up her lovely quilt with her dirty attire. "I ran the whole way back."

"You? Run?"

"Surely I am capable of a little exertion when the need arises." Viola tried unsuccessfully to curb the defensive tilt of her words.

"You have yet to tell me how the need arose."

"*He* is back!"

"'He' who?" Ruby asked, raising an eyebrow in question.

"Lord Haversham!"

"Lord Haversham passed on over three months ago. My mother wrote me about the sad news in her latest letter. You must be mistaken."

"Not the *old* Lord Haversham . . . the *new* Lord Haversham!"

"Brock Haversham has returned from service? Oh, dear!"

"Oh, dear is right."

"You must calm down. What do you mean by, 'he is back'?" Ruby asked. "I was unaware that the two of you had met."

"We had not met before yesterday. He arrived, unannounced, to inquire into Foldger's Foals. He had the audacity to barge into my office and demand to know how a woman came to own a stable." Vi fell back onto the quilt, her concerns about soiling the delicate cover forgotten.

"While I have not been in his presence in over fifteen years, that does sound like him. Why did you not tell me at last meal yesterday?" Ruby's bottom lip jutted out sullenly.

Ruby had known the Havershams as children, Vi recalled. Of course she would know the eldest brother.

"I was quite preoccupied," Vi said to soothe her

friend's hurt feelings. "I completed all the paperwork for the sale of eight foals and put together this outfit, in the event he demanded to see me."

"Where did you acquire such a hideous dress?"

"I borrowed it from Cook, and Sarah altered it to fit."

"And those boots? Good gracious, they must be three sizes too large."

"Daphne was wearing them this morning. She was more than willing to trade them for a pair of kid gloves and enough coin to buy a new pair of boots in town," Vi continued as she sat forward on the bed to remove the loathsome boots.

"The upstairs maid? Whatever will she do with kid gloves?"

"I care not what she does with them."

"I assume Lord Haversham departed as soon as he found out who you are, so why is it unsafe for us to attend our tasks at the stables?"

"Do you think me mad?" Vi said.

"Sometimes—"

"Ruby St. Augustin, I will have you know that I—we—have worked too arduously to have our livelihood, and that of so many others, collapse over a chance meeting between myself and a member of the *ton*."

"Then do tell how you managed to acquire a sale from the very man who has all the right to despise your very existence." Ruby's booted toe tapped a rapid rhythm, a severe expression darkening her normally serene face.

"I did what any person in my shoes—err," she looked down, ". . . boots would do. I told him my name is Lady Posey Hale."

"Lady Posey Hale? Wherever did you come up with such a name?"

"That does not matter. What matters is that I never lay eyes on the man again!"

"Is he as handsome as I remember?"

"While I do not know how handsome he was, he does cut a very dashing figure presently," Vi admitted reluctantly. Her hands rose to cover her cheeks, sure they had returned to their crimson color from a few minutes before.

"Maybe we should sneak over to the stables so I can have a peek."

"We most certainly will not sneak back to the stables, until Connor has come to assure me that no danger remains."

"That is very wise," Ruby admitted. "It wouldn't do to have your name circling around the gossip mills again." She retreated into the room and sat at her writing desk. "Mother has not written of Brock's return to Kent. I wonder if I should write of it. It would be very nice to inform my mother of something before she is aware."

"She is most likely in London this time of the season." Viola had long wondered about the relationship between Ruby and her mother. Mostly, why she insisted on Ruby attending Vi for all these years instead of acquiring a suitable match in London. If her dear friend wondered the same, she'd never mentioned anything to her. "Maybe she will send for you this year."

"I gave up hope on that long ago, Vi. Besides which, I must stay here and make sure you do not get yourself into another unfortunate situation."

It had been many years since Vi's one and only

'unfortunate situation.' Although her father seemed to believe she'd find herself in another one if left to her own devices. "You cannot think I would put myself in a situation like that again."

Ruby raised a brow in question.

"Well, I did not seek out this current predicament, as you well know, and stop looking at me thus." Vi stood from the bed and walked to the fireplace and back. She felt caged in her own home, helpless to rectify her current debacle.

"He will leave shortly and not return, correct?"

"Yes. Connor offered to deliver the foal to his country estate when I deem them ready." The thought of not seeing him again should have soothed her discomfort, but a prick of disappointment flared instead.

"Then you truly are not in any type of situation. He will leave and we will stay here. That he has returned to England means naught to us," Ruby said. She rubbed her hands together as if removing any dirt that clung, and showed her clean hands to Vi. "And it will give Connor the excuse to stop in London for you. How long has it been since you received a letter from Mrs. Hutton?"

Vi thought for a moment. How long had it been? "A few months, I suppose."

"Then it will be wise for Connor to stop in and check on her and the children," Ruby said. "It cannot be too far out of the way for him."

"I have a much smaller donation this quarter, I fear."

"Do you truly believe the children care how much you are able to send?"

Vi wished she could send more, do more for them

all, but with business slowing recently she would be limited in her contributions to the orphanage for the time being. "I guess not." Although, Lord Haversham's purchase certainly would add to the amount.

"When will Connor be departing with the foals? I have a few scarves and mended coats to send with him."

The sooner the better, as far as she was concerned.

Yes, the problem would depart shortly and they would return to business, as usual. Viola had no plans to return to polite society, even if they'd accept her back, so there was nothing to fear.

"Ruby, thank you ever so much." Vi worked to suppress the emotions bubbling just below the surface of her ever-composed countenance.

"Whatever for?"

"For being here after so many have forsaken me." A tear slipped down her cheek and she quickly dashed it away. It would do no good crying over her past mistakes. She'd tried that route, and it had solved nothing. It was better to accept her lot in life and make the best of it.

"Now, Lady Viola Oberbrook, wipe that grim look off your face and be proud of all you've accomplished, while not having to worry about a bunch of pompous nobodies looking over your shoulder. You've changed—not a member of the *ton* would even recognize you now."

Vi didn't know if she believed Ruby's words, but she hoped they were true.

CHAPTER THREE

Connor focused on his friend as the man took the empty seat across from him. His lean, almost-feminine form folded easily into the sturdy wooden chair, and Connor noted that Hamp's appearance hadn't changed in all the years they'd known each other. He still had the boyish look of his youth, his hair the darkest ebony with nary a grey strand to be seen.

"I do not understand why you insist on meeting at this insufferable tavern, as if I am someone who frequents these types of establishments." The man's gaze flitted around the crowded room.

You are the only thing that is insufferable here. Connor couldn't help but take in his surroundings. The tavern was a respectable place, as far as country taverns went. The family who ran the public house and inn kept a clean yard, edible food, and tidy rooms. People in the area didn't ask for more. "Unlike yourself, I seek to keep our dealings a secret. People here are not prone to gossip, as I meet many business clients herein."

Both men paused when the barkeep's daughter arrived to take their drink order.

"Right nice see'n ye, Mr. Cale," she said and turned her smile on Hamp. "And you, m'lord, always be a pleasure to serve ye." She winked.

Connor swore she licked her lips. Subtlety was not Darla's forte, and her father well knew it. It was a wonder the barkeep hadn't sent the girl to live with relatives further removed in the country, but seeing as she drew in a crowd, Connor was willing to bet that they overlooked her indiscretions.

"It is always a pleasure to be in your company as well, Miss." His friend's lecherous smile mirrored Darla's.

"We will both have scotch," Connor said and waved his hand in dismissal.

With a small pout of her painted lips, Darla moved back toward the bar and her father.

Hamp watched as she sauntered away, her hair moving in time with her ample hips. Connor guessed his associate wasn't so against this particular establishment after all.

Connor noticed the man's perfectly tied necktie and impeccably tailored riding coat and a pang of jealousy surged through his body like a bolt of lightning. There had been a day when he had dressed similarly, when women had looked at him the way Darla lusted after this man—as he had always hoped Lady Vi would look at him. One day, he promised himself, she would—and it would be too late.

"I can only be away for so long. What did you need to discuss?" Connor asked, shifting Hamp's focus from the girl.

Reluctantly, his business partner returned his attention to Connor. "You should learn to enjoy life a bit more."

"I do not enjoy life because I do not bed the local barkeep's daughter?" Connor heard the tiredness in his own voice.

"That is only one way you do not enjoy life. Remember when we used to run about town?" Hamp laughed. "Those were good times. Now, you work yourself to the bone for that ungrateful girl."

"You should not complain about my employment with Lady Viola." Anger infused Connor's voice. Taking a calming breath, he continued. "If not for Foldger's Foals, we would not have been able to successfully start our—"

Darla returned with their drinks and cut off the conversation.

"Here is ye drinks, boys." Lust dripped from her lips, and she directed her words at Connor's companion. "Ye better be find'n me before ye leave."

"I always do, my sweet," Hamp said.

The door to the tavern swung open and Connor trained his eyes on the new arrivals. He didn't recognize the pair dressed in well-worn breeches and overshirts.

"I be waiting for ye, m'lord." The girl leaned over the table to better display her assets as she wiped a bit of spilled ale from the table.

"Darla," the barkeep called, a gruff expression on his weathered face. "Some new customers do be need'n a drink."

She glanced over her shoulder with a huff before turning one last smile on Connor's companion and moving to the recently arrived pair.

"Has Lord Featheringdon contacted you yet?" Connor asked to attract Hamp's attention again.

"Yes, I received a letter from his man of business with the post yesterday. He is sending his stable master to acquire a few foals." Hamp knocked back his scotch in one large gulp and his face pulled into a grimace. "Is this scotch or horse piss?"

"We are not in your exclusive club in London—"

"Speaking of London, I am in need of more money . . ." The man's voice trailed off as he waited for Connor to offer up more coin.

"I have siphoned off as much as possible without her noticing. There is no more money to be had."

"There is always coin to be had. If I am to impress potential clients in town, I must have money."

"Have you blown through your inheritance already?" Connor could not help but ask. His curiosity about Hamp's financial status had grown over the last year. "From what I hear, your mother is living quite comfortably on her stipend."

"Do not question me about my financial well-being. This is about our business." He tilted his tumbler back and drained his glass, his knuckles white as he grasped the glass a bit too tight.

Connor had struck a nerve. He must remember his longtime friend could only be pushed so far—Hamp was not a man Connor wanted to be at odds with. "There is little money coming in and much more leaving to feed and pay the last remaining staff."

"So, she is close to shutting down?" Hamp asked.

"Very close."

"And you have copied her client list in its entirety?

"Of course." Connor pulled a folded sheet of

paper from his coat pocket. "All thirty-six clients and their direction."

He made to grab the parchment from him, but Connor shifted the list out of his reach.

"This is not yours. Yet."

"Why ever not?"

"It is too soon yet to contact anyone. Another fortnight and it should be clear that Foldger's Foals will be no more. It will be far easier to persuade most of her clients to purchase from us then."

"I knew there was a reason I aligned myself with you." He raised his hand to signal for Darla to bring him another scotch. "Another?" When Connor shook his head, the man held up one finger in the direction of the bar.

"I only think it is important that we are not too obvious in convincing her clients to instead purchase from D & C." Connor lowered his voice as another man sat at the table closest to them. "We cannot risk a client going to Lady Viola."

"I doubt there is much she can do at this point. I guess she could travel to London and spread word of how you deceived her, but then she would only be exposing herself."

He despised when Hamp was correct. It irritated him even further when he knew it.

"Is this all you wished to discuss?" Connor asked.

"I needed to verify that you and I were still working toward a common goal."

Darla shimmied up to the table and set down the man's drink. "Will that be all, gentlemen?"

"Yes," Connor responded before the man could draw out their useless meeting any longer. "How much do I owe?"

"Don't ye be worrying 'bout that, Mr. Cale. Ye friend more than pays the tab." She giggled and moved on to the men at the next table.

"I do not mind working off the tab," he said with a wink.

That'd be the only thing the man had ever earned in his life, Connor couldn't help thinking.

Connor stood. "You have not changed, my friend. If there is nothing else, I will be on my way. I must return to feed the foal." He dropped a curt bow and turned to leave.

Before he took a step, the man grabbed his arm, halting him.

"I need more money to continue in London," he spoke low.

"I plan to travel to London soon myself. I will bring you funds then."

"Make sure you do, or I will be forced to quicken the downfall of Foldger's Foals."

Connor made no comment, seething at the impossible position he'd been put in. But if it was a choice between Lady Vi or his own return to society and respectability, he knew he wouldn't hesitate. Connor would choose his own needs above all else.

CHAPTER FOUR

Brock strolled into Haversham House and nearly fell to his knees. It was hard to enter this place without memories flooding his mind. Memories of his beautiful mother, heavily pregnant with the twins. Or his young brothers sliding down the main balustrade during their games of pirates. Of his father, voice raised in anger over the improper escapades of Winston and Cody.

Eventually, his thoughts always came back to *her*-- Lady Viola Oberbrook. How he despised the woman! Lord help him, and everyone around him, if he ever came face to face with that Siren. He was unsure of what had become of her, and he had no desire to inquire as to her current whereabouts. He knew the unpredictability of his siblings, their tendency toward rash decisions and their scorn of consequences, but why had only his brothers suffered that day? With both dead, the blame should have fallen on her shoulders, no matter the unfairness of that fact.

"My lord." His butler bowed before him. "May I

relieve you of your overcoat?"

"Thank you, Thamston. Please have water brought up for a bath. I'm afraid after two days in the saddle I smell worse than the stable I visited." Brock shrugged out of his coat and started for the stairs.

"My lord?"

"Yes, what is it?" He stopped mid-stride, turning back to Thamston.

"Mr. Jakeston awaits your presence in the front parlor."

"Well, why did you not say so sooner?" Brock changed direction and headed to the closed door off the main foyer, throwing it wide to greet his oldest friend. "Harold! I distinctly remember saying I'd send word when I returned from Hampshire."

His sudden appearance startled his friend, who looked to be dozing off in an overstuffed chair, his feet resting on an ottoman. Mr. Harold Jakeston snapped up straight and lifted his booted feet from the delicate, cream cushion of the ottoman. "I apologize for lurking when not invited." His hair stuck out at odd angles and his eyelids were heavy with lack of sleep.

Brock snorted. "You are always welcome in my home, my friend. You look exhausted. Another row with your father?"

"Is it that obvious?" Harold rubbed the sleep from his eyes.

"Not to someone who doesn't know you as well as I. They would assume you always look this downcast and bleak. Has Thamston or Miss Styles been in to offer you refreshments?" Brock asked.

"No, no. I did not seek to impose upon them." Harold flung his hand in front of him, warding off

Brock's concern.

"Is it the vicar debate again?"

"Whatever else would it be?"

"You must come clean and tell him you have no intention of following in his footsteps." Brock moved to the sideboard and poured two healthy fingers of brandy.

"But as the third son, I have no other options. Without a shilling to my name, the path may well be forced upon me." Harold's hand swiped at the hair falling across his forehead.

"Have a drink. Everything will appear better after."

Harold relieved Brock of a tumbler. "No sherry?"

"The situation calls for something a bit stronger, would you not agree?"

Harold nodded and tipped the glass to his lips, draining the amber liquid.

"Another?"

"No, thank you." Harold moved back to his napping chair and sat, his overly stressed body crushing the cushion under its weight.

"I will be traveling to London soon to start my quest for a bride," Brock said. "I insist you accompany me. Maybe we can marry you off to an heiress. Then you would not have to worry about your father or his vicarage."

"It is almost too much to hope that things would transpire thus." The tension melted into despair and he sank further into the chair.

Brock tilted his own drink to his lips and pondered his friend's predicament. He hadn't thought about Harold accompanying him to London before, but it would be advantageous for them both. Harold could get away from his father, and Brock would not be alone during his first foray into society in over fifteen years. He had been no more than a lad when he'd chosen the career path of a military man, against his father's wishes.

As Harold seemed lost in his own thoughts, Brock surveyed the room in which they stood. His parents' last portrait hung regally above the fireplace. The downward gaze of his mother's eyes hid the grin that sought to overtake her face. She'd just found out she was again pregnant, after many years of trying. His father immediately commissioned the painting.

His father, the fifth Earl of Haversham, beamed with pride behind Brock's mother. Neither had any way of knowing that in seven months' time she would be dead and his father would be tasked with raising twins, with only the help of a twelve-year-old Brock and a household of servants.

And now, they were all gone: His mother, his father, and the unborn boys just thought of in that painting. If it hadn't been for Lady Viola Oberbrook, his brothers would still be alive; his father would never have died of a broken heart. She had taken his family.

"Are you not listening to me?" Harold chided.

Brock tamped down the inner rage that constantly boiled at the thought of Lady Oberbrook, and turned away from his parents' portrait. "I apologize. My mind was elsewhere. What did you say?"

"I asked how it went at Foldger's Foals. Did you find their stock of good quality?"

Oh, he'd found something of quality there, although he wasn't sure it had anything to do with the livestock for sale. "I was quite satisfied with the animals I saw."

"How many did you return with?"

"They are not ready at the moment. In a fortnight, I will return and bring home eight foals." While Mr. Cale had insisted on delivering the animals to Haversham House, Brock had expressed his desire to collect the animals himself. Would he gain another glance of the fair Lady Posey? His hopes were high on that front. "Until then, I will work on repairing the stables here. You are welcome to stay and help."

"That may be just the thing I need."

"I was going to bathe and get a fresh start in the morning, but we might as well start now," Brock said. "Before your father says play time is over."

# # #

Days had passed and still Vi had found no solution to her problems. An increase in sales and a decrease in wages would not help at this point. She sat upon a tightly cinched bale of hay and listened as Alexander, her strong, well-trained stable lad, pronounced each phrase as she'd dictated to him moments before. The boy, truly on the cusp of manhood, had been with her for years. She knew he had more to offer than his mangled arm showed. Capable and sturdy, he worked twice as hard as most of her men, his disability notwithstanding. She wished she'd had his insatiable drive at his age.

"'May I take your coat, my lord?' How'm I do'n, Lady Vi?"

Vi looked up to see Alexander, stopped before her. "I apologize. What was that?"

"My lady, you be alright today?" he asked.

"That is, 'how am I doing?' and, 'My lady, are you all right today?' And yes, Alexander, I have only been very busy as of late." Vi watched as Alexander nodded and turned back to his work, continuing to recite his recent lesson.

The boy was smart, and worthy of a better life than Vi could ever give him. One day, he would be a stable master at a grand country estate or butler in a fashionable part of London...if only he'd dedicate himself to his studies. When he had become too old to stay at the orphanage, Vi had quickly taken him in and put him to work. She'd been happily surprised that his disability did not limit his physical abilities in the slightest.

"Very good," she praised him. "Now, please recite Pope's *Essay of Man.*"

"Again, my lady?"

Vi knew the work she demanded of him was mentally exhausting, but she hoped one day he would thank her. "Yes. Until you can recite the whole poem, with perfect pronunciation, you will say it every day." She smiled in encouragement. "You almost have it perfectly memorized."

"I jus' don't be get'n—" he started.

Vi stood and swept the hay from her skirt, considering her words before she spoke. "Alexander, I have told you many times. To work in a grand house, for a noble man and his family, you *must* carry yourself at their level."

Alexander stared blankly at her.

"Do you remember the day you were told you would have to find different lodging? And a job to pay for your own food and housing?"

"Yes, ma'am."

"How did that make you feel? Alone? Desperate?

In need?" she asked. These exact emotions had stuck deep within her; they lived in her every waking moment and darkened her slumber each night. She knew them firsthand.

Alexander pondered her question for a minute before responding. "Like I was good for nothing. I be scared to think about those workhouses and what happens to people like me there."

She knew she was being overly hard on him, but she needed him to understand the consequences if he didn't try his best, especially knowing she would not be able to take care of him for much longer. "I am here to show you, to teach you, that if you believe in yourself you will never be alone or destitute. No workhouse will be in your future."

They were so very different—from completely different worlds, yet they were also mirror images. She an ex-lady of the *ton*, and he a discarded boy. There was so much she yearned to teach him, wisdom she wished she'd had at his age. She wondered if she would have heeded the advice herself.

"I don' be know'n what a cripple like me could do for nobody."

His words brought tears to her eyes. With only one functioning hand, Alexander was still more proficient than any stable boy she'd ever employed. He had a way with the animals that defied the laws of nature. It was as if they understood each other's needs on the most basic level.

He cared for them.

"You are much more than your disability, Alexander." She took the hand that hung lifeless at his side and massaged the damaged skin. "You are

43

intelligent, caring, compassionate, hardworking…"

Alexander lowered his gaze, as if embarrassed by her praise.

She continued, hoping to drive her point home. "You are so much more! And you will have so much more as you grow older and use the skills the good Lord gave you. One day, I promise, you will have a home and a family of your own. And, if you work hard now, a means to support them. You will never have to be alone."

He lifted his sorrow-filled eyes to meet her. "I do be appreciating all you have done for me."

"That was almost perfect, but it is not 'do be appreciating.' Try, 'I do appreciate,'" she corrected, lightening the mood. "Now, Pope's *Essay on Man*."

Alexander nodded and his deep voice filled the empty stables with the words of his namesake, Alexander Pope:

> *Know then thyself, presume not God to scan*
> *The proper study of Mankind is Man.*
> *Placed on this isthmus of a middle state,*
> *A Being darkly wise, and rudely great*

She let the words drift over her. They settled like a heavy cloak, coating her in memories of her past and the harshness of mankind. Not just society, but her harshness as well. Society had only punished her as she'd deserved.

> *With too much knowledge for the Sceptic side,*
> *With too much weakness for the Stoic's pride,*

He hangs between; in doubt to act, or rest;

She'd been weak, still was. She only hoped that one day she would gain the knowledge and strength to right her wrongs. Could she humble herself to mankind to renew her body and soul? Seek forgiveness for what her youthful naiveté had caused? Cody and Winston had not been born only to die. And neither had she.

She'd preyed on those two young men, egged them on, and ultimately caused their deaths. If she were to be judged today, would she be found wanting? Had she corrected any of her errors?

Had she any hope of correcting her past? Perhaps she should not push Alexander to persevere when, in truth, she'd been the one to give up. She had yet to face her sins and make amends; instead she cowered in the country resigned to her fate.

The thought of soaring again, of not being afraid to admit her mistakes and gain her pardon from any and all who would give it, breathed wind into her sails. But she knew only one person who could grant her the forgiveness she sought.

Brock Spencer, Lord Haversham, held her future salvation in his hands, though he did not realize it. She hoped the day would come that she could ask for that salvation.

Alexander continued solidly, pushing to finish when he paused. Clearly, searching his mind for the correct pronunciation of a word.

"The word is 'absolution,'" Vi cut in. Even as she said the word, a heavy weight settled upon her shoulders.

She was a fool. A fool to think anyone would

forgive her and remove the cloak of shame she'd worn since fleeing all she had known in London. Truly, a fool to think she ever deserved the right to ask for Brock's absolution.

# # #

Brock surveyed the progress they'd made over the last several days. He'd been hesitant to undertake the repairs on the estate himself, but was glad he had. There was something comforting about being busy again. This was the type of life he was used to, and craved—one that showed his worth. He did not look fondly on the idle hands of his English countrymen who were born to privilege.

"What next, Brock?" Harold asked, similarly studying their handiwork.

He ran his hand through his hair in the hopes the sweat he'd worked up would keep it out of his eyes. "Why don't we tend to the tack room? It will be important that the saddles, horse blankets, and leather are kept dry from the elements."

"Fine. You still haven't told me why you are in such a hurry. You haven't properly mourned the loss of your father, and you've rushed into rebuilding the estate—the very estate you couldn't get far enough away from when we were younger."

Harold was an inquisitive and intellectual man, and Brock had known it was only a matter of time before his friend would question his haste to move forward.

"I seek to prepare my home for a family, to once again fill the halls with laughter. If I can't achieve that in the near future, at least I'll be occupied with the horses. Training and the like." He feared he'd shared too much, opened himself to the jests of a hurried marriage and the rumors of financial destitution, which could not be farther from the truth.

"I see," was Harold's only reply as he started toward the tack room.

"What in the blazes do you mean by that?" Brock followed closely on his heels.

"Not a thing. Do you not plan to hire someone to run the stables for you, to train the new foals?" Harold inquired as he entered the tack room.

"Whatever for? I am completely capable of the job, am I not?" Did his truest friend think him weak? Lacking, in some sense?

"Why yes, some would say overly capable. But with that responsibility weighing on your shoulders, however do you plan to meet, woo, and marry a chit in London?"

The man had a good point, one Brock hadn't pondered as yet. Images of Lady Posey invaded his mind: her dark hair—would it hang down her back if released from the severe knot she kept it in? Her blue eyes, as clear as the seas along the French coast... But most of all, her presence itself. While they'd only met on two brief occasions, he was positive she would light any room she entered. "I will manage."

"I have no doubt that you will."

Brock lifted the stack of new wood and carried it into the room, dropping it at Harold's feet, against the far rotting wall. "Enough talk. We sound like two old dowagers chatting over afternoon tea." He grabbed a hammer and knelt by the section of wall in the most disrepair.

Before Harold could respond, Brock heard footsteps behind him.

"Well, well, well. So nice of you to improve my inheritance, cousin."

Brock's head came up and the hairs on the back of his neck rose. "If it is not my well-connected cousin, Mr. Rodney Swiftenberg." He added extra emphasis to the 'mister' before his third cousin's name. "To what do I owe this honor?"

"I've merely come to check on my forthcoming asset," Rodney replied. "I do hope you are not emptying my coffers to repair this shell of a stable."

"I would never dream of squandering your life blood, cousin. You remember Mr. Harold Jakeston, do you not?" Setting down his hammer, Brock stood to face his cousin.

"Ah, yes, your childhood shadow. How could I forget the meek and meager vicar-to-be?" Rodney responded in his usual condescending manner, nodding in Harold's direction.

Brock didn't venture a look at his lifelong friend, but a distinct heat came from Harold's direction. It was tempting to react in a violent way—to grab his cousin by the throat and slam him against the rotting wall of the tack room, or use the man's creatively tied cravat to wring his scrawny neck.

Instead, he smiled.

Rodney sought a reaction at every turn when they were growing up, and that hadn't changed.

"You'll never let it go that Harold and I excluded you from our adventures as children."

"That is untrue. Winston, Cody, and I were very content to seek out our own adventures," Rodney said.

There was truth in his cousin's statement. Only a year older than Brock's twin brothers, Rodney had kept himself entertained at their expense. When cook's pies had gone missing or a full chamber pot had been launched over the railing from the second story, landing in the foyer and coating Mrs. Pearl St. Augustin in fecal matter, Rodney had been present but quick to blame the incident on the twins. His father had indulged the trio at every turn. His proclamation that 'boys will be boys' still rang in Brock's mind.

"Do you plan to stay on at the estate? Harold and I could use another set of hands to finish this project before we set off at the end of the week." He hadn't seen Rodney since his return to England, and he found it suspect that his cousin should appear now. Brock had learned upon his return that Rodney hadn't even seen fit to show his face at his uncle's funeral.

Could he blame his cousin for not attending a funeral that he, himself hadn't attended? Brock liked to tell himself that if he'd known his father had passed, he would have made the journey home, taken the time to see to all the details and to honor his father.

"I had planned to spend a few days restoring my constitution. The season can be quite draining, if you recall." Rodney leaned against the door jamb, eyeing the room in which Brock stood.

His cousin hadn't worked a day in his life, never needing to provide for himself or his family. Brock assumed he'd been upset to hear the heir to Haversham House had returned, alive and suitable to inherit.

Kneeling once again, Brock ripped a half-rotted board from the wall, tossing it over his shoulder, aiming for Rodney. "Be of some help, cousin, and fetch me the satchel of nails outside the door."

"And taint my new Hessians? I think not."

"I'll retrieve them," Harold said, leaving Brock alone with his cousin.

"That's a good little boy," Rodney taunted.

Brock leapt from his crouched position and fairly flew across the small room. He itched to wrap his hands around Rodney's perfect, pale-colored neck. "Cousin! I will warn you only this once. Do not disrespect guests in *my* home. Do you understand me?"

"Do you not mean *our* home, dear cousin?" The ignorant man held his ground and dared challenge Brock.

"You may have been allowed to live here by my father, the Lord rest his soul, but I am not the compassionate man he was." Brock took a step closer, forcing Rodney to retreat. "This stable, the Hall, and everything else entailed to the Haversham title belongs to me and me alone. You are permitted here and at my other residences because I see fit to allow you entrance."

Rodney took another step back, his foot catching on a length of wood, and he tumbled haphazardly to the ground.

Brock continued forward to tower over his cousin, driving his point home. "Until the unfortunate time that I pass, deprived of an heir, you will not be known as anything more than Mr. Rodney Swiftenberg." He found bullying in any form distasteful, but his cousin needed to learn his place now, before Brock allowed him too much leeway. At that point, it would prove difficult to rein the man back in.

"I apologize for giving you the impression that I take for granted all your father has done for me since my own mother and father died," Rodney backpedaled. "I do not mean any disrespect."

A bit of his anger fled at Rodney's words. Rodney had seen many hardships in his life as well, losing his own father at a young age and then his two best friends and cousins.

He had not been the only one to suffer with Brock's brothers' passing.

Brock offered his hand and his cousin grasped it. His clammy hand almost slipped from Brock's. With a small tug, Rodney lurched to his feet and brushed his palms down his trousers to remove the straw that clung to the material.

"If you do not plan on assisting Harold and me, you can return to the main house. We will meet you for supper," Brock said.

"Yes, I could use a bit of time to freshen—"

"Will we be needing all of these?" Harold lugged a brown satchel full of nails into the room. "I can feel the blisters now."

"What are your plans here, anyway?" Rodney looked between the pair.

"Brock is readying the stables for the foals arriving soon," Harold answered before Brock could stop him.

"Foals? When do they arrive?" Rodney inquired.

"They are not arriving. Harold and I will leave in a few days' time to collect them and bring them here." Brock wanted Rodney out of his hair—the sooner, the better. If that meant he and Harold would have to leave the estate as well, then so be it.

"Brock, but I thought you said—"

Brock silenced Harold with a glare. "There has been a change of plans, I thought I told you at the noontime meal? Something has come up, and we must travel back to Foldger's Foals to collect the horses."

"Foldger's Foals in Hampshire? I haven't had the pleasure of visiting a horse ranch in many years. I do believe I will tag along."

Brock's worst nightmare looked to be coming true. "You do realize the journey is over five hours on horseback?" he asked in hopes of discouraging him. "The trip may require us to stay a few days. The inns in that part of the country are quite primitive."

"I have no obligations until the ball at the Duke of Essex's townhouse a fortnight hence." Rodney cast a sly smile in Brock's direction, clearly enjoying the discomfort he caused his cousin. "I do believe a jaunt to the country will be a bracing way to pass the days."

CHAPTER FIVE

Vi entered the foyer and made her way to the grand staircase, her half boots leaving a trail of mud on the freshly scrubbed floor. Exhausted, her body craved a warm bath and a nap before supper was served. The muscles in her neck clenched as her foot hit the first step. Her calves strained to lift her heavy boot up to the next.

"Miss," her maid, Sarah, called from behind her.

"Sarah." Vi sighed. "Just the person I hoped to see. Please have my bath drawn and inform Cook I'll be a bit later than is the norm for my meal." She turned her attention back to the task at hand, traversing the stairs and somehow making it down the never-ending corridor to her room.

"Yur pa requests yer immediate attendance in his study," Sarah continued.

"My father? What is he doing here? The season is not yet over." It had never been favorable to Viola when her father arrived unannounced at their country estate. Most years, he'd come in hopes of convincing her to accompany him back to London. Each year, he'd left disappointed to finish the season's festivities without her.

"He don't be explaining hisself to the likes o' me, Miss."

"It was a rhetorical question." Viola sighed again. She might as well get this over with, find out what he wanted and help him on his way back to town. "Thank you. I will attend to him posthaste."

Sarah curtseyed and scurried in the direction of the kitchen.

Vi had only managed to scale two stairs, but the trip back down was even more painful, if that were possible. The newest bunch of foals were a feisty, unmanageable lot. With Connor away from the stables more and more—seeking out new clients—the training and care of the horses fell to her. They'd had to let several stable hands go over the last few months.

Thankfully, her father's study lay only a few paces down the hall. She shuffled her feet across the floor, moving at an unbearably slow but steady pace.

As she drew close to the partially opened study door, voices drifted out to greet her. The situation was worse than she'd expected. The Dowager Duchess of Darlingiver had accompanied her father, Lord Liperton. The couple had been linked for over fifteen years, but rarely traveled together.

Vi halted outside the door to listen. While eavesdropping was an unbecoming trait in a young lady of the *ton*, she'd left that life long ago—which had only caused her talent to rust a bit.

". . . but John, my dear. This is verily too much to

ask of me," the Dowager Duchess groaned. "Do you not see that I have my hands full with my own wayward son? I think the boy spends his allowance before his solicitor has even drawn him a cheque."

What could her father, a man who had everything, ask of this woman?

"While I've agreed with you for many years, the time has come. Her situation will not change unless she confronts it and makes them change their mind." Her father's voice rang with determination. "Besides, the current Lord Darlingiver is a fine young man, a little spirited, but that spirit will even out with time."

This could not, would not, be good. Her father was obviously set on his course of action here at Foldger's Hall.

"It is my reputation on the line, my lord."

"That I understand. It has weighed heavily on my mind, but Viola has changed," her father continued.

"If you do say so," the older matron replied.

What did the Dowager Duchess know about how she'd changed? The woman had sponsored her coming out during her introductory season, and at the first hint of scandal had distanced herself from Vi and her father. In fact, Vi didn't remember seeing the woman for close to five years after she'd left London for Foldger's Hall. How dare the duchess speak ill of her without even knowing her?

Vi concentrated on calming herself. It wouldn't do to see her father after all these months with a scowl on her face. Looking down, her sturdy work dress was stained with mud, hay stuck to it in spots. There was naught she could do about it now. Her father requested her presence and she didn't seek to anger him further by making him await her arrival.

Plastering a serene smile on her face, she pushed her way into the room. "Father, how lovely to see you! And Lady Darlingiver, it has been too long." Vi first hugged her father where he stood in front of the massive fireplace, then turned to curtsey to the dowager, who sat upon a small settee.

Her neck tweaked at the pose and her feet trembled, but she didn't give in to the protests of her overworked body or let her socially acceptable smile falter.

"My dear Lady Viola," the older woman gushed. "You look lovely as ever, although a bit unkempt." The dowager's hand rose to cover her nose.

"I sincerely apologize for my attire. I only just returned from the stables and I fear I am in need of a long soak," Vi ground out between clenched teeth. Again, her smile never wavered. If there was anything she'd learned in her short time in London, it had been how to 'grin and abide,' as her father said.

"My dear daughter! Look at you," Lord Liperton said as he moved from his place across the room.

"Father—"

"You are fairly as dark as a Frenchman! This will not do in the least."

What? Viola brought her hand up. It was true, her skin had gained a sun-kissed glow. But dark as a Frenchman? Of all the absurd things her father could have said, this was one she hadn't expected.

"How do you expect to find a suitable husband when you appear to have just returned from the continent?" he asked.

Vi looked between her father and Lady

Darlingiver, unable to form a response.

"Most unbecoming. See, John. Nothing has changed," the older woman huffed.

Viola found her voice. "I suppose it is advantageous that I am not, nor plan to be, in the market for a husband." It appeared they were jumping into the heart of the matter that had drawn her father to his country estate before the end of the season, and away from his duties in Parliament.

"Do not be silly, my girl." Her father stood between Vi and the dowager, as if he needed to intervene in an attack between the women. Which was preposterous, since Vi measured a whole six inches shorter than her portly father, and the dowager towered over the duke, his head only reaching her well-toned shoulder.

"Listen to your father for once, Lady Viola."

Listen to her father? The woman had no clue if and when Vi had listened to her father over the years. "I do well to always hold my father's words in the highest esteem, my lady."

"Have a seat," her father said, motioning to the settee next to the dowager.

Viola opted for a leather-covered desk chair close to the study door. If she needed a quick escape, it would be convenient.

"Viola," her father continued, taking the seat Viola had declined. "I've been thinking—"

"Obviously."

"Do not interrupt your father, young lady," the dowager again cut in.

"Viola . . ." her father started over.

"I told you, the girl hasn't a refined bone in her

body. She has been laid to fallow out here in the country and is not fit for town life," the woman wailed. "I suspect even my son would be hard pressed to introduce the girl around."

Her father took the old lady's hand in his own, rubbing it in comfort. "Give her a chance, Evie."

Evie? Never had her father addressed the woman so informally. Their relationship had most assuredly progressed since Vi last spoke with her father. She almost felt as though she'd intruded on a private moment between the pair.

She wondered what the dowager's son, Hampton, had to do with her return to town.

"May I be excused to freshen up? We may continue this discussion over dinner, mayhaps."

"I think not." Her father's voice rose in anger.

"Go on, John," the dowager prodded.

This was too much! They acted as if Vi had exiled *herself* to Foldger's Hall. "Father, please say what you wish to say."

"As you well know, I've long held that you need to acquire a husband—"

"And against my wishes, your father has enlisted my support," Lady Darlingiver interrupted once again.

"Evie, your support and understanding over the years has kept hope alive."

Viola wanted to throw something at the pair, if only to get her father to spit out what he wanted to say. How many times must they go through this? They would argue and then he would return to London, not to be seen for several months before he saw fit to try yet again to convince her of her need for a husband.

Her father adjusted his place on the settee, sidling

closer to Lady Darlingiver, if that were possible. "I think it is past time you return to society and find a husband. It will not do to continue playing with horses here."

"You think I play with horses?" Vi sputtered. "I've run a very successful foal ranch for going on eight years. I do not merely 'play with horses.'"

She needed to calm down. She counted to ten before continuing. "Besides, if memory serves, it was you, Lady Darlingiver, who convinced me to leave London in the first place."

"At the time, your father and I thought it best—"

"Why should I return now? I have built a life for myself here. I have people who depend on me."

Her father raised his hands before him, palms up, as though pleading for her attention. "I'm not a young man, Viola. You must marry and secure your future. I will not be able to indulge you forever."

"Indulge me? Father, Foldger's Foals is completely self-supporting."

"Yes, but if something were to happen to me the estate will go to my cousin, Gerald."

"But not Foldger's Foals. That property is not entailed to the dukedom," Vi countered.

"Be that as it may, your secret would spread and your livelihood would be gone," he continued.

Blast. Her father had a point. She needed a different angle. "Do you think I do not see the gossip rags?" she said. "I'm not so far removed from the *ton* or their idle gossip."

"It is true, your name still graces the pages of many papers. But your return will cease the gossipmongers. You are a different person now."

Lady Darlingiver stiffened beside her father.

Obviously, the woman didn't hold the same opinion. Maybe Vi could find an ally in her.

She refocused her attention. "Lady Darlingiver, in your esteemed opinion, do you feel that I can successfully reenter society?"

The woman darted a glance at Vi's father before speaking. "That will depend solely on your behavior, my dear."

That was a safe answer; clearly, the woman wasn't willing to take the fall for Viola again. Not that Vi could blame her. The dowager had gained entrance to the finest homes in London during Vi's disastrous season. She'd been introduced to the most eligible and worthy bachelors, and Viola had made a mockery of her.

"I appreciate your honesty, Lady Darlingiver, and I do not seek to impose on you. It would be a great undertaking to reintroduce me to society." Viola hoped to impress upon the woman's need to maintain her stellar reputation before the *ton*.

"Evie does not mind the challenge." Lord Liperton turned to his partner. "Do you?"

"My lord, Lady Viola makes a very good point."

So they were back to formalities. This boded well for her cause.

Lady Darlingiver continued. "It will indeed be a great undertaking. And while I'm not opposed to the challenge, I am unsure how successful it will be."

Her father leapt from the settee and stood before Viola.

She craned her neck to look him in the eye from her seated position, her muscles fighting the angle.

"Let me make myself very clear, Viola. You will marry and marry soon! Heaven help me, I don't care if you marry Connor, but marry you will!"

Viola wondered why images of Lord Haversham popped into her mind at that very moment.

CHAPTER SIX

Lord Haversham had avoided his cousin's threatening stare for the last several hours. Unfortunately, this also meant not making eye contact with Harold, who rode on the far side of Rodney.

"Must you set such a fast pace, cousin?" Rodney held the pommel as his legs flopped against the horse's flank, his feet having lost their purchase in the stirrups long ago.

The ride to Foldger's Foals had started with Rodney poised as the dandy he was, his maroon riding coat hanging over his bright yellow breeches in the most fashionable of ways. That had been hours ago. Now, his yellow too-tight pants were smudged with dirt and his hair bounced to and fro to the rhythm of the horse's steps.

Brock found it hard not to laugh at the obvious discomfort Rodney had insisted on putting himself through. "As I said before we left, we are expected and I don't wish to keep them waiting. Do not worry, the drive is over the next ridge."

"Why would I be worried?" Rodney straightened in his saddle. "The journey has been delightful thus far."

"The way you're clutching the pommel tells a different story," Harold chimed in with a laugh.

Brock slowed his pace to an even trot, knowing they'd soon arrive. Lady Posey wouldn't be expecting him for another few days, but he could not stand another day in his cousin's presence. He'd thought when actually confronted with the reality of several hours in the saddle, Rodney would change his mind and flee back to London like a rodent before the storm. That had not been the case, much to Brock's disappointment.

"Is that the drive there, dear cousin?" The chipper tone of his cousin's voice proved how wrong he'd been.

Perfectly trimmed boxwoods bordered each side of the well-traveled lane leading to the stables. Although nearly the dinner hour, the ranch hummed with activity. Stable hands rushed here and there carrying feed and other supplies.

"Fear naught, we have arrived." Brock turned Sage down the drive, Rodney and Harold following suit.

The trio pulled their mounts to a stop outside the well-maintained stables and dismounted. Two young boys rushed out, taking the reins of all three horses, and led them into the covered stable yard without a word.

"Gentlemen, you are early!" a voice called from behind them. Brock turned to see Connor Cale ambling over from the office.

"Mr. Cale, may I introduce my cousin, Sir Rodney Swiftenberg, and Mr. Harold Jakeston."

Connor issued a curt bow in Rodney's direction. "It is a pleasure to have you both here at Foldger's

Foals, welcome." Next, he inclined his head to Harold. "Are you in the market for foals, as well?"

"They have only accompanied me to retrieve mine," Brock said.

"Well, welcome all the same. They are a feisty lot and the extra hands are appreciated." Connor turned from the men to the pasture on the far side of the stables. "Lady V—Posey is working with the young, as we speak. Would you gentlemen like a gander at our training process?"

Brock nodded, noticing Harold did the same. Rodney looked like he wanted a hot bath and possibly a stiff drink. "We would, thank you. Wouldn't we, Rodney?" He poked at his cousin.

"Indeed, indeed. You are correct, as always, *dear* cousin. I must endeavor to gain as much knowledge as possible to efficiently run *my* stables," Rodney countered.

"Are the foals not going to Haversham House, my lord?" Connor's confused stare moved from Brock to Rodney and back again.

"Forgive my cousin. He is a little too eager to claim his inheritance." Brock's penetrating stare settled on Rodney, daring him to speak out of turn again. "Let us have a peek. Do you employ a stable master or horse trainer?"

"Ah, no my lord. Lady Posey prefers to handle the foals herself."

"What?" Harold asked beside Brock. "I'm not the man-about-town, but this sounds highly irregular for a lady of the *ton*."

"As you will see, Lady Posey is anything but a traditional lady of the *ton*. Have a look for yourself."

Something about the flippant comment made Brock stiffen.

Connor turned and headed around the far side of the stable. "Right this way. We have a training area in back."

As they rounded the back of the stables, Brock stopped dead in his tracks. Before him stood Posey, dressed in breeches as she put a foal through its paces on a long lead rope. The young colt went from a walk to a trot to a gallop with an artful grace, requiring barely a word from its mistress. While Lady Posey held a long whip in one hand, Brock sensed she had never used it on a foal, or any creature, before. The whip tapped a rhythmic motion on the ground beside her; as the tapping increased so did the speed of the foal.

"Amazing!" Brock hardly noticed the word exited his mouth.

"Yes, our foals are superbly trained."

Was the man daft? Brock wasn't staring in awe at the foal, but at the sight of the most beautiful woman he'd ever had the pleasure of gazing upon. The breeches hugged her toned legs as if they'd been tailored to fit her body alone. But that was impossible! What modiste in her right mind would create a pair of breeches for a woman?

"This way, gentlemen. There is a better vantage point over here." Connor moved to stand closer to the enclosure that held Lady Posey and the foal.

"Is that a woman out there?" Harold's brow furrowed.

"Undoubtedly a woman, you buffoon," Rodney countered, slapping Harold across the back, causing him to stumble.

Harold's hands shot out to stop himself from colliding with the railing.

Brock bit back a harsh reprimand that would have more than likely embarrassed his cousin and opted for another cold stare, which only gained him a smirk and raised eyebrow from Rodney.

A soft clicking sounded from the pasture. Relaxing his posture, Brock turned from his cousin and back toward the heavenly creature effortlessly commanding the foal. She'd stopped the young beast and gently pulled it in her direction. Brock waited, his breath held, at what she'd ask of the foal next.

"As entertaining as this is, I think I'd enjoy a sip of tea or a nice scone," Rodney addressed Connor. "Might there be a place I can freshen up?"

"Of course," Connor said. "My apologies for not offering sooner. Where are my manners?"

"No harm done," Brock stated. "Rodney and Harold, why don't you go with Mr. Cale, and I'll consult with Lady Posey on the preparedness of the foals? I will meet up with you after."

Harold looked from Brock to Rodney and back again. His eyes said quite clearly that he wanted nothing less than to be in a room alone with Brock's cousin.

"I'll not be long," Brock said, hoping to soothe Harold's unease. He only sought a few minutes alone with Lady Posey.

Harold nodded and moved to follow the retreating forms of Rodney and Connor as they made their way to the stable's office.

The clicking continued, drawing Brock's attention back to the pasture. Lady Posey called the animal back to her once more. She'd cast the lead rope and whip to the side. As the animal came to a halt in front of her, she reached out and took its head between her hands and softly nuzzled the foal's velvet muzzle.

The breeze carried a song his way. The familiar melody brought memories crashing into his mind.

"I saw a fair maiden, sitting and sing, she lulled a little child a sweet lording," Lady Posey sang softly.

Brock's mind filled with images of his mother as she sang him to sleep, his small frame cradled against her body. He hadn't heard the tune in how long? Twenty-nine or thirty years? How time had flown. Life always changing, rarely moving in the direction he'd hoped.

He pushed the memories back where they belonged and cleared his throat. It wouldn't do to sound choked up when he spoke with her.

Lady Posey's head raised and she looked in his direction, bringing her hand up to shield against the glare from the late afternoon sun. "Connor?" she called.

Brock ducked under the top railing of the fence and slipped his leg over the bottom. "No, Lady Posey. It is I, Lord Haversham."

"My lord! We hadn't expected you for a few days yet." She rubbed her hands down the front of her pants and started in his direction. The young foal followed as if it were a pup.

"Alas, I could not tarry another day to inspect the progress of my investment." *Nor wait another hour to see you*, he wanted to add. He trained his eyes to the ground to avoid tripping on the rocky, uneven soil.

"While I understand your concern, you must remember I've been responsible for training foals for nearly eight years. I assure you that my staff and I are quite capable of accomplishing our duties." She stopped a few feet from him.

"It is not as you think, my lady." Why did Brock always feel he had to soothe her ruffled feathers? "I only mean that I greatly anticipate the addition of your foals to my own stable. That is all."

Lady Posey's head tilted to the side, as if judging the truthfulness of his words.

The foal moved in close and nudged her lower back, seeking attention. "If you will await Connor in my office, I will send him round to finish any outstanding paperwork."

"I have already met with him. He actually led me here."

Her eyebrow shot up in question. "He did?"

"Yes, he is preparing refreshments as we speak."

"Lovely," she mumbled. "Allow me to return Star to her stall and I will come round to the office."

She made to walk away when her booted foot caught on an uneven clump of earth, causing her to stumble. Brock's arm shot out. Before he knew what was happening, he had encircled her waist. The rough material of her clothing rubbed against his forearm and he drew her to him, halting her downward trajectory.

With her body pulled firmly against him, she only reached his chest. Her labored breath swept across his neck, drawing his mind to the pounding drumbeat that started there and echoed everywhere else. The intimate encounter was unexpected.

But he intended to use it to his advantage.

"My lord, thank you ever so much for the assistance." Her body stiffened. She attempted to push against his chest, but his arm was wrapped around her tightly, trapping her to him.

He looked down, shifting the brush of her breath so that her sweet exhale washed over his face and her almond-shaped blue eyes came to focus on his. His gaze traversed lower, where her heaving chest strained against the cotton material of her brown tunic.

Did her body have the same electric response as his own? Lightning had surely forsaken the heavens to course through his body.

She wiggled in his grasp, but didn't utter another word of protest. Not that he was capable of hearing her speak with the blood crashing through his veins, creating a loud humming in his head.

How long had it been since he'd kissed a woman? Not the doxies who followed his troop of men, no—Lady Posey was far above their class. While she smelled of the earth and hard work, she was every inch the lady those women could never be.

His head lowered slowly, so as not to startle her, and he settled his mouth against her soft lips. Suddenly, she no longer pushed away from him, but rather leaned in. Brock accepted her slight weight against him and moved his lips against hers, coaxing them to match his movements.

Faintly, he registered her hands moving from his chest to slide up his sides, her fingers digging roughly into his shoulders.

Brock needed to be closer to her, yearned for her to be one with him. His hands ached to move from her back lower to her round posterior, to grasp her firm flesh and hold her body securely to him.

As if from afar, a foal whinnied and reality returned.

Brock trailed his lips from her mouth to her ear and down her neck before pulling away.

Posey sighed. He held back from capturing her mouth once more, certain he would never release her again. Instead, he moved his hands to her hips to stabilize her and stepped back.

As he watched, her eyes snapped open and her face flushed an endearing shade of pink that spread from her cheeks down her neck—the slender neck his lips had caressed only moments before. Her hands fell from his shoulders to rest at her side, unsure and awkward. "I must seek out Conn—Mr. Cale and see if he needs assistance," she whispered. She averted her eyes and her back stiffened once more.

"Until then, my lady." Brock took a step back and bowed low as she turned and stumbled to the gate leading into the back of the stable. The only thing that looked better than her toned legs in her skin-tight breeches was her firm, round derriere.

A smile pulled at his lips as he visualized her working around his estate. Her leaning over to nail in a wayward board that had come loose, or scooping grain into feed buckets as they completed their morning chores.

Without warning, the portrait of a smiling Posey cradling a young son to her side, Brock standing proudly behind them, replaced the family portrait in his estate foyer.

This was the type of woman he could marry—nothing like the chit his brothers had fancied.

Lady Posey was anything but idle and vain.

# # #

This was exactly *not* what Viola needed. She'd only that morning convinced her father and Lady Darlingiver of the futileness of their visit. Shortly before luncheon, she'd packed them into her father's coach and sent them on their way back to London for the remainder of the season.

Now, she had Connor leading Brock out to the pasture and then leaving him there to watch while her stable master prepared refreshments. They definitely had a few things to discuss after their guest departed.

And that kiss! What had she been thinking, lingering in his embrace for so long? She hadn't been thinking. She'd been caught in the moment; her heart rate still beat erratically. She paused outside the stables to catch her breath. Her hand came to rest against her bosom. Her breasts expanded and contracted against the rough material of her tunic.

What was wrong with her? She'd been caught off guard—that was all. She simply hadn't expected to see him outside her training ring. With a deep sigh, she continued inside.

As she walked into the stables, Star close on her heels, Alexander appeared at her side.

"Can I be help'n you, m'lady?"

"That's 'my lady,' Alexander."

"Yes'm." The boy bowed his head.

"Alexander, we've gone over and over this. It is, 'Yes, my lady.' You will never be hired in a fancy stable in London if you do not speak properly."

"I understand, my lady."

"Much better. You will be round for your lesson after the evening's feeding, correct?"

"I would never miss a lesson, my lady," Alexander said as he bowed and then moved toward Star's stall door, his crippled arm hanging loose at his side. "In, girl."

She watched in disbelief as the foal moved easily into the stall and Alexander closed the door behind her. Other than herself, only Alexander showed such skill with the foals. She was certain he would prove a superior stable master in one of London's finest homes, if only the *ton* could look past his deformity and see his heart, his drive to succeed after such a harsh beginning. If they couldn't, of course, Alexander would always have a home at Foldger's Foals and her father's adjoining estate, Foldger's Hall.

"Please double check the water pails in each stall after you brush Star down."

"Of course, my lady."

She turned and started toward her office—and certain exposure, she was sure. Brock's unexpected arrival had ruined her plan to be conveniently away from the stables the day he returned for his horses.

The blasted man had destroyed everything.

Not only had he returned unexpectedly, but he'd also dared to kiss her. As much as Vi would like to pretend it hadn't happened, she already felt something awakening within that she'd suppressed many years ago. Love was not in her future. One little kiss would not change that, no matter how her heart fluttered at the thought.

As she approached her office, she heard voices through the open door. Male voices. Several—as in more than two—male voices. She could not fathom who, other than Connor and Brock, would be in her office. They weren't expecting any other clients. She slowed and peeked in the door.

"Here she is now, gentlemen."

Bloody hell!

Connor moved around her desk toward the door. The men loitering in her office also turned in her direction. One was dressed as if he'd just left a musicale in one of London's many drawing rooms. The man's yellow pants were offensive to Vi's eyes. Thankfully, she hadn't encountered the man outside, or she might have been blinded by the light he gave off. Brock and the other man were dressed more appropriately considering their task.

"Let me introduce Lady Posey Hale." Connor stood at Vi's side and faced her guests. "This is Mr. Rodney Swiftenberg, Lord Haversham's cousin."

The dandy bowed in her direction, his eyes scrutinizing her face. "Lovely to meet you." He paused in thought. "Although I must confess I feel we've met before. Do you travel to town often?"

"It is a pleasure, Mr. Swiftenberg. I have not had the enjoyment of attending a season in many years." Viola eyed the man similarly, certain they'd met before but unable to place where.

"And this is Mr. Harold Jakeston," Connor continued.

"Lady Posey." Mr. Jakeston issued a bow lower than was customary. His dirty-blond hair fell to cover his eyes. His hand swept over his forehead, efficiently pushing the wayward lock back into place, revealing amber gold eyes.

"Welcome to Foldger's Foals. Are you here to acquire a few of your own?" Viola asked in confusion.

"We are merely here to help Haversham remove his horses to his stables," Mr. Swiftenberg chimed in.

"That's wonderful, but you are early. There are still a few foals not ready to leave." Vi moved through the men to the safety of her desk, not venturing a glance in Brock's direction. She was sure her face would burn in yet another blush if she dared.

"I hope to collect the foals that are ready—"

"That will not be necessary," Vi stated, changing her mind abruptly. "They will all be ready today."

"Are you certain?" Connor questioned her. "You just said—"

"Of course, Mr. Cale," she interrupted. "You won't mind accompanying Lord Haversham back to his estate to make certain the transfer is smooth?" She was shocked she'd come up with a plan with barely a thought, but this would handle Brock's problematic presence. She could not have him hanging around the area for Lord knew how long. What if her father decided to return and try his hand at convincing her to travel to London?

That would be a disaster of epic proportions.

"I'm sure that will not be necessary—" Lord Haversham started again.

"My lord, you are a busy man and I do not seek to waste more of your time. Mr. Cale can accompany you to ensure the younger foals adjust to life on your estate." Vi turned to Connor, hoping her discomfort would be attributed to her busyness. Surely the stable master couldn't guess that she was squirming at the memory of Brock's lips pressed firmly against hers. "Please ready the foals. Lord Haversham has a long journey in front of him."

She kept her eyes firmly on Connor, for fear that every person in the room would see straight through her ruse.

"We will help prepare to leave." Lord Haversham nodded in Mr. Jakeston's direction.

Viola felt the pressure leave the room as Connor, Brock, and Mr. Jakeston filed out. Only Mr. Swiftenberg remained. Again, Vi had the feeling she'd met the man before, but she couldn't place him. *If* they had met at a ball or the opera years ago surely, he'd not remember her.

He too moved toward the door, as if to follow the other men out.

Vi sank into her chair and lowered her head into her hands, propped on her desk. She needed a few minutes to compose herself. Her fingers itched to touch her still-swollen lips. Ever since her first encounter with Brock, nothing had gone as she'd wanted or planned.

Instead, she heard the door shut and the lock moved into place with a deafening click.

She lifted her head from her hands.

"Well, well, well. I'd always wondered what happened to you." Mr. Swiftenberg didn't turn, but kept his back to her.

Realization dawned in the next instant. Morning fog . . . gun shots . . . *I assure you there has been no mistake made this day.* His clothes were different now, but his arrogance was the same as she remembered.

"Did you think I would not recognize you? Tsk, tsk. It has not been so many years—"

Vi's eyes narrowed. Would she be able to intimidate him into silence? She had to convince him to keep her secret.

"Lady *Viola* Oberbrook." Swiftenberg pivoted from the door and bowed in her direction. "I am unsure I can say it is a pleasure to make your acquaintance again, but at least you haven't caused any innocent men to lose their lives this day."

"You must be mistaken—" Vi stood from her chair. The plea in her voice was unmistakable, even to herself.

"Believe me, I sincerely wish I was mistaken." Mr. Swiftenberg—Rodney—strolled across the office and around her desk, his pace agonizingly slow, until they were toe to toe. "I want you to stay away from my cousin."

"Do you think this was my plan? To ever again come face to face with a member of your family?"

"You have always been a conniving, scheming wench!"

Vi drew back at the venom in his voice. "I want nothing to do with Bro— Lord Haversham. I only want him to collect his foals and be gone." Her hands shook, her legs ready to give out beneath her.

Rodney spun around on his heels and his hand flew to his head, pulling through his immaculate hair. "I do not need you complicating things for me at this juncture. I am so close!"

"Close to what?"

"This was not supposed to happen. None of this was supposed to happen." The man appeared to be coming unhinged.

"Whatever are you talking about?" Vi asked.

"I am talking about *my* estate, *my* title, and *my* inheritance!" With each 'my' his finger jabbed into his chest.

"You think I invited him here? That I want to drag out my past?" The questions rushed from her lips, but Rodney gave no indication he heard or comprehended a word she spoke. "Please, do not tell him who I am!"

"I fear I have no other option but to expose you." Rodney paced in front of Vi's desk. "He is interested in you. Why else would he hurry back here so quickly, other than to see the beautiful Lady Posey Hale?"

"Impossible . . ." But even as she protested, she pictured Brock's form fitted perfectly against hers.

"Impossible that he is infatuated with you? Or impossible that he cannot recognize the woman responsible for his beloved brothers' deaths?" Rodney laughed.

A chill crept up Vi's spine. Her secret was close to being exposed. The life she'd built since that day—the day that would be forever branded into her very being—would be ripped from her. "I will not entertain his interest, nor do I plan to return to society. Ever."

"The bell of the ball doesn't wish to be the center of attention again? Please! Things cannot change. People do not change."

"I have not attended a ball in eight years. Regardless of what you think, I have changed."

"Highly unlikely." He stopped his pacing and confronted her where she sat in her desk chair.

Life as she knew it was slipping from her grasp. If she were publicized as the owner of Foldger's Foals, her father would follow through with his threat to sell her stables and return her to a life of idleness. A life filled only with needlepoint and the occasional visits from family members. Only more appalling than this was the many she would be unable to continue helping.

A part of her considered the flip side of the coin. Maybe she *did* owe it to Brock and his family to pay retribution for the sins committed against them. The sins she alone was responsible for. Was it not Brock's right to punish her as he saw fit, regardless of whatever penance she may already have paid?

Could repenting lessen the weight on her soul?

Perhaps the time had come for her to confess her sins. Instead, she asked, "What do you want from me?"

"I want you to stay away from Brock. After today, I want you to act as if you've never met the man."

"Done." Why did a piece of her rebel at this agreement?

"No, you will take this one step further. If he tries to contact you—which I have no doubt he will do—you'll ignore his correspondence. Rebuff any advances he might make in the future." Rodney's posture straightened, his confidence returning. "Yes, this will suit me just fine."

"Whatever you want. But please, remove yourself from my office. I feel I'm a bit under the weather and wish to rest a spell."

Rodney nodded. "That is perfect. I will give the men your regrets at not attending us at our departure."

"Say as you wish."

A satisfied smile spread across his face. "Until . . . never, Lady Posey Hale. I have thoroughly enjoyed our conversation." With a bow in her direction, Rodney turned and unlocked the door, flinging it wide on its hinges.

CHAPTER SEVEN

"There you are."

Viola raised her head from the desk, where it lay cradled in the crook of her arm. She blinked a few times to clear the sleep from her eyes. How had she fallen asleep?

"You did not come back to the house for luncheon and I worried," Ruby continued as she entered the office, her lavender day dress moving fluidly around her legs. "But now I see why missing a meal was agreeable to you."

"Whatever are you going on about?" Vi rubbed her palms against her eyes. "It seems I fell asleep."

"Have you been crying?" Ruby's hands came to rest on her hips. A stance Vi had become very familiar with over the years.

"No, I have not been crying—"

"Do not lie to me, Viola Oberbrook! Your eyes are red and swollen, so unless you have been rolling around in the hay barn, you have indeed been crying."

Vi had long been unable to keep anything from Ruby. "Do not worry overly much. I am a bit burdened with the financial situation of Foldger's Foals is all." Which wasn't a complete lie, but would move Ruby's concerns in another direction.

Ruby's hands fell from her hips and she embraced Vi. "I knew the situation was worrisome, but not this dire. We will have to apply ourselves to finding a solution."

"That is exactly what I need to do." Vi did need a solution, but not to the problem Ruby suspected.

Ruby sat in the chair opposite Vi. "Now, who are the men gathering the foals from the pasture? There is a fellow gallivanting about in a set of yellow pantaloons!" Ruby raised an eyebrow. "I did not think you expected another client until next week."

"That, dear friend, would be Lord Haversham, his cousin, and Mr. Harold Jakeston." She debated how much to tell Ruby. It was senseless to have both of them worrying about Rodney's threat. "They arrived early to transport the foals to Haversham House."

"Did he come for the foals or to see you?"

The girl was a perceptive one. "Do not be mad." Vi glanced behind Ruby and out the only window in the room. "They are returning. Do you think we can slip out and back to the estate without notice?"

Ruby stood and turned toward the window. "I fear not. They are headed this way. Our best option is to hunker down in here. Who did you say the other man with Lord Haversham is? He looks vaguely familiar." She approached the window to gain a better view.

How would Ruby know Rodney? Heat moved to

Vi's face. "The man in the yellow is—"

"No, no. Not him. The other gentleman." Ruby's nose was about pressed to the glass. "The tall lanky one."

"Ummm, I believe he was introduced as Mr. Jakeston. No title and no residence given." The tension in her body eased a bit, although her body remained alert.

"Jakeston . . . Jakeston. The name is oddly familiar."

"Seems that everyone is oddly familiar nowadays."

"What do you mean by that?"

"Not a thing, not a thing." Vi waved off the comment.

"You are acting peculiar today."

"I'm doing no such thing!"

Ruby turned from the window. "Looks to me as if they are preparing to depart."

"Are you certain?" Vi stood and moved to have her own look out the window.

"I may not own a ranch or train horses, but they seem to be mounting their steeds with young foals in tow." Ruby turned a sarcastic smile on Vi.

"Your wit shines brighter than a certain pair of ocher breeches." Vi gazed out the window. "I have never taken you for a fool."

"I would hope not. Now, let us sit. It would not serve you well to be caught watching Lord Haversham as he departs. One might think you will miss him." Ruby regained her seat.

"One would be utterly mistaken to hold that delusion as truth." Vi glided back to her desk as nonchalantly as possible. It would not do to have her friend worrying that she would run off to town after a man.

Now, where had that thought come from?

For the first time, Viola noticed a small basket on the edge of her desk. "What have you brought?" she asked, easing into her seat.

"Just a spot of cheese and bread. As I said, I worried when you did not return for luncheon. I do know how you despise missing a meal."

"It is not that I fear missing a meal, but that I work hard."

Ruby retrieved the basket and spread their bounty between them. "It is no secret how hard you work."

"If memory serves, you do not take kindly to skipping a meal, either," Vi teased back. She tore a chunk of bread from the loaf between them and paired it with a bite of cheese. Popping it into her mouth, she couldn't help but remember that meal long ago when Ruby had first come to her. It had been Vi's darkest hour, alone at her father's country estate for nigh a year with little company but the servants and Connor. She'd been in need of a friend—someone to instill hope that the future held something, anything, for her. The utter despair and isolation had nearly driven her mad. If her father hadn't insisted she remain in the country, she would have foolishly fled back to London and faced down the society that had shunned her. Alas, she'd been broken—had not been ready then, and she feared she might never be ready.

Cursed shouting and the nervous neighs of a foal shook Vi from the bittersweet memory of her past.

"Whatever is that noise?" Vi—food forgotten—rushed to the window, Ruby on her heals.

"If not for his yellow breeches, I fear there would be a full moon on display in the middle of the day," Ruby said over her shoulder with a laugh.

Rodney lay on the ground next to his horse, his tawny clad arse facing Viola's office window. Lord Haversham's newly acquired foal pranced nervously about the fallen man.

Viola rushed to the door.

"What are you doing?" Ruby called behind her.

"My foal. One may be hurt. I must help calm them." Sunlight blinded Vi as she rushed into the stable yard and utter chaos. Hooves flew when one horse bucked its hind legs, only to cause another delicate young colt to rear up, its slender-but-lethal feet clawing at the air above Brock's head. Neighing, another foal nipped at the flank of the rearing horse.

Viola rushed into the storm toward Brock, who was caught in the middle of the fray.

To her surprise, he reached out and snagged one of the bridles and then a second, reducing the horses' range of movement. With two foals calmed, Viola turned to assess the remaining danger. On the far side of the commotion, Alexander also sought to soothe the horses. Vi relaxed a bit and slowed her pace as she approached the frightened animals.

"Apple . . . Pixie . . . Gunther," she whispered. Three small heads turned her way as the three foals closest to her settled down. "Come!"

The trio hesitantly walked in her direction as Alexander grabbed the harnesses of the remaining foals. All three animals at her side, Vi turned a menacing stare on Connor as he attempted to help Rodney up from the ground.

"We make a good team, you and I." The words were whispered in her ear, and goose pimples immediately rose on her arms.

Brock stood at her shoulder, two harnesses attached to two wild-eyed colts in hand.

"There would have been no occasion for such dangerous teamwork if Mr. Cale had been doing his job properly," Viola scolded, addressing Connor while keeping her gaze safely away from Lord Haversham. "You do realize the danger you put both these men and the horses in?"

"I apologize for the disruption." Connor held the flailing Rodney under his arms in an attempt to get the man back on his slightly heeled boots as they slid out from beneath him.

Rodney sunk back to the ground with a "Humph!" He kicked out his foot in irritation, catching the hoof of Brock's horse with his wooden boot heel as he made to stand once more.

As if to return the insult, the horse stepped back and right onto the toe of Rodney's black boot. A howl of pain rent the air as Rodney tugged his foot free. "You mangy—"

Vi ignored the chaos even as Lord Haversham looked on, smirking, from his own mount. "Whatever happened?" she demanded, looking from Connor to Rodney and on to Lord Haversham.

"Why, I never—" Rodney started.

Not waiting for a reply, she spoke to Alexander. "Remove the foals. I will call for them once this situation is under control."

Lord Haversham handed his reins to Mr. Jakeston, who had also dismounted. "I apologize for my cousin's ineptness in the saddle, Lady Posey."

"My ineptness?" Rodney screeched.

"Do you realize one of the foals could have severely hurt themselves or another of the animals in this frenzy?" She hoped her menacing stare burned a hole right through him.

"I assure you we—"

"Do not assure me of anything, my lord," Vi shot in his direction. "The first thing you must learn about these animals is that they are easily excited. When in a group, that excitement will quickly turn to fear, which in turn incites them to either fight or flee."

She couldn't help but wonder if her flight from London was similar to the spectacle that had just played out in front of her. Like her foals, she'd run at the first sign of danger, incited by her father's rage and embarrassment—just as one horse's rearing had caused another to buck. Would she have the same reaction now, or would she stand and fight, even if it meant admitting her faults to one and all?

"Do you believe I am an ignoramus who has no skill with horses? I will have you know I led a cavalry of forty soldiers on horseback against Napoleon himself. I am versed in the art of calming horses," Brock said coolly.

The statement caught her off guard. Vi had known he'd participated in the war against the French, but as an active soldier? She'd envisioned him ensconced in an encampment far from the dangers of death or maiming. "My apologies, my lord. I was unaware of your history, and concerned for my animals." She took a step back but kept her eyes firmly trained on Lord Haversham.

"Do you not mean 'my' animals?" he asked. "If

memory serves, you have a fat sack of coin sitting upon your desk."

She'd never had a hard time letting her colts go. That was the nature of her business, after all. "I stand corrected, my lord." Her words were said through gritted teeth. True, he had paid—and handsomely—for the foals, but deep down, they were still her babies. She'd cared for each and every one of them since their births.

Ruby cleared her throat.

"Ah, pardon my rudeness. This is my companion, Miss Ruby—"

"Pleased to make your acquaintance, my lord," Ruby cut Viola off. She lifted her skirt and curtsied to Brock.

What was she thinking? If she'd shared Ruby's last name, Lord Haversham would have surely made the connection to his country estate. Thankfully, Ruby was in command of her wits.

"The pleasure is mine, I assure you." Brock bowed to Ruby, but kept his eyes on Vi. "May I introduce my cousin, Mr. Rodney Swiftenberg and my friend, Mr. Harold Jakeston."

"How do you do, gentlemen," Ruby stated with all the grace and poise of a regular lady of the *ton*.

Mr. Jakeston stared at Ruby in a most peculiar way, just as Ruby had eyed him from the office window. Did the two indeed know each other? It was quite possible Rodney did not need to fear Vi would announce her true identity, but that Ruby would be the one recognized by Lord Haversham or Jakeston.

"Now that the required introductions have been made, I assume you are in a hurry to begin your journey home, my lord," Vi said, in hopes of breaking the odd staring match currently under way between Ruby and Lord Haversham's friend.

"Have we met, Miss Ruby?" Jakeston asked.

The man would not stop.

"I do not presume so." Ruby averted her gaze.

"Connor, please instruct Alexander to bring the foals round again——"

"I beg your pardon, but you look like one I once knew. Where do you hail from?" Jakeston continued.

"Again, you must be mistaken." Ruby avoided the question.

"My family's parsonage lies on the Haversham estate. Do you have family in the area?"

Yet again, Vi's deception was in danger. Why had she run from her office to assist during the commotion? She cursed her foolishness. Surely Connor could have handled the foals.

"I find myself in a hurry to return, cousin," Rodney spoke up. He was the only person present who wished her identity to remain a secret almost as much as herself.

"Of course," Brock said. "Lady Posey, thank you for the fine stock."

Vi sighed in relief. "My lord, thank you for your business. I trust with the help of Mr. Cale, your return trip should be smooth."

"I do not foresee any troubles." Brock took the reins of his horse back from Jakeston. "Let us be on our way, gentlemen."

Several minutes later, Viola and Ruby watched the group depart down the lane, Connor and the foals in tow.

"I fear we were almost discovered." Vi crossed her

arms across her chest.

"We? This is your deception, not mine."

"You were quick to cut me off when I nearly revealed your family name," Vi countered.

"It was for your sake, not my own. I do not agree with lying, but I do understand why you must."

"Do you know Mr. Jakeston?"

"Yes. He and I grew up together with Lord Haversham and his brothers, but shortly into my eighth year my father insisted I act more the lady. Then started my years of dresses, tutors, and training in all things a woman should know. It has been many years since I've thought of him," Ruby said with a sigh.

"Why ever would you think of him?" Vi prodded. Was there a man and a relationship in Ruby's past that Vi wasn't privy to? She'd never known her friend to speak of anyone. Maybe this explained the lack of communication between Ruby and her family now.

"I was not thinking of him in particular, but of all of them. I did spend my childhood amongst a horde of boys." Ruby winked at Vi, lightening the mood. "Now, let us not think about boys any longer, and finish our repast."

"Indeed." Viola wouldn't push her friend. The possibility of Ruby turning the tables and questioning her about Brock might lead Vi to explore her own uncomfortable connection to the man . . . and the kiss she could still feel on her lips.

CHAPTER EIGHT

The sun sat barely above the horizon as Brock wearily locked the final foal in the last available stall in his newly renovated stables. The ride home had proven uneventful but chaotic. It was without question in his favor that Mr. Cale had been able to escort them most of the way.

"Shall we return to the house? I find myself in need of a bath and a substantial meal," he asked Harold.

"A meal would not be remiss."

"I think you need a good scrub more than the food." Brock laughed at the hurt expression on his friend's face. "We can only hope Rodney has retired for the evening. The man is a good-for-nothing dandy if I've ever encountered one."

"Ha! He's changed for the worse since he's been unable to ride the coattails of the twins."

The reminder of his brothers' deaths sucked the jovial mood from Brock. It seemed he couldn't go anywhere without someone mentioning them. He'd enjoyed the day at Foldger's Foals, being so occupied that no one brought up the tragedy of his past. It was unlikely Lady Posey or Mr. Cale knew his painful family history; neither looked as if they'd attended a season in London in recent years—if ever. Now, Miss Ruby was a different story. Harold assured him on the trip home that he knew the girl, but couldn't place her.

"Brock."

Brock shook himself from his thoughts.

"Something always seems to bring up the past—"

Brock held up one hand to silence him. "Don't. I must engage in conversation about them with others, but not you . . . we have so much else to discuss."

"Such as?"

"Such as our trip to London to find me a suitable bride. It is time the estate is again filled with laughter and pounding feet!" Brock slung his arm around Harold and steered him out of the stables and toward the main house.

"We did have fun running amuck, did we not?"

"That we did, my friend!" They took the steps two at a time. The front door swung open before Brock had the chance to reach for the knob. "Good evening, Buttons! Please have Cook prepare dinner for two and have it waiting in my study in one hour's time."

"Certainly, my lord," the short, portly butler responded as he bowed his head. "I will also have warm water sent up for you."

"Very good. Send some to Harold's room as well—but do not waste the warm water on him." Brock laughed.

"Very kind of you," Harold said. "If I sought to be mistreated, I would head home to my father."

"I will have water brought up." Buttons turned on his heel and started for the kitchen.

"You've scared my poor butler with your complaining," Brock teased.

"As if we haven't scared our fair share of servants over the years. Remember that time—" Harold stopped walking mid-sentence, his brows drawn together in confusion. "By gawds! I figured it out!"

"How to get away from your overbearing father? I could have told you—"

"No! How we know her."

"How we know who? You are not making sense."

"Miss Ruby! She is Ruby St. Augustin." Harold smiled, a look of pride crossing his face.

"St. Augustin? How do I know that name?"

"How can you not remember? She's the chit from the estate next to yours. The ragamuffin who constantly followed us about as children." The satisfied look didn't leave Harold's face.

"Well I'll be a poppy's colored feathers! You just might be right. But however did she end up all the way in Hampshire? 'tis a long way from Kent."

"True. I expected the girl had attended a London season and was quickly swooped up," Harold continued. "While her family did not come from money, her father was in possession of a title."

Brock began up the main staircase to his bedchambers, Harold at his side. "Did you fancy her?" he couldn't help but ask. The girl was nothing but a fuzzy memory of a dirty child with stringy dark hair scampering after them as they embarked on adventures around the estate.

"Would it have mattered if I did?" Harold sighed.

"She was far out of my class. Her father's a baron, for heaven sakes."

He often wondered why Harold held such a low opinion of himself, but then he visualized Vicar Jakeston, all full of hell's fire and brimstone. Their trip to London would do both of them good. "She would have been lucky to have you as a husband, my friend."

"Whatever you say, Brock." Harold stopped in front of the door to his guest chamber. "I will meet you in the study in one hour."

"One minute late and I'll have Cook's meal eaten." Brock again laughed and continued down the hall to his own door.

It was unfortunate the way Harold's father treated him, as if he had not a single upstanding qualification in life. While Brock had done everything in his power to escape his distant, sometimes absent father, his friend had been left with a man who'd continually and without mercy crushed Harold's will. His friend had needed him, but Brock had been too concerned with his own troubles to be bothered. He'd not only run from those troubles at home, he'd abandoned his best friend when he'd needed him most.

He only hoped that, as with the newly renovated stables and high expectations of his London trip, Harold would also flourish anew. Brock meant to see his friend happy and carefree once more.

CHAPTER NINE

"Thank you, Parsons. That will do." Brock looked into the mirror at his reflection. His cravat was tied perfectly and his Hessians shone in the dim light of his dressing room. After years as a soldier, he'd become accustomed to never seeing his reflection. He'd been satisfied with the lack of looking glasses available in the soldier encampment, because it gave him ten years without staring into his mother's eyes . . . his eyes. He did not have to see his dark-chocolate wavy hair, also the mirror image of his deceased mother.

And in turn, if Brock was away from home he didn't have to see the hurt, the sorrow and pain, in his father's eyes every time he looked at his eldest son. Brock's parents had been a love match between two members of the *ton*, both from excellent lineage. He often wondered what the outcome would have been if both his parents hadn't been born to wealthy, powerful families. Would his mother have forsaken her wealth and privilege to live a meager existence with his father?

Or would his father have married his mother is she'd been a lowly maid? In Brock's dreams, they would have been together no matter the circumstances of their birth.

"Brock?" Harold called from his bedchamber. "Are you ready to get this infernal evening underway?"

"Infernal evening?" Brock exited his dressing room to find Harold lounging before the fireplace in his chambers. "You seemed to enjoy yourself last evening."

"I enjoy being anywhere my father is not, but these clothes are confining." Harold stood and pulled at his artfully tied cravat. "And look at this cane! Of all the absurd things. What man would willingly carry this thing around when they can walk perfectly without assistance?"

"Ha! You have spent too much time among the common folk in Kent." Brock moved to the sideboard and poured himself a healthy tumbler of scotch. "Pick your poison," he said.

"Do not get me started on my aversion to spirits!" Harold threw himself back into his seat as if he were a child of five refusing to go to bed. "I positively do not understand the allure of getting utterly sloshed each evening and losing a fortune at a card table."

"I do believe you'd make a wonderful wife, my friend. Would you like a nice glass of sherry to start your evening?" Brock barked with laughter. He'd not tease his friend thus in the company of others, but when it was just the two of them, Brock enjoyed tormenting the man.

"Sherry I can handle. Sweet and light. Everything that scotch and whiskey are not." Harold sat forward expectantly.

"It is unfortunate for you that I would not stock sherry in my private quarters. Shall we be off?" Brock asked, then gulped down his tumbler of scotch.

"If you wish." Harold rose and followed Brock out of the chambers and down the stairs.

When they gained entrance to the main foyer, Buttons was ready with their overcoats. "My lord, your carriage waits."

"Marvelous." It was time he got his priorities in line: wife, estate, family. Would there be room for vengeance once his home and stables were full once more? The never-ending drive to see justice done hadn't ebbed since his return, but he needed to focus on moving his life forward, regardless of whether that meant never seeing the past righted. "Please inform Parsons not to wait up for me. I sense the evening will be a late one." Brock slipped into his coat and winked at Harold, who dragged his cane behind him. The night air was punctuated only by the thump of the cane as it hit each step.

# # #

Though the evening was growing late, Vi remained behind her desk at Foldger's Foals. She'd hoped things with the business would change, perhaps even improve as fast as they'd declined. Alas, her financial situation had taken another turn for the worst. She smoothed her hand across the day's post that had arrived shortly before the evening feeding. Now resting on the cool surface of her desk, the two letters held completely different messages, but both signaled doom.

She dashed a wayward tear that had escaped without her notice. Tattersalls had written to void their longstanding agreement with Foldger's Foals. The letter, written in a man's heavy hand, stated they wished to seek out "more affordable foals" closer to London.

She pushed the paper out of her sight, uncovering the second letter—this from her father, begging her to reconsider her decision to stay in the country.

Her head dipped to her hands, propped on the desk. Helplessness coursed through her. Before being shunned by the *ton,* she never remembered feeling like she'd been set adrift at sea, unable to swim and with neither a paddle nor life-saving device.

With the way things were progressing, she'd have no other alternative but to travel to London or stay completely idle at her father's country estate. Neither option suited her in the least.

Foldger's Foals had been the premier breeding ranch for almost as long as she'd been in business. Ironic, but she'd never viewed the *ton* fickle in their opinions when it came to business. Now, it seemed that many had decided to buy elsewhere with little or no explanation. It should not wound her so, but she felt abandoned all over again. As if she was being shunned for a second time.

Enough!

She straightened in her seat and squared her shoulders. "I will not fail," she uttered to the empty room. She, with the help of Connor, would discover the reason for the decline in clients and set things to right. She had no other options available to her.

An image of Lord Haversham flitted through her mind: His strong arms, his deep laugh, his smile. Had she ever seen him smile or did she only dream of it, a gleam lighting his eyes? Had he thought of her after he left? Most assuredly not. He was now a man about town. No doubt he was currently waltzing at a grand ball dressed in London's finest.

She sighed and collected the letter she'd shoved across the desk in her moment of weakness. *Tomorrow*, she thought to herself. Tomorrow was a new day, and she would figure out the problems facing Foldger's Foals.

# # #

Brock loathed the idea of telling Harold he'd been correct. So far, the evening had been a tedious affair filled with money-hungry, matchmaking mothers with less-than-suitable, often downright homely daughters. A part of him had assumed he would waltz into a ballroom, pick out a gorgeous young debutante, court her, and marry within the year. Alas, the young women who raised his blood pressure immediately had him running for the hills with their insipid conversations and lack of . . . Well, he was unsure what they lacked, but he was certain something was missing.

More than once, he found himself wondering what Lady Posey would wear to a ball such as this. Would her dance card fill quickly? Did she have the permission of Almack's to waltz? Would she even care to gain the approval of a group of stuffy elderly ladies long past their prime?

"What are you smirking at?"

"Naught of importance." Brock pushed off the wall he'd been leaning against and took the drink Harold held out to him. "How are you faring this evening? Better than myself, I hope."

"I must admit, Lady Garnerdale stocks the most

delicious sherry I've had the pleasure of tasting. Do you think she'd mind if I take a bottle home?"

"We will never know because if you dare ask such a thing you will not make it out of this ball alive." Brock looked into the glass he held. "This isn't sherry, is it?"

"Of course not. Although I will have to keep that in mind next time I play your nurse maid and fetch you a drink."

While he'd been away, Brock had missed the easy companionship he and Harold shared. It still surprised him that they'd been able to rekindle their friendship as if a day hadn't passed since their youth.

"Have you placed your name upon any lucky young woman's dance card?" he asked Harold.

"Come now. After setting sights on you, none will give me the time to even be introduced properly," Harold sighed. "I fear I'm doomed to return to the vicarage and live a solitary life."

"Solitary? I'm sure you'll spend much time tormenting me and my family. I'm sure my children will love their Uncle Harold."

"Your wife as well, no doubt." Harold waggled his eyebrows.

"Ha! I only hope you're wrong on that account. Now, let's meet some young ladies so we are not doomed to spend eternity together, just the two of us."

"Would that be so awful?"

"Unbearably awful, my friend." Brock slapped Harold across the back and his friend's sherry sloshed from his cup and landed on the floor. "You'd better hope our hostess didn't witness that. She is quite particular about her ballroom floor. And where is your cane?"

"I hid it behind the potted plant over yonder. I've tripped on the blasted thing three times this evening—and that was before the band had the opportunity to warm up."

"Make sure you retrieve it before we depart." Brock surveyed the crowded ballroom. Pale-colored dresses swirled to and fro as women adorned in outrageous head pieces moved to the music in the arms of dandified men of the *ton*. Finding a suitably appealing wife would be harder than anticipated. Everywhere he looked he pictured Lady Posey; handing her a sherry, talking to a man of the *ton*, or moving to the strings of a waltz.

"Do not look now, but our hostess is headed our way with a lovely pair of girls in tow," Harold said beside him.

"Let us hope she did not witness your faux pas and is here to throw us out." Brock smiled when Harold paled. "Buck up, Harold. It appears she is about to introduce us to two young eligible women."

"I surely hope they are not both for you," Harold mumbled.

Brock smothered his grin as Lady Garnerdale skidded to a stop in front of them, the two ladies behind her almost running her over. "Lady Garnerdale, this ball is quite the success." He bowed to their hostess, elbowing Harold in the stomach when he failed to follow suit.

"Umph! A pleasure, my lady."

"Lord Haversham! It is an honor to have your attendance at my little party this evening," the matron gushed. "You have been too long gone from polite society."

"Someone had to vanquish the evil Napoleon. Do you not agree?"

"My lord, I would not presume to know anything about the complexities of politics."

"Indeed," Brock replied.

Her eyes rounded at his lack of manners and mention of such a manly topic, but she composed herself quickly. "My lord, may I introduce Miss Gylinanda and Miss Hylinanda Unkers." She motioned to the females cowering behind her. "Where did you two go?" she asked as she swung around to find the girls directly behind her.

"A pleasure, Ladies," Brock answered, looking at the pair for the first time. Twins! And they couldn't be any older than sixteen, barely out of the school room.

Harold snickered beside him at Brock's obvious discomfort.

"And may I introduce the esteemed Mr. Harold Jakeston. He resides at the estate adjoining my own." It wasn't a bald-faced lie. Harold's home was within close proximity to Haversham House; they did not need to know that Brock actually owned the vicarage and the land on which it sat.

"Mr. Jakeston. I was unaware of your relationship with Lord Haversham. Indeed, it is a pleasure to meet a dear friend of my lord." Lady Garnerdale honored Harold with a slight incline of her head and her hand came to the ornate headpiece perched securely upon her upswept hair.

"Lord Haversham. Mr. Jakeston," the twins echoed and dropped into curtsies fit for a king.

"Ladies, what a pleasure. Is it presumptuous of me to request a dance for myself and my friend?"

A shower of giggles erupted from the twins.

Lord help him survive this confounded evening, he thought.

"Lovely young Ladies such as yourselves most likely had your whole dance card spoken for shortly after you arrived," Brock prodded.

Another episode of giggles lit the air. "We do indeed have available dances this evening, my lord," the pale-orange clothed twin replied, her fan covering her mouth.

"Wonderful! Shall we?" he asked as he extended his arm to the twin brave enough to speak, leaving Harold with the girl ensconced in a dress closely resembling the shade of vomit.

"Indeed, this is wonderful," Harold mumbled.

Brock heard the strings of a cotillion strike up and was relieved he'd not be required to engage in chit chat with Miss Gylinanda. Or was he escorting Miss Hylinanda? He was hard pressed to decide if it mattered.

CHAPTER TEN

Brock watched Harold twirl the miss in the putrid dress around the dance floor for a second time that evening. If his friend did not watch himself, come tomorrow morning he'd find himself ensconced in the girl's father's study discussing a marriage settlement. He'd barely had a moment to speak with Harold after their hostess discovered he was endowed with an estate. Lady Garnerdale had led him about the room meeting one debutante after another. Brock could not complain, as this left him to his own devices, the matchmaking mothers seemingly intimidated by the scowl that had cemented itself on his face shortly after dancing with another insipid chit.

"Oh, dear heavens!" Lady Garnerdale called behind him.

If the woman thought to introduce him to another sorry excuse for a lady he would pull his hair out. While he was at it, he might just rip the headpiece currently perched on her head and stomp it beneath his feet.

He turned to stop the woman before she started the next round of introductions, and froze.

The hostess rushed away from him to intercept a man and pair of ladies as they traversed the crowded ballroom in his direction. Brock craned his neck to see around her.

Was that . . . No, it could not be! But was there any other explanation for Lady Garnerdale rushing across the ballroom?

The Duke of Liperton! None other than the father of one Lady Viola Oberbrook.

Brock searched the ballroom for any sign of the girl responsible for his brothers' deaths. Not that he'd a clue what she looked like; he would not be able to pick her out in a morning room over tea, let alone a crowded ballroom.

Bringing his eyes back to his hostess, Brock watched as Lord Liperton fled, leaving his two female companions behind. The man did not even pause to retrieve his overcoat as he exited the ballroom and possibly the house entirely.

"Was that Lord Liperton?" Harold asked from his side.

"It most certainly appeared to be."

"Do you suppose he saw you?"

"I do not think he would beat such a hasty retreat if he had not." Brock looked over at his friend and then at the dance floor. "What happened to your dance partner?"

"She split a seam and also beat a hasty retreat," Harold said. His monotone voice and flippant hand gestures made the announcement sound as if his friend encountered this issue often.

Brock was tempted to laugh, but feared it would sound the delusional crackle of a deranged man. His hands shook and his heart beat erratically over his near-encounter with Lord Liperton.

"Do you think they might have rushed off to the same place?" Harold asked.

"Do you mean the ladies retiring room?"

"I suppose not."

"I think I am going to go after him. We have not had the pleasure of meeting or discussing his daughter's hand in my family's misfortune." Brock made to move toward the direction the Duke had fled, but Harold grabbed his arm.

"Is that truly wise?" Harold raised an eyebrow, and his grip on Brock's arm tightened. "Put it behind you."

"Put it behind me?" Brock felt the words echo between them. He couldn't expect Harold to understand the loss of a brother—both of his lived and breathed. He couldn't expect him to know the guilt, the emotional anguish, of returning from war to find one's father dead. Not only emotionally dead, as he'd been after his mother's death, but cold and in the ground.

Brock had expected to return home to make amends for abandoning his father while the old man dealt with the loss of his beloved wife. Then, he'd failed to return to lay his brothers to rest, further compounding his overwhelming guilt and grief.

Brock took a breath. He could not fault his friend for his inability to grasp the pain he'd held inside for far too long. "Yes, you may be correct, my friend," he said. He gave the only answer Harold could understand—the answer indicating that Brock was willing to try and move past the weight lying heavily upon his shoulders.

"Besides, our esteemed Lady Garnerdale is making her way toward us now."

Indeed, the woman was headed their way. He shook off Harold's hold.

"Well, well, well. These women are certainly out of the school room," Harold commented, his attention directed to two matronly women presently accompanying their hostess. "Wait—"

"What is it now?" Brock asked.

"That is our neighbor, Mrs. Pearl St. Augustin— Miss Ruby's mother. Imagine the coincidence. We see her daughter in Hampshire, and now Mrs. St. Augustin in London—"

"Will you pipe down?"

Harold had the nerve to look affronted.

"Who is the older woman with her?"

"Am I able to talk now?"

"If you get to the point," Brock said.

"I do not have a clue."

For the first time in their long friendship, Brock wanted to strangle his friend. "We should prepare to find out, because they are almost upon us."

"My lord." His hostess curtsied, her headpiece nearly disengaging from her head. "May I introduce Lady Evienne Darlingiver?"

"My lady." He bowed over her extended hand. This was something he did not miss about polite society: all the bowing and formalities. "A pleasure."

"My lord," Lady Darlingiver gave the appropriate response.

"And this, Lord Haversham," the hostess continued, "is Mrs. St. Augustin. I hear you are already acquainted."

"It has been many years, Mrs. St. Augustin." Brock bowed while she dropped into a curtsey. "Our country seats are close."

"That is marvelous, my lord." Lady Garnerdale noticed Harold standing to Brock's left. "Oh, Mr. Jakeston, are you also acquainted with Mrs. St. Augustin? Your estate must also be—"

"Indeed," Brock cut her off before Harold's story was compromised. "We grew up frolicking in the pastures between our family homes." He looked to Mrs. St. Augustin in hopes she would not let slip the fact that Harold's family was employed by the current Lord Haversham, as had been the past three generations of Jakestons.

"In that time, there were many children gallivanting about the countryside." Mrs. St. Augustin sounded slightly peeved at the fact.

"This is true," Harold spoke up, addressing their hostess. Turning to Mrs. St. Augustin, he said, "We had the pleasure of seeing Miss Ruby not a fortnight ago, at the estate of Lady Posey Hale."

"Lady Posey Hale? You must be mistaken." Mrs. St. Augustin turned a confused look at Lady Darlingiver, who in turn shook her head.

Brock felt that a whole conversation passed between the ladies that neither he nor Harold was privy to. Strange. "I assure you, it was indeed her," he assured them.

"Oh, Lady Danderland!" Lady Garnerdale fairly shrieked, startling two ladies in conversation a few feet away. "Do excuse me. I must speak with Lady Danderland."

The group watched as their hostess made her way

across the ballroom in pursuit of a lady who clearly did not wish to be caught.

Brock returned his attention to Mrs. St. Augustin with his most charming smile. "I dare say Miss Ruby is much as I remember her as a child. Do she and Lady Posey have plans to attend part of the season?" He could not help inquiring about Lady Posey.

"I believe not, my lord. Will you excuse us, as well? I fear I am not feeling quite the thing."

The women clasped arms and started away before Brock and Harold could wish them good evening.

"I dare say that was as close to the cut direct as I have ever seen," Brock mumbled. "Harold, I believe it is time you collected your cane."

"Finally. I thought this evening would never end."

"Have them bring the carriage round and I will meet you in front. I am going to retrieve something before we are on our way." Brock eyed the lords and ladies surrounding him in an attempt to locate their host and hostess. Both were occupied with various members of the *ton*.

Brock strolled casually around the ball room, skirting dancers. He passed by the refreshment table and continued on toward the hall beyond the card room. He glanced over his shoulder to make sure no one tracked his movements. As he thought, no one paid attention to him as he crept down the corridor leading not only to the retiring rooms, but also to Lord Garnerdale's study.

When he reached the end of the hall, he turned away from the ladies retiring room door and in the direction of the men's toilet and the study. He kept his pace unhurried when he heard a group of ladies exit the retiring room behind him. When they continued toward the ballroom, Brock increased his speed and entered the door at the end of the hall, closing the door securely behind him.

A musky, thick smell invaded his nose. Peering around the smoke-laden room, Brock searched for anyone lurking in the shadows. Convinced he was indeed alone, he moved to the sideboard and slid open the cabinets below. Bottle after bottle of premium scotch, brandy, and whiskey lined the shelves. He carefully removed several bottles in search of his real goal—a bottle of Madeira for Harold.

"You must have at least one bottle," Brock mumbled. He feared he'd reach the back of the cabinet and not find what he sought. Crouching on his haunches, he pulled out a tall, slender green-tinted bottle and examined the label. "Aha!"

Brock quickly restocked the liquor cabinet. As a last thought, he pilfered a bottle of scotch for himself. It was the least his hostess could do after subjecting both men to the likes of the Unker twins. The door slid back into place on a well-oiled track.

Now, he only needed to exit the study without anyone noticing. He placed his ear against the closed door and listened for voices in the hall. Hearing none, he grasped the door handle and eased the barrier open a crack. The hall was deserted. Brock slipped out, a bottle tucked securely under each arm. If all continued thus, he would be able to traverse the hall and instead of reentering the crowded ball room, he'd slip out the front door to the safety of his awaiting coach.

A smile lit his face at the lark he'd pulled off—not that the Garnerdale's would even notice the absence of two bottles of spirits. Brock looked forward to the surprise on Harold's face when he handed him a premium bottle of imported Madeira.

Moments before he'd made his escape, hurried footsteps sounded from the direction of the ballroom. Brock ducked into the men's retiring room. It was most likely several ladies rushing to the women's room to repair a ripped dress; perhaps Miss Unker's unfortunate incident had repeated itself. At the return to silence in the hall, Brock eased the door open a crack and peeked out.

Two ladies stood in the hall where the corridor from the ballroom ended, their heads leaned together in conversation. Brock couldn't be certain with their backs to him, but the lemon-colored dress appeared to be that of Lady Darlingiver. He assumed that her company was Mrs. St. Augustin.

As Brock strained to hear their conversation, Lord Liperton crept down the corridor and joined the ladies' conversation. What could they possibly be talking about? Meeting in a darkened hall did not bode well for the direction of their chat.

"If I had known he was in town, I would have stayed at Foldger's Hall." Lord Liperton raised his voice enough for his words to reach Brock, his arms gesticulating wildly.

Lord Liperton appeared to calm when Lady Darlingiver laid her hand against his arm. The connection between the pair was apparent, even from a distance.

"What do you mean, he has been to Foldger's Foals?" Liperton took a step back from the ladies. His voice peaked, giving off the impression of a female screech. "I knew I should not have allowed Viola to remain on that ranch. It is bloody—"

Something knotted in Brock's stomach.

"Now, do not get your knickers in a bunch, Lippy." Lady Darlingiver's voice rose to be heard over Liperton's increasingly alarming tone.

If they thought Brock cared that he had seen Miss Ruby residing in the country, they were wrong. He'd hardly given the miss a second thought. Now, Lady Posey was a completely different story.

"Why ever not? This is possibly the worst thing that could happen."

"She did not give her real name." It was Mrs. St. Augustin's turn to soothe Lord Liperton.

"Thank the heavens the girl holds a bit of sense inside that head of hers."

Brock stilled himself from barging into the corridor to confront the trio, demanding answers. It wasn't true; it couldn't be. He had kissed her, enjoyed bantering with her... Dreamed about her!

"It has been eight years, Lippy. Surely he has dealt with the tragedy and moved on. There is no reason we should fear he suspects anything." Lady Darlingiver stepped closer to Liperton once again. "We had a lovely chat."

Brock couldn't listen to another word, but kept his ear pressed firmly to the door, not wanting to miss a single syllable.

"He did not mention me?" Lord Liperton asked.

"No. Now, let us enjoy our evening. Pearl watched Mr. Jakeston leave several minutes ago, and I am sure Lord Haversham was close behind him."

Brock peered through the slit in the door.

Lady Darlingiver offered her arm to Liperton.

"Shall we return to the ballroom? I would so enjoy a glass of sherry before we continue on to Lady Estque's ball." It was hard to miss the woman's smile in the dim hall; her teeth gleamed, catching the pale light from the candles lining the walls.

Brock slipped out of the deserted men's room after their steps receded down the long hall. His mind was abuzz with conflicting thoughts. All he sought was to escape this house, and slip into the safety of his awaiting carriage. With his stolen bottles of spirits again clutched under his arm, he fled down the hall, not bothered with his seemingly hurried pace and what that appearance gave off to others. His steps echoed off the walls, deafening to his own ears.

The woman had deceived him. Deliberately and without remorse. Lady Posey! He wanted to laugh out loud at his own stupidity. Cry at the girl's ability to hurt him, even after all these years. Lady Viola Oberbrook had misled his family again; thankfully, she'd dared to fool him and not his weak-minded brothers or elderly father. The fact hit home—there was no one else for her to fool. Only him alone, and she had succeeded marvelously.

She'd drawn him in with her charm. Lied to his face. Taken his coin. Kissed him shamelessly in the pasture. Since that day, it was almost all he could think about. She'd given him hope for a future, full of love and companionship, maybe not with her but with someone. For the first time since his mother's death, he'd truly thought a life of happiness was within his grasp.

Now, that dream had been dashed to the ground.

As he approached the end of the hall, Brock forced

himself to slow a bit to allow the footman to assist him into his evening coat, though his blood boiled just under the surface. If the scarlet-clad footman noticed Brock juggling the pilfered bottles of Madeira and scotch, he did not comment. He was overheated, certain his face was the color of the Garnerdale's livery attire.

The cool evening air as he left the house soothed his raging mood. It helped that his carriage indeed waited outside. Brock looked around, but Harold was nowhere to be found. He hoped the man waited inside; otherwise, he may well be left behind.

"Simeon," Brock nodded to his own livery man.

"My lord, I trust you have had a pleasant evening." The man nodded in return. "Where to next?"

"Home," Brock commanded. His voice rang harsh above the noise of departing guests. His evening out may be ending, but he had many plans still to make this night.

CHAPTER ELEVEN

The dust flew from Sage's hooves and sweat dripped from his mane. Still, Brock pushed him harder, toward the woman capable of fooling every male member of his family. Toward a confrontation he was not sure he was prepared for—could ever prepare for. He'd never planned to face the woman responsible for all that had gone wrong in his family.

Never had he dreamed he would also fall for her charms.

Upon arriving home, he and Harold had indulged in their stolen spirits and Brock had hatched the plan to confront the woman. He would demand answers—answers his father had never gotten. Against his better judgment—and Harold's drunken protests—Brock had ordered his steed brought round at the first sign of daylight.

As soon as it came, he'd ridden hell bent in the direction of Hampshire. He barely noticed the rain pelting him as he ducked low over Sage's neck.

He crested the final hill and the lane came into view. His blood pumped through his veins and his teeth clenched in determination.

How *dare* she! She'd made his family into fools time and time again. He would not let her get away with it once more. She may have tricked him at first, but no more. He was not, and never had been, a fool. He'd partly blamed his twin brothers for being dolts and allowing a woman to pit them against each other. He pushed the notion from his mind that she'd also had him pining away this past fortnight, dreaming of taking her lips to his own in the pasture... Comparing the ladies he'd met in London to her.

The ironic part was that he still thought of her as Lady Posey Hale.

Sage turned on the empty lane and Brock dug his heels in to spur the horse forward once more. The pasture and grazing patch were deserted of both horse and man due to the chilly rain pounding the earth. Water had begun to pool on the rutted lane and he slowed his horse's pace, afraid of the beast turning an ankle. It was unacceptable to injure Sage in his recklessness and haste.

The stable and office came into view. The windows were shuttered against the cold and the doors to the stables had been pulled shut. The place appeared abandoned.

He pulled Sage to a stop and the horse's feet slid on the muddy ground. Brock vaulted from the saddle, landing in a puddle of mud that sprayed his Hessians.

No stable boy came to take Sage's reins. Brock flipped them across his saddle, certain the horse was too exhausted to go far.

For a moment, he wondered what he'd expected to find here: A bustling yard, horses prepared to journey to their new homes? Or possibly Lady Viola awaiting his arrival, an apology at the ready? He'd found none of that—quite the opposite. The place still appeared well maintained, but void of any activity. The neighing of foals couldn't even be heard in the distant pasture.

The emptiness, loneliness, and barrenness of the space overtook him. Suddenly, reality struck. What did he think he'd accomplish with his hell-bent ride to the country?

He forced himself to continue. No matter that what he'd found here was the same seclusion, the same desolation, he'd experienced since his return. He was here for a reason. Brock focused his attention on the office door and the woman he was certain sat behind it.

He threw the door open wide and barged into the room. An empty room, as it turned out, void of any living thing. It looked the same as when he was last here: ornate desk and luxuriously adorned paintings and chairs.

Somehow, it felt different.

Now, he knew that it housed the play business of a selfish, petty girl, not the confident and in-control woman he'd believed Lady Posey to be.

On the desk, he spotted two open letters. He only hesitated a moment before invading her privacy. She did not deserve such luxuries. He grasped the two envelopes and ripped them from the desk. One was addressed to Foldger's Foals, from Tattersalls in London. He threw that one aside, not interested in her business dealings.

The second letter also came from a London address. Lady Viola may not reside in London, but she was obviously still very involved in the social scene she had so enjoyed as a young debutante. The return address listed Dover Street, a very fashionable part of town. Was the letter from an old lover? Or perhaps a current one?

Unable to help himself, he slipped the letter from the envelope. He unfolded the crisp, cream parchment and began to read.

My Dearest Viola,

I hope this letter finds you in good health. I grow weary of your absence here in London. I miss you more than words can express. I understand your hesitancy to return to polite society, but with myself at your side you will not fail. I love you and miss your ever-delightful disposition. I beg you—

From there, the letter had become unreadable. Large drops of liquid had landed upon the parchment and the ink bled into undecipherable smudges.

He stilled himself from ripping the page and burning the pieces.

He'd held out hope that the woman had changed, that he would confront her and he would be shown her new nature, but it appeared that she still lead men on, raised their hopes only to dash them in the end. A part of him felt sorry for the poor bastard awaiting her presence in London with such hope and love. Brock moved around the desk and searched the drawers for a piece of paper and a nub with which to write. Hastily, he wrote down the return address. If the opportunity arose, he planned to warn the man. Maybe save him the heartbreak Brock himself had borne these last eight years, and rehashed the night before.

Lady Viola deserved no man's love or acceptance. She was as deceptive and manipulative as she'd ever been. He re-folded the letter and shoved it back in its envelope, placing it under the letter from Tattersalls. Then, he turned to search the grounds for her.

The door to the office shut against the rain, he checked on Sage and then headed for the stable door. He grasped the handle and slid the door open enough to squeeze in. Just because he took offense at their mistress, he would not be responsible for any young foal falling ill due to exposure.

The interior of the stables was dim due to lack of the sunlight that had shone through the open windows on his previous visits. A fresh pile of manure stood recently raked in a corner, and new straw lined the stalls.

Brock pulled open the nearest stall. The water bucket appeared recently filled, and the feed bucket held a small amount of uneaten oats.

Where was the young, crippled boy who manned the stables?

He closed the stall door, making sure to securely latch the lock, and left through the back door, toward the training pasture. The rain had let up since he'd been in the stables. Now, a light fog had settled across the vast fields beyond. From his vantage point, the property stood deserted.

He knew her father's estate was close. Had it been a few hours earlier, before the effects of his drunken night had worn off, he would have knocked on every door within a five-mile radius in search of Lady Viola's deceitful hide.

His rage ebbed as he continued his search of Foldger's Foals. Without a soul to take his anger out on, his temper cooled. Why had he traveled all this distance to confront her? He was not the man to rave, scream, or belittle a person, no matter how much said person deserved the put down—and Lady Viola deserved the put down of a lifetime.

With one last peek into Lady Viola's office, Brock recognized that the time had come to depart. He returned to Sage and swung up into the saddle, the damp leather soaking his riding pants through. The journey back to London would be less hurried, giving him ample time to consider his options. There was one thing he knew for certain: This was in no way over. There must be retribution for his family's suffering.

# # #

She was tired of the pitying glances the servants turned in her direction. The *tsk, tsk* from Cook. The sorrowful expression on her maid's face. Viola'd had to depart her father's estate, no matter how dreadful the weather was. She had been willing to ruin a good pair of shoes in the many mud puddles along her trail from the estate to Foldger's Foals.

Did she think she could keep the financial failings of her business from the people she saw every day? Cook's son had had to look for work at the local tavern, because Vi could not continue to pay his salary and afford him a place to live. Her maid had lost her latest love interest when the cook's son had departed the day before, fearing he would return to his drinking and womanizing ways.

The worst part had been seeing Alexander off to London that very morning, escorted by Connor. The boy had pleaded with Vi not to send him away, to give him another chance. He'd done everything short of crying to convince her to change her mind. They hadn't completed his lessons, he'd said. No lord would want a cripple working for him, he'd argued.

The anguish in his words nearly brought her to tears.

But he didn't realize that she was sending him to London for his chance at a better life. His new employer, Lord Drake, was a fair man who had no reputation for mistreating his staff. She knew his stables were topnotch, since the man had purchased most of his stock from her.

Vi never wanted to see Alexander go, for fear the world would treat him poorly, but go he must. He must forge his own life and destiny; carve a path for himself. She wanted more for him than what she had. A life in the country was something she'd resigned herself to, but Alexander should have more: The chance to meet and marry a woman he loved; the chance to have a family.

The only thing she took comfort in was knowing he would work in a respectable home not far from her father's townhouse on Dover Street. Alexander had left knowing that if any trouble arose, if he was ever mistreated, he could seek shelter at the townhouse of Lord Liperton.

Shortly after luncheon, Vi donned her warmest dress, complete with a lavender shawl to keep the rain from soaking her clear to the skin, and she'd escaped. She made her way through the vine-covered gate separating the two properties and hopped over another puddle.

The sound of hooves in the distance caught her attention. Viola watched as a lone horseman rode down the lane, beyond shouting distance. Had she missed a potential client? That was impossible. The last appointment of the season had passed the day before without anyone showing up. She thought about running after the retreating figure, waving her shawl to get the man's attention, but what good would it do? Foldger's Foals was officially a failure. All that was left was to tell her father.

Now, she not only had many people depending on her in London, but also a dozen young foals she needed to feed, with zero income with which to do it. The oats and hay would disappear with no money to purchase more.

Connor believed he could find buyers for the remaining foals during his trip to London. It was advantageous that the trip be used for not only settling Alexander into his new employment, but also might earn enough to keep her business from complete ruin—or so Connor said. In truth, she knew she could not employee Connor for much longer. Did he sense this himself? Viola was unsure if the man had anywhere else to go. A part of her hoped he looked into other employment while in town.

Viola resolved to write her father about him. The Duke of Liperton held many friends in London, and maybe one was in need of a loyal man of business.

Large, cold raindrops splattered her face, shaking her from where she stood, watching the man ride into the distance. If she did not seek shelter, she would catch her death of cold.

No, hailing the retreating horse man would solve nothing.

CHAPTER TWELVE

Brock reclined in the overstuffed chair and gazed at the fire before him. The flames licked at the dry log and reflected off the wall behind him. He'd arrived in London only an hour before and, after trading his drenched clothes for proper evening attire, he had rushed out of his townhouse to avoid Harold. The last thing he needed at the moment was his friend's level-headed study of the situation.

Not fit for societal interactions, Brock had made his way to White's, where he currently sat with a bottle of scotch in one hand and bourbon in the other. He'd waved away the man who offered him a crystal tumbler. He preferred his liquor straight from the bottle in situations such as this. Although, he could not remember being in such a situation before. In fact, the last time he'd imbibed this quantity of alcohol, he'd been mourning the loss of his twin brothers.

Strange how such things tended to come full circle.

He took a large swig of scotch; the amber liquid

burned a path down his throat. He'd obviously not consumed the proper amount if it still burned going down.

The entire ride back to London, his thoughts had been absorbed with the need to understand how Lady Viola had hidden her identity from him—and from society as a whole. He'd conferred with several business men before seeking out Foldger's Foals. No one had linked the shunned Lady Viola Oberbrook to the operation. The woman had probably deceived the good people of England for the last eight years. Could he let it continue?

Images of the woman singing softly to the young foal after a hard training session invaded his mind, unbidden. At the memory, he again recalled his mother lulling him to sleep as a child. How he wished this woman had not turned out to be the only one he could never be with, let alone stand to be in the same room as.

He sighed.

The sweet girl his foal seemed to adore was indeed the cold-hearted wretch responsible for his family's demise. How could they be one and the same? Alas, the love letter he discovered on her desk proved she'd not changed.

"Ah, dear cousin. Lord Hurst was indeed correct," Rodney spoke behind him.

"Leave me be, Rodney," Brock called over his shoulder. "I find myself not in the mood to spar with you this evening." He continued to stare blindly into the flames of the fire.

"Spar with me?" Rodney sounded affronted. "I only seek to find what has sent my dear cousin so far into his cups."

"That," he said, lifting his cup in mock salute, "is none of your business. I bid you good night."

"I ventured by your townhouse today and was shocked to learn you had departed London on course to Foldger's Foals once again. Has a certain young lady caught your eye?" Rodney laughed and moved around the chair Brock lounged in, taking the seat next to it.

He straightened in his seat and focused on his cousin. "You knew?"

A deep laugh issued from Rodney.

Brock threw one of the half-drunken bottles. It narrowly missed Rodney's head, smashing against the wall behind him. "You bloody son of a bitch!"

"And you call yourself a man of war with that aim? Tsk, tsk," Rodney said, eerily calm in the face of his cousin's fury.

"I will ask you one last time. Did you know the woman we met with was Lady Viola Oberbrook?" Brock held his cousin's stare. He may no longer wear the uniform of a man of war, but he certainly would kick Rodney's arse from here all the way to the continent and back again if he continued this charade.

"Does it truly matter if I knew?"

"Cousin, you walk a thin line." Brock tightened his grip on the remaining bottle, not wanting to waste more alcohol when he would probably again miss his mark. "Of course it matters. That woman is responsible for the deaths of my brothers and your supposed best friends! Did you even mourn their loss, or did you only see it as bringing you two steps closer to my title?"

Rodney signaled a servant for a tumbler of brandy.

Brock waited until the servant had left them before he continued, not seeing the need to lay out his family drama before the prying ears of the help. "Answer me." His whispered command echoed through the room.

"You demand an answer from me?" Rodney tilted the tumbler to his mouth. "I was here. It was I who helped your father bury Winston and Cody, my *best* friends. It was I who watched your father's slow decline in health. His heart broke a bit more each day. And all while you frolicked with your soldier gents."

"There was nothing enjoyable about my time serving His Majesty. There was death and sorrow and depression where I was, as well." Brock forced himself to relax into his seat when two gentlemen sat in a pair of chairs across the room.

"Be that as it may, I was here and you were not." The glass returned to Rodney's lips as he drained the amber liquid.

"When did you know it was her?" Brock asked again.

"The second I laid eyes on her."

"And you did not tell me. Which makes me wonder why that is." Brock had imbibed such an enormous amount he was unable to keep his inner thoughts to himself. Verily, it was long past time he made his way home.

"What I would entertain knowing is how exactly you discovered who she truly is."

"I do not doubt you would like to know this." Brock pushed himself from the chair and stood. His legs lacked stability. "Unfortunately, I do not have the time or energy to waste here with the likes of you."

Brock grabbed his cane from where it leaned against the table at his side, and made for the exit.

"Dear cousin, one question before you depart."

He turned to face Rodney. "Of course."

"Whatever are you doing in London after you and Harold worked so diligently to repair the stables and stock new foals?"

"That is a question I *do* have time to answer." Brock grinned. "I am here to obtain a wife, so that the eventuality never occurs that you inherit my title." He laughed bitterly as he departed the room. The urge to peek over his shoulder to see Rodney's reaction was great, but it was an urge he would rather die than indulge in.

# # #

The sound of water being dumped from buckets woke Brock. He laid face down in his bed, his quilt covering his fully clothed form. Rolling over, he opened his eyes to light streaming in from nearly every window in the room. His head protested and his pulse beat strongly behind his eye sockets. To relieve the extreme heat that had settled on his body, he pushed the covers off to see his boots still laced tight. What the bloody hell had he done last night?

"I see you are awake," Harold said.

Brock moved his head in the direction of Harold's voice. His friend lounged against the door frame to Brock's dressing room.

"What in the blazes happened last night?" Brock asked.

"No one knows for certain, but Cook found you asleep on the front stoop when she left for the market before dawn." Harold raised an eyebrow. "I had hoped you could tell *us* what happened."

"I arrived back from Foldger's Foals and decided

to have a drink at White's." A bottle or two was more like it.

"And . . . ?"

"I imbibed quite a large quantity of scotch—"

"I gathered that from the smell of you."

"Rodney showed up and we argued—"

"Naturally," Harold interrupted again. "Kindly skip to the part about sleeping on the front stoop."

"I left White's . . . but that is the last I remember." Brock rubbed his aching forehead and rose to sit. "How did I get to my chambers?"

"Your valet and I carried you, of course."

"Why am I still wearing my boots?" Brock threw his legs over the side of the bed and placed his booted feet on the floor.

"We are not *that* good of friends." Harold laughed. "Now get up. Your bath is ready."

In the corner farthest from Harold stood Brock's copper bathing tub, filled to the brim with steaming water. "You will not remove my boots, but drawing my bath is within our friendship?" It was Brock's turn to raise a brow. He stood and removed his evening coat.

"Ha! If it had been up to me, I would have doused you where you slept. Are you ready to tell me what transpired that had you rushing to Foldger's Foals yesterday and then returning only to drink yourself into oblivion?"

"She duped me."

"Who duped you?" Harold moved from the doorway to sit on the bench at the end of Brock's bed.

Brock pulled his shirt over his head and started next on removing his boots and pants. "Lady Viola Oberbrook," he said as he leaned over to untie his laces and simultaneously hide his heated face.

"Lady Viola duped many people, but that is behind you. You must forget about her and move on with your life. Dwelling on her and her actions will not bring back your father or the twins."

Brock straightened and slid his feet from his boots. "No—the woman is still engaging in foolish behavior. She is simply doing it now under the name of Lady Posey Hale."

"You jest," Harold said in disbelief.

"I assure you, I am quite certain they are one and the same person." Brock pushed his pants down over his hips and let them drop to the floor.

"Bloody hell." Harold averted his gaze a second too late.

"Bloody hell is correct. As I pilfered your bottle of Madeira at the Garnerdale's ball, I overheard Lord Liperton speaking with Mrs. St. Augustin and Lady Darlingiver." Brock paused and looked at Harold as he stepped into his tub. "You are aware that Liperton and Lady Darlingiver have been romantically linked for several years?"

"On the contrary, I was unaware of this." Harold kept his eyes averted.

"Indeed they are. She called him Lippy! Can you imagine?"

"You are straying from the topic. What sent you hell bent toward Hampshire and then into your cups, culminating in you forgetting how to open a door?"

"I am getting there!" Brock submerged himself in the steaming water. "Do quiet down, my head feels as if a trumpet master has been playing all night long."

"And whose fault is that?" Harold asked, again

training his gaze on his friend. "You know I have little sympathy for—"

"I was leaving Lord Garnerdale's study," Brock continued, cutting him off, "with a bottle of Madeira under one arm and scotch under the other, when I heard hurried footsteps and then hushed conversation in the hall. Liperton had not fled the house as I'd thought, but merely hidden, proving the coward I believed him to be."

Harold waved his hand and Brock continued.

"As it should happen our dear playmate, Miss Ruby, has been the companion to one Lady Viola Oberbrook, daughter of the Duke of Liperton these last seven years at Foldger's Hall. Did I mention that Foldger's Hall abuts to Foldger's Foals?" Brock asked.

"Just as your estate borders mine?" Harold crossed his arms over his chest.

"Are you comparing that woman's lies and deceit to my attempts to rescue you from your father's clutches?" Brock glared at his friend as he rubbed a sponge thick with suds over his chest.

"Not in the least. I do find it ironic, however. So tell me, did you rush to Hampshire and put Lady Viola in her place? Did you shout at her? Did she apologize for leading your brothers on a merry goose chase?"

Brock wished any of those things had occurred. "She was not there," he mumbled, in hopes Harold wouldn't jump on the opportunity to question his decision to seek her out.

"Not there, you say? And naturally you rush back to London to drink so much you cannot make it through your front door. I understand now."

His friend's judgmental tone grated on Brock's

nerves.

"What do you plan to do now?" Harold stood and made his way back to the door. "Let us hope that no one saw the aftermath of your heavy drinking. I do not care how much you have in your coffers, marrying a drunkard is not the path most respectable fathers would willingly send their daughters down."

"Point taken."

"I will await you downstairs in the breakfast room." Harold closed the door quietly behind him.

As annoying as Brock might find it at the moment, his friend was correct: What was his plan? He only wished he knew. He'd acted out of anger and hurt when he'd rushed to the country, and then again at White's. If that affected Harold's chances of gaining a respectable bride, Brock would not forgive himself.

Regardless, he could not let Lady Viola get away with what she'd done.

Brock massaged the sandalwood-scented sponge up his arm and over his shoulder as he contemplated his next move. A part of him wanted to return to his estate and put his thoughts of finding a wife and seeking retribution for his family behind him. So many people he'd encountered since his return had thought his brothers' deaths *were* behind him.

If Harold had the slightest idea how this weighed on him, his friend would likely bash him over the head and keep him locked down at his estate until sensible thought returned.

The key to the return of his sanity lay in the acknowledgement of fault by only one person: Lady Viola Oberbrook.

For the first time since his return, Brock thanked

the Lord above that he hadn't come face to face with Lady Viola.

The element of surprise was still in his favor.

CHAPTER THIRTEEN

The life of an idle lady of the *ton*, ensconced at her country estate, grated on Viola's nerves. More than once, she found herself longing to throw her needlepoint at the wall.

The walls! Yet another thing she could not stomach. Who in their right sensibilities selected salmon for the color of their walls? The sitting room desperately needed renovation, but she'd spent so many years at Foldger's Foals that she had not bothered with her father's outdated estate.

With time on her hands, she found herself falling into previously enjoyed pastimes. The desire to renovate rooms, redress her father's staff, and modernize Ruby's wardrobe were strong. But that was not her any longer. She had changed. She was no longer the debutante of the season, to be doted upon by all things breathing . . . No, she was the aging daughter of a duke.

She sighed.

"Whatever is the problem now, Vi?" Ruby asked

from her seat on the far side of the table where they had laid their thread colors.

"If I must look at these walls for one more second, I fear my stomach will relieve itself of the delicious sandwiches we had at morning tea."

"Would you prefer we move outside?"

"Outside, my chambers, the kitchen . . . They are all the same." Vi threw her needlework to the table and slumped into the sofa.

"Sit up straight. You will wrinkle your dress, and you know how Sarah abhors ironing them out."

"Is it really vital that I sit up straight?" Vi took her bad mood out on her friend. "To be honest, I may start ironing my own wardrobe. Goodness, I do have the time." She'd been in a foul mood for days now, but she knew that punishing Ruby with her disagreeableness would not help.

Ruby ignored Vi's outburst and continued with her needlework.

"I am sorry. I do not know what has come over me these last few days," Vi said.

"Do you think I do not know what your problem is?" Ruby finally set her work aside and met Vi's gaze. "Are you so delusional or oblivious that you cannot see?" Before she could speak, Ruby continued, "You are no longer the type of female to sit idly by and let the days pass. You refuse to go to London as your father requests, but have nothing to occupy your time here."

To her chagrin, Vi recognized that everything Ruby said was true.

"And you refuse to release Connor of his duties, so the few things to attend to with the foals, he is handling. If you want my opinion—"

"I'm not sure I do," Viola said. She had not seen Ruby this agitated, ever.

"Oh, but you will have it." Ruby stood from where she perched on the edge of the sofa, her hands on her hips. "You need to get your arse out of this house. You have never been one to give up. Why now?"

"I have tried—"

"Truly? Are you sure you've put one-hundred percent into making Foldger's Foals successful?"

Vi nodded. "I have spent countless nights thinking of all our options."

"That is my point! You have spent time *thinking* about the problems, but what have you actually done?"

Viola didn't understand the passion flowing from her friend. Ruby would have a place here with her regardless of the state of Vi's business.

"Maybe it is time you journey to London—"

"I am in no need of a husband," Viola fairly shouted.

Ruby leaned over the table, her finger jabbing the air in front of Vi. "Why are you so petrified of attracting a husband? There are more than marriage-seeking men out there. There are business men. Stop and think about the benefits of a trip to town."

If Vi was of the opposite sex, she would have let forth an explicit phrase—or two. Ruby was right. She hadn't thought of a trip to London to further her business. "While I see your point, how could I sneak into London without alerting my father?"

"Now, that is something you should be thinking about." Ruby regained her seat and her composure, picked up her needlepoint, and returned to her work.

How was it possible for the woman to be up in

arms one minute and quietly working the next? How she envied her friend's acceptance of her lot in life.

"Come in," Ruby called without lifting her head.

Viola hadn't heard the tap on the door.

"My lady." Sarah entered the room. "This came in the post today and Mr. Cale requested I bring it to you posthaste."

"Thank you." Vi took the missive. Lord help her if it was another letter from her father imploring her to come to London.

"Who is it from?" Ruby didn't bother looking up.

Viola turned the letter over in her hands. "It is from a London address I do not recognize." Hanover Square. . . . She racked her brain for an acquaintance or old friend who lived in that area of town, but came up with none.

"Well, open it!" Ruby set her work aside and stared at Vi expectantly.

"It is not every day we receive unsolicited letters from London. Maybe it is a new client."

The front of the envelope had been addressed to Lady Posey Hale. Her stomach sank, and she feared her luncheon would indeed make another appearance.

"Why the look of doom and gloom?"

"It is from Lord Haversham, addressed to Lady Posey Hale."

"I knew we hadn't seen the last of Brock. He was rather smitten with you."

Vi looked up, wishing she could forget about the letter. "Smitten? What do you know of smitten?"

"Not much as it applies to myself, but I did grow up with Brock and his siblings—" Ruby managed to look contrite when Vi winced at the mention of Cody and Winston. "I do apologize, but I will not coat the situation in sugar to make it more agreeable to you."

Vi waved her hand, signaling Ruby to continue.

"I do despise it when you wave your hand at me like that."

She waved her hand in Ruby's direction again defiantly.

Ruby huffed but continued, "I was going to say that I grew up with Brock, and I remember a time he was smitten with our dairy maid. He took to showing up at our estate and following her about. My mother finally had to send him on his way."

Vi couldn't refute the similarities in the situations. Brock—when had she started thinking about him as Brock and not Lord Haversham?—had arrived early to gather his foals. He'd also followed her out to the pasture and watched her for Lord knew how long. Now, a letter from him. A part of her wanted to squeal like a girl straight out of the schoolroom, but the practical woman knew the letter could hold nothing but bad tidings and disappointment.

Ruby cleared her throat and stared. "Open it."

"Does it matter what the letter holds? All of my dealings with the man have been a ruse, and when he finds out he will hate me more than he already must."

Her dear friend moved to sit beside her and put a comforting arm around her shoulders. "I think it matters greatly to you what this letter holds. Give it to me, and I shall read it." Ruby plucked the letter from Vi's hands and ripped the envelope open.

Vi's hopes of shredding the letter, as if she'd never received it, were dashed as Ruby smoothed the parchment out in front of her.

She watched closely as Ruby's eyes scrunched in confusion, widened in surprise and then a smile spread across her face. "I must read this to you." Delight infused her tone.

"Are you sure it is something I want to hear?"

"Most assuredly, Vi."

Viola wasn't so sure, but was hesitant to say no. "Very well." She rubbed her hands down her olive-colored dress nervously. Why did she make to rub her hands clean every time she had a bout of anxiety?

Ruby cleared her throat and spoke in a deep voice. "*Lady Posey Hale--*"

"Do stop that!"

"Oh, all right. You are quite stiff when your deceit is coming to a head." Ruby paused and started to read again, "*I have come into contact with several men seeking to expand their stables. Your attendance in London is requested to meet with said gentlemen. Please send word of your arrival date.*" Ruby re-folded the letter and replaced it in its envelope.

"That is all?" Vi asked and sat back in her seat. When had she moved to perch on the edge of the sofa? If Ruby had read one more sentence, Vi might have ended up on the floor.

"Did you expect more?" Ruby raised an eyebrow.

"You know exactly what I expect!" The woman was insufferable.

"I am unsure what more you want. That is all he wrote."

"Do not play coy with me. Lest you forget, I perfected the art of coy long ago. How did Bro—Lord Haversham, sign the letter?" Part of her wondered why she cared. The other part knew it would speak volumes.

Ruby took her time extricating the letter from the

envelope once more and smoothed it out. "Well, that is odd. He signed it, 'Sincerely Yours, B'."

Viola's eyes widened.

"I am unsure how to chasten you. Do you prefer Lady Viola or Posey? You do have feelings for him." Ruby grasped Vi's hand, crumpling the letter as their fingers intertwined. "Oh, when do you plan to leave?"

"I will do no such thing . . . I cannot do such a thing!"

"But this is exactly that thing we have been talking about. A way to save Foldger's Foals."

"The cost would be too great."

"What other choice do we have? If you plan to keep Foldger's Foals open and keep your dependent's funded, you must go."

Viola stood. She needed to move to release the pent-up agitation that threatened to cripple her. When she disengaged her hands from Ruby's fingers, Brock's letter stuck between her own. It was true: She needed to keep her business afloat. She had many people depending on her. Then again, she never anticipated returning to London to face the people who had sent her fleeing in her youth. The *ton* didn't believe people could change, as she had. Could she sneak into London, attend the meeting, and leave just as silently? Would she know the gentlemen? There were too many risks involved.

She paced from the sofa to the fireplace and back again before another knock sounded at the door. "Come in," Vi called.

Connor strolled into the room and bowed slightly to Vi and then Ruby. "Ladies. I trust your day is going well."

His tone irked Vi. He sounded almost jovial as she and Ruby debated the fate of Foldger's Foals.

"I have finished the chores on the ranch. Is there anything else you require of me?" Connor asked.

An idea sparked in her mind. Why had she not thought of it before? "As a matter of fact, I do have another assignment for you."

"Anything, my lady."

"I will need you to travel to London and meet with a few potential clients."

"Vi—" Ruby started.

"Of course. I have been eager to return to London and check on Alexander at his new post."

Vi avoided eye contact with Ruby, her disapproval evident from her heavy breathing. "I will need you to leave immediately. Is that a problem?"

"No. I will go prepare." Connor executed another small bow to both women and turned to leave the room.

"Connor?" Vi stopped him and he turned back to face her. "I will need you to drop off an envelope for me while in town."

"My pleasure."

He left the room.

Viola turned to Ruby and knew from the look on her friend's face that they had much to discuss. "What?" Vi asked.

"Why ever would you send Mr. Cale when I know you wish to see Brock?"

"Because I am not willing to risk everything I have attained in the last eight years for the chance to be in a man's presence for a few hours. Need I list all the other reasons I cannot travel to London?" Viola held up her open hand, fingers outstretched, and counted off her reasons. "Number one: I gave him a false name. Number two: Not one person in polite society would entertain my return to town, and number three— Rodney." Vi shut her mouth so quickly she bit her lip.

Ruby's eyes narrowed. "Rodney . . . Mr. Swiftenberg? Whatever does that dandified man have to do with your decision not to meet Brock in London?"

"Did I say Rodney? I meant—"

"You are a terrible liar."

Vi sighed and sank into the chair next to the ornately carved fireplace. Curse Ruby for knowing her so well.

"What are you not telling me?" Ruby asked.

"Just as you know Brock, Harold, and Rodney from your childhood, so do I have a history of sorts with Rodney." She only debated for a moment before deciding to tell Ruby everything. There was no real reason she hadn't told her the day everything happened; there was certainly no point in holding back now. "Rodney was there that day."

"Are we talking about *the* day? You've made it clear you never wish to speak of that day."

It was true, Viola had hoped leaving London and starting a new life would put that dreadful day behind her, but wherever she went, her past was not far behind. She'd spent the last eight years running from what she'd done.

Vi's silence must have encouraged Ruby to continue her line of questioning. "Did he speak with you the day they came here? That is highly improper."

"Yes, we spoke privately, but the only improper thing that occurred was him threatening me to stay away from his cousin."

"He obviously knew you did not seek Brock out, and had no future plans to cultivate your relationship with him." It was Ruby's turn to rise from her seat and pace.

"Well, of course that is what I said. We both know the man will hate me if he ever learns my true name. . . . If I were him I would hate me, as well."

"Tis sad, is it not that, people do not believe in the power of change?"

"Some days I wonder what the point of changing was—except I could not have lived long with myself."

"Do not pity yourself—it's unbecoming. I do hope you put Rodney in his place."

"There was no point in it. I hope to never see that insufferable man again." Viola picked up her needlepoint and set back to work.

Never seeing the man would be too soon, indeed. And she most definitely never planned to see Rodney again, his wrath was not something she'd anticipate experiencing. Connor would do a fine job of representing Foldger's Foals in London, after all, his livelihood depended on the business' success just as much, if not more, than Vi's did.

She'd never truly thought of what Connor would do without his position and salary. Did he have a family home to return to? A savings, even a meager one, to help him get by until he found another position?

Connor must know how important this meeting was to them all.

CHAPTER FOURTEEN

Brock watched as his stable hand put the young foal through its paces, starting with a walk and moving into trot, gallop, and eventually a run. There was barely room in the small grassy area at the back of his London townhouse, but they managed. The transitions were smooth, with nary a hitch. The entire crop of young had exceeded his expectations thus far. How the woman gained such acclaim for her stock, he now knew.

"My lord?"

He turned to see a stable lad, envelope in hand, and head bowed.

"Yes, Charles," Brock said. It had been difficult convincing his staff to be at ease in his presence. He was not a harsh man, which he had learned was a rarity nowadays in society.

"You tol' ye valet to bring you ye post as soon as it got here." The boy held out the envelope.

He'd been expecting a reply from Lady Viola for the last several days. For his plan to be executed, he had to get the insufferable woman to town. "Thank you." Brock broke the seal and removed the letter, written on pale pink parchment.

"Beg'n ye pardon but may I be go'n, my lord?"

"Of course. We would not want the stable master thinking you are tarrying in your duties now, would we?"

Charles straightened in surprise, but when Brock followed his statement with a wink, the boy relaxed and hurried on his way.

Brock returned his attention to the letter in his hand.

As he read, his mood darkened and he couldn't help the explicit phrase that fought its way out. "Bloody, unbearable woman!"

"What has Lady Viola done to anger you now?" Harold asked behind him. "I cannot think over much, as she is not even in the same shire."

"I would not be so sure her person cannot cause my foul mood just because she is hours away." Brock handed the letter to Harold.

"Ah. You are upset because the woman will not rush to London at your beck and call." He looked up at Brock and handed him back the letter. "She may be the cause behind your family tragedy, but she is no fool. She has successfully kept her identity hidden from everyone she does business with, it is not logical for you to expect her to travel here to meet with new clients."

"I am sick of your insight into the human mind." Brock pushed past his friend and headed through the garden, back to the house. Why could things not go as he planned? Life in London was very different from his life as a military man. His men had done what he commanded, in exactly the manner he commanded it done.

Harold hurried after Brock, his footsteps quick to catch up. "What will you do now?"

Brock stopped and Harold almost crashed into him. "Is it not obvious? I have to organize a meeting with potential clients for Mr. Cale to meet with."

"I was unaware you actually have people interested in purchasing foals . . ."

"I do not, but I am fairly certain we can collect a few 'clients.'"

"We?"

"Of course." Brock started for the house again. Again, she'd found a way to elude him. "Mr. Cale should arrive on the morrow. That gives me the next few hours to figure this out," he called over his shoulder.

"I will get my coat and we will be on our way."

"Oh, I do not plan to look farther than my own home." It was not as though he needed to actually find someone willing to spend the money needed to buy foals; Brock only needed to produce a few people who *appeared* willing.

"This should indeed be interesting."

# # #

"My lord, are you positive we are allowed within White's?" Buttons, Brock's butler, spoke for the three men currently ensconced in one of White's private rooms. They all held tumblers with two fingers of scotch apiece and sat perfectly upright.

This was in complete contrast to Brock, who'd downed two tumblers full in short order. How could he have ever thought this would work? His butler, valet, and stable master masquerading as gentlemen of the *ton*. He had been so sure of his scheme on the coach ride from Hanover Square.

Brock eyed his servants and noted their obvious discomfort. "It is quite fine. You are in the company of an earl, who would dare question my choice of companions?" He hoped his voice held conviction, because he was unsure of the protocol when bringing guests into his gentlemen's club. "Do have a drink and relax or we will never pull this off."

"As you wish, my lord," Parsons said.

"And please call me Haversham for the duration of the evening." Brock looked between the three men—his London stable master, Jeffers; Parsons, his valet, and Buttons.

At Brock's insistence, all three men sipped their scotch and nervously eyed their surroundings. He could imagine their awe at being entrenched in the plush and luxurious inner sanctum that was White's. Many men only dreamed of attaining an invitation past the front doors. While Brock had given up the finer things in life when he'd traveled with his military group, he had been raised amidst wealth and privilege—no matter how hard he'd tried to forget it.

Booted feet sounded and then two male voices could be heard outside the room.

A soft knock sounded and the door swung open.

"Lord Haversham, I am so glad you and your associates were able to meet with me this evening," Mr. Cale said.

Brock stood and shook the man's outstretched hand. "Of course. I am sure you are eager to return to

Hampshire."

"That I am, my lord."

"Then shall we get started?" When Mr. Cale inclined his head, Brock moved on to introductions. "May I introduce Lord Parsons, Mr. Buttons, and Sir Jeffers. And this, gentlemen, is the representative from Foldger's Foals."

The men shook Mr. Cale's hand in turn and looked to Brock for their next move.

"Let us sit." Brock and Harold had decided to avoid further confusion on his servants' parts; they would keep their surnames. This meeting would not be overly long, and added complexity was not needed. As far as he knew, Mr. Cale was not a man of the *ton* and a few made-up aristocrats would not be noticed.

Thankfully, Mr. Cale had come prepared and navigated the men through the requirements for their respective stables.

Brock had had the foresight to instruct each man on their lineage and estate location, all safely more than a day's ride from Foldger's Foals, situated in remote villages unknown to most outside their particular regions.

"Sir Jeffers, what do you foresee yourself needing foal for?" Mr. Cale asked.

Jeffers cleared his throat, glanced at Brock, and took a sip from his tumbler before answering. "I am looking for carriage horses. I travel frequently between London and my properties. The journey is long, and I find my horses do not last as long as one would hope."

Brock nodded for him to continue.

"My—Lord Haversham has spoken your praise." Buttons faltered.

"We have the finest stock in all of England, or so Tattersalls is wont to say." Mr. Cale laughed, not recognizing the slip. "Thank you gentlemen for meeting with me. I would enjoy your visiting Foldger's Foals if you are ever in our area."

"Oh, for certain." Parsons spoke up.

"Well, gentlemen. You have our directions. Please let me know if I can be of any help when the time comes for you to purchase." Mr. Cale shook each man's hand in turn and executed a bow in Brock's direction. "I will leave you to your evening."

"We are departing as well, we will walk you out." Brock hoped to look engaged in business as they left in order to discourage any conversation with others in the club. "Right this way." He stepped in to walk beside Mr. Cale, his men leading the way. "Thank you for traveling to London on such short notice. I believe where business is involved you must strike when the iron is hot, as they say."

"Lady Posey is very grateful for your recommendation." Mr. Cale smiled.

Brock was unsure what about the man irked him, but while in Cale's presence the urge to frown at his overly jovial attitude was overwhelming. It quite possibly had more to do with the woman Mr. Cale worked for. "I enjoy seeing businesses receive what they deserve." Brock returned the man's smile.

They traversed the newly crowded main room and made their way to the front. Men lounged, drank, and played cards in the many nooks the club featured. Cigar smoke hung as heavy over the room as the early morning fog was wont to do across the English countryside. A servant swept the front doors open and a familiar voice called to Brock.

"Gentlemen, please hail our coach. I will be right out," Brock said to his servants, and turned to greet his ever-present cousin. "Good evening, Rodney."

"Brock, was that—" Rodney tried to look over Brock's shoulder to get a glimpse of the men departing with Mr. Cale.

Brock quickly shifted to the left to block Rodney's view. "You are correct. Mr. Cale traveled to London to meet with a few potential clients."

"No, I thought I saw someone else I recognized." Eyebrows raised in suspicion, Rodney relaxed his posture. "I do hope you have not invited *her* to London."

They both knew the *her* to whom Rodney referred.

"I would not dream of that." Brock hadn't paused long enough to dream about inviting her to town, but had hurriedly posted the letter to her—the one resulting in Mr. Cale's presence. "I must be going. Ladies to meet and balls to attend."

He'd never tire of rubbing it in Rodney's face that he, Brock, held the fate of the Earldom in his hands. If he chose to marry and have children, then Rodney's grasp on the title would slip further and further away.

"Good day, cousin." Brock took the coat a servant held out to him and exited his club, the doors closing silently behind him.

CHAPTER FIFTEEN

Connor exited White's with the gentlemen Lord Haversham had introduced him to, pausing on the walk outside. "It was a pleasure to meet you, Lord Parsons, Mr. Buttons, and Sir Jeffers." Connor looked at each man in turn. "I do hope to conduct business in the future."

Even as he said it, Connor kept envisioning the scene he had stumbled upon at Foldger's Foals just a few short days before: Lord Haversham and Lady Vi, wrapped tightly in each other's embrace in the pasture. Haversham had had no right to kiss her—she was meant for him! Even her father had expressed his agreement to their union.

"Good day," the men chimed, stiffly.

Odd, the men didn't act as most men of the *ton* did. In his not-too-distant past, men of the upper class had taken pleasure in emphasizing his lower station in life, always finding the opportunity to showcase their superiority.

"Please give Lord Haversham my regards. I must be off to another meeting before I return to the country."

"Of course. Do enjoy your time." Lord Parsons looked around nervously.

Had he forgotten how to hail their carriage? It was not his concern either way. Connor turned on his heel and headed down the street. When he arrived at the corner, he turned left, following the walk. His partner waited in his coach to take himself and Connor to their next meeting.

Connor entered the carriage and took the seat facing the rear.

Hamp sat deep in the seat facing forward, his face covered in the shadows of early evening. "That was a fairly short meeting. All well?"

"It went well, although I am unsure if the men are truly interested."

"What makes you think they are not?" the man asked.

He couldn't pinpoint the exact reason for his thinking. "They seemed to be uneasy, as if the expenditure of coin was out of their norm."

Hamp sat forward, his hard jawline no longer covered in shadows. "But you were able to pass one of them the card I gave you?"

"I am not an ignoramus or incompetent, Hamp." They had known each other for years, Connor thought irritably, and still the man thought he was inferior and unable to fulfill his part in their business arrangement.

Rather than respond, Hamp sat back in the shadows and rapped the side of the carriage with his cane, signaling the driver to depart.

"Thank you for providing me with transportation while I am in town," Connor said to ease the tension.

"Do you have the money you promised?"

He should have known the man had an ulterior motive for taxiing Connor between meetings. It seemed everything always boiled down to money. "As I told you, there is not much money left to be had—"

"Not much, but some . . ." The man cut in.

"Hand it over!" Hamp's voice verged on a whine.

He wondered how much Hamp had drunk so far that evening. From the smell inside the coach, he'd started early and continued nonstop until recently.

"You realize you are stealing food from children's mouth by taking this money, correct?" Connor kept the envelope tucked close and out of Hamp's reach.

His friend laughed. "In all the time you have known me, do you think I give one fuck about children and if they are well fed?"

Doubt hit Connor hard. It took all his will not to tuck the envelope back into his coat pocket and exit the moving coach. He'd spent years certain that Lady Viola deserved all that would eventually befall her. She'd toyed with him for years, but he'd never been prepared for his vengeance to spill over on innocent children. This would be the last time Hamp would benefit from him taking money that rightly belonged to the orphanage.

Connor pulled the envelope Lady Viola had asked him to deliver from his pocket and handed it over. "This is all. Any other money, we will have to earn from selling our own stock."

"By 'we'—" The man raised an eyebrow in question. "—you mean 'you,' correct?"

CHAPTER SIXTEEN

Brock jumped into the coach before someone had the opportunity to follow him out of White's or hail him on the street. He took the forward-facing seat, the anxious visages of his servants staring back at him. The scene was a bit comical, with all three men crammed on the one velveteen bench. The evening attire they wore would certainly be wrinkled beyond repair. The three were stacked into the tight spot, their wide eyes gazing about uneasily. Sardines ready for the tin.

The coach shifted and they pulled onto the busy street, bound for Brock's townhouse. "Wonderful job, gentlemen," Brock said by way of greeting to the men.

Buttons, his butler, craned his neck to look at Parsons before speaking. "My lord—may we refer to you as 'my lord' now?"

"That is preferable."

"Well, my lord," Buttons started again, "will this be an ongoing occurrence? Not that I am complaining about the fine clothes and night away from my duties,

157

but…" His voice trailed off as uncertainty crossed his face.

"I assume my request is rather confusing to you, and I do not foresee another episode such as tonight." He had been oblivious to his staff's interpretation of what had been transpiring—why Brock needed to hire his own servants as friends and acquaintances. He hadn't been lord long enough to command or ask certain things of his staff, and it was understandable that they might question his judgment. "We will return home and the three of you are free to spend your evening any way you see fit."

All three men nodded, and a look of relief was exchanged.

What Brock wouldn't do to live the unburdened life of a servant.

As they traversed the crowded streets of London, Brock realized he had spent the majority of his day free of the weight that acquiring justice for his family entailed. He had not hatched a new scheme to bring Lady Viola to London, nor contemplated ways to bring down Foldger's Foals. He had focused solely on this meeting with Mr. Cale, and he'd pulled it off wonderfully.

The men continued to exchange glances as Brock contemplated his next move.

"My lord?"

"Yes, Jeffers." The men clearly had something they wanted to discuss, but were hesitant to speak. "Please speak freely." He feared he'd frightened his staff by requiring them to dress as gentlemen. Had it been cruel to show them a life they would never lead?

"When I shook Mr. Cale's hand, he spilled me a

note." Jeffers produced a folded scrap of paper. "It says—"

Brock grabbed the note, ripping it from Jeffer's hand, startling him into silence. The note was more of a calling card than a letter or missive. "I will be in town until tomorrow. Please call on me at your convenience to discuss a better purchase of superior-stock foals. I will reside at Smythe's Guest House for the duration of my stay," he read aloud. "What in the blazes?" He flipped the card over. "D & C's Fine Foals?"

"I was confused as well, my lord. I was under the impression we were meeting with the man from Foldger's Foals," Buttons said.

"We did meet with Foldger's Foals," Brock mused. "That son of a bitch!"

The men sank into their seats as if to distance themselves from Brock's outburst, uncertain how to take his expletive.

"Relax, will you? My words are not directed at you." His servants did not seem to believe him. "For heaven's sake! Buttons, you have known me since I was a wee lad. Am I a cruel man?" Brock tried a new tactic.

Buttons didn't respond for what seemed like a lifetime and the realization struck that his servants, in fact, did not know him. They had once known the hurt and sad child who'd lost his mother; they remembered the carefree youth who tramped around the estate with his two younger brothers in tow, but they were unfamiliar with the man he'd become.

"Jeffers . . . Parsons, you have not known me as long, but I am sure that other servants talk." Brock looked between the three as the coach slowed before his townhouse.

Brock sighed. His door swung open and steps were set down for him to alight. There was naught more he could say; it was out of his control what his staff thought of him. Perhaps in time he could change their opinion or at least soften their reserved nature around him. If he was unable to find a wife and sire an heir, it would be only him and his servants for the duration of his life. What a dreary thought.

"Enjoy the rest of your evening," Brock said and departed the crowded coach to retire to his empty suite of rooms. He took the steps two at a time and paused for his front door to open. He'd neglected to remember that his butler was just now departing the coach behind him.

Grasping the handle, Brock pushed the door open and headed up the staircase to his chamber. He'd never had the opportunity to feel lonely surrounded by the men he commanded; there had always been plans to evaluate, sick and injured to tend to, and disputes to mediate.

Thankfully, he had much to think about. Most importantly, why Mr. Cale appeared to be working for another business whilst sabotaging Lady Viola and Foldger's Foals. A war waged within him by the time he reached his door. She deserved any misfortune that should befall her, but he found himself unaccountably piqued that someone should take advantage of the woman in such a way. Could he suppress his honorable nature and forsake his integrity by turning a blind eye?

"Damn."

"Only home a few minutes and you are already cursing? I take it your meeting did not go as planned." Harold sat in front of Brock's fireplace, a crystal flute in his hand—filled with sherry, no doubt.

"You are becoming a might too comfortable entering my bed chambers. We would not want the staff getting the wrong idea now, would we?" Brock raised an eyebrow in question, hoping to dissuade further talk on the subject of his meeting.

Harold started, straightening in his seat.

Brock's bid at humor and distraction failed. "Whatever is the problem? I met with Mr. Cale, introduced him to several potential clients, and then we left. No one the wiser."

"Then why the horrid mood?" Harold pressed.

The man was too perceptive. "Our good Mr. Cale slipped one of my men a business card as we departed."

"So . . .?"

"So, the card invited my men to meet him at a future time to discuss a business transaction unrelated to Foldger's Foals." Brock slipped out of his coat and collapsed onto the chair next to Harold, the warmth from the fire penetrating his booted feet.

"Interesting." Harold raised his glass of sherry to his lips.

"It is, indeed."

"What do you plan to do?"

"Why do you assume I would do anything?"

"As a man of worth, it is highly unlikely that you would allow a woman, no matter your feelings for said woman, to be taken advantage of."

"It is a pity that my servants do not view me in the same light." Again, he tried to change the subject. He was shocked when it worked.

"Give them time, Brock. You have been absent for over fifteen years. You were nothing more than a lad when you fled."

"I did not flee."

"Truly? Did you bid your father farewell?"

Brock shook his head.

"Your brothers?"

Again, he shook his head.

"It is hard to believe that the only person you told was I—under the cover of night, no less. You know, it took your father months to find out how you paid for your commission." Harold laughed.

"So I heard."

"He was livid you'd sold your mother's jewels."

"They belonged to me to do with as I pleased."

"I understand that. Your father did not."

"What did he expect me to do? Continue to live on the estate, spend the season in London, holiday in Bath . . . and all the while plagued with the twins. They were the spitting image of my mother." His gut tightened at his flippant remark about his brothers. Truth was, he'd give anything to have them underfoot now. Brock stood from his chair and poured a tumbler of scotch. With one large gulp, he swallowed the liquid and slammed the tumbler on the sideboard. "I could not spend every day continually reminded of the mother I lost."

"They lost their mother, too."

"I know that!" Brock turned to face Harold, sure his anger and regret was evident on his face. "But they did not know her. She did not tuck them into bed, ever. She did not sing them to sleep. They were unaware of all they had lost. I was not." His war-worn hands scrubbed at his face and through his hair.

"You still had your father."

Brock worked to calm the pounding of his heart. It had been years since he'd thought of the rejection and loneliness of that time: His father busy with infant twins and Brock left to his nurse maid. Yes, his father had still lived, but he had rarely bothered with his eldest son. Never again had Brock had someone to tuck him into bed or regale him with tales of far-off lands. Instead, it had been up to Brock to take care of his brothers as they grew older and their father became more distant. The heartache of losing his wife had worn heavy as the years passed, and he preferred to spend more and more of his time in London.

"Brock?"

"Yes, you are correct. I did have my father . . . at least his person." If not his mind nor heart.

"He did the best he knew how."

"Undoubtedly."

"Be glad that he did not rule with an iron fist, as mine does."

"At least I would have known he was about," Brock countered.

An uncomfortable silence fell over the room. At last, Harold sighed. "What is our plan now?"

"I wish I knew." The statement had never been truer. He had no clue what his next move would be or if he even had another move to make. Maybe it was time he focused his energy on finding a wife and integrating into society instead of ruining Lady Viola. But how could he give up on the rage that had fueled his very being for the last eight years?

"There are always the Unker twins." Harold waggled his eyebrows.

Both men laughed, the tension in the room

dissipated.

Even as they relaxed, however, Brock's mind returned to his predicament. Ruin Lady Viola, or forget her and at last begin to live his own life? And if he did that, could he in good conscience ignore Connor Cale's clear sabotage of Foldger's Foals? Conflicted and not desiring to dwell any longer, Brock sought to lose himself in the company of his friend once more. One way or another, he knew a decision must be made soon.

CHAPTER SEVENTEEN

"Why are you hiding out here?" Connor walked into her office, a look of concern on his face.

Her fingers brushed away the wayward tear clinging to her cheek. Vi hoped the redness had faded from her eyes. "I have nowhere else to go." Her sigh sounded overdramatic, even to her own ears. "How did the meeting go?"

"Efficient change of subject. You are lucky I cannot help but indulge you at every turn." Connor bowed and his hair flopped in front of his eyes. "The meeting did not go well, I fear."

Another setback. "But Lord Haversham wrote that it was imperative to meet with them posthaste," she mused. She'd been hopeful that these men would turn into clients—preferably, clients with deep pockets.

"I'm sorry."

The look of pity on his face made her sick to her stomach. It was truly over.

Connor had always been supportive and

understanding. Along with Ruby, he knew all her secrets... and stuck with her still. Over the years, she'd wondered what it would be like to marry him—to let him take care of her. Would he be a good, fair husband and father? She dismissed the thought. One day he would make an excellent husband, but not *her* husband. It had nothing to do with his advanced age, for his youthful rugged handsomeness had only matured since they'd met, lending him a distinguished look. Her father had hinted the union would please him.

Was it time for her to think about what would please others, instead of herself? She feared that time had arrived, yet she could not justify settling—not that attaching herself permanently to Connor would be settling. It was only, she'd never anticipated marrying anyone. While she kept her regret hidden, deep inside that spot where she kept things she couldn't change, it clawed at her every so often. While she would have no family of her own, she *did* have her father, Ruby, her staff and her horses who all depended on her. She told herself that their companionship and love was no different than that of a husband and children.

She didn't let herself dwell on the eventuality of her father's passing, or the transfer of the estate and title to his cousin. The thought that she'd be forced to sell her ranch and live off the generosity of a relative who was more stranger than family, was also something she kept tucked safely deep within.

Yes, regret was not something she had time for.

"If it pleases you, I will feed the stock before I retire for the day." Connor's words shook her from her reverie.

"A few more things before you go." Vi squared her

shoulders. She'd more important things to worry over. "Were you able to deliver the envelope?"

Connor dipped his head. "Yes. I handed it to Hutton as you asked."

"Thank you. I understand the area is not the most affluent part of London and at times unsafe—"

"No need to explain yourself." Connor waved a hand in dismissal.

"Well, thank you all the same. Now, tell me more about the meeting."

Connor sat in the blue gilded chair in front of Vi's desk. "There was something off about the men. While they listened intently to what we had to offer, they seemed uncomfortable and nervous—"

"Nervous how?" Vi asked.

"A bit uncomfortable. I may be making this something it is not, but they glanced quite frequently at Lord Haversham for what seemed like approval before speaking. It was odd for men of the *ton*."

It was out of character for any man, at least in her experience.

"I was unable to arrangement any further meeting."

"You did what you could." Vi stood to signal the end of their conversation before asking nonchalantly, "Did Br—Lord Haversham inquire as to my well-being?" She had thought of nothing else the two days Connor had been away. She hoped Brock had inquired, as much as she dreaded the possibility that he would.

Connor eyed her suspiciously and turned his head in thought. "I do not remember him mentioning Lady Posey."

"Well, that is as it should be," she said to cover her

interest. "It would not do to have London abuzz with fresh gossip. People may wonder about who indeed owns Foldger's Foals." Now that things were over, it would be ironic for word to spread.

"Indeed, it would not." Connor's chair creaked as he stood and moved to the door. "I will eat and return in the morning. Please do not stress over much."

The door clicked shut behind him and Vi gazed out the window at his retreating form. She'd never wanted to put herself in such a position again; the lying was a trait she'd abhorred in her younger self. It was hard to convince one's self that one had changed with all the deceit swarming around.

Mere moments after Connor had disappeared from view, her office door burst open. Vi's stomach jumped to her throat in surprise when Ruby rushed in, breathing hard.

"Vi! There you are." Ruby bent at the waist and placed her hands on her knees.

"Here I am. Whatever is the matter?" Vi's hands went naturally to her hips in Ruby's usual pose.

"It is your father—"

"What about him?" Her voice broke slightly on the last word.

"He is at the estate and wishes to see you immediately." Ruby swallowed large gulps of air as her breathing calmed.

"It cannot be so important that they sent you rushing over here."

"But it is…they carried him into the house from the carriage. Lady Darlingiver will not stop her pacing." Ruby straightened, her hands wringing with her own worry. "She says he fainted at a ball last evening."

Vi sprung into action, blowing out the numerous candles lighting the room, and grabbed her shawl from the hook behind her desk. "Let us be off."

Ruby grasped her skirt, lifted it nearly to her calf and dashed out the door, Vi close behind. They navigated around the many puddles in the stable yard and made their way to the path that led to her father's estate.

Her father was not a young man. He had shared his concerns about his health and Vi's unmarried status many times over the last few years. In fact, she could remember twice in as many months.

They flew through the gate separating the properties and moved quickly up the steps and into the foyer, the butler pulling the door wide for them to enter.

"Where is he?" Vi's voice echoed in the cavernous room, bounced off the walls.

"This way, Lady Viola. He is resting in the parlor." Smith, the butler, attempted to lead the way, but Vi found herself with zero patience. Walking in a ladylike manner was out of the question.

The skirts of her dress brushed against the man when she slipped past him. The familiar hall of the house rushed past as she hurried out of the foyer, down the hall, and finally into the parlor.

"Father—"

"Lady Viola, do quiet down!" Lady Darlingiver's voice cut Vi off. "He is resting. The journey here was an arduous one." The woman huffed where she sat on a chair pulled up close to the lounge her father reclined upon. Her veiny hand grasped Lord Liperton's limp fingers.

The strong, rotund figure that had been her father

just a fortnight before had been replaced by a frail, sallow-complexioned man she hardly recognized. "Whatever happened?"

"We attended the Everheart's ball last night—their youngest daughter was introduced to society—and your father was discussing politics with several gentlemen." The dowager's voice rose as her story progressed. "I left him for only a few moments when a servant rushed to alert me that Lippy, I mean your father, had fainted dead away." The woman released her father's hand to push a lock of hair from his closed eyes.

"I sent for his doctor as soon as we arrived at his townhouse. Doctor Durpentire gave him approval to travel here."

The name struck Vi as oddly familiar.

Vi pulled up her own chair and sat next to the woman she'd spent more time in argument with than civil conversation over the last ten years. "Why did you bring him here? He must need rest. You could have sent for me."

"I did not bring him here to you." The woman's face clouded in confusion. "We traveled here because we are now away from the prying eyes of society. If we had remained in town, I would not have been able to stay and attend to him—it is just not done."

This was the Lady Darlingiver with whom Viola was familiar.

Vi pasted a smile on her face. "I do so much appreciate you caring for my father while he is in town. If you had not attended the ball with him last evening, I fear what could have happened to him." If the woman detected Vi's sarcasm, she did not let on or take the bait.

"I cannot agree with you more, my dear." The

dowager released her father's pale hand again and took hold of Vi's as if to soothe her.

Since the opportunity arose, Vi grasped her father's hand with her free one and gently squeezed.

"Viola? Is that you?" her father mumbled. His head lolled to the side and his eyes parted slightly.

Vi pulled her hand from Lady Darlingiver's clammy clutch and stroked the side of her father's face. "I'm here, father."

"You came?" A hint of surprise could be heard in his voice. "You finally came to London." His eyes sprang open and he pushed the cloth that covered him away.

"No, Lippy. I brought you to Foldger's Hall." The dowager moved in closer.

Her father pushed himself into a sitting position. "Will you both give me a bit of air? It is quite stuffy in here without the pair of you leaning over me as if I am on my death bed."

Both women sat back in their seats to give him room. Viola feared another fainting spell.

"Why are you both staring at me thus?"

"What happened last night?" Viola asked. Concern laced her voice.

Lord Liperton looked about the room, but focused on nothing. "Ummm, well . . ."

"You were at the Everheart's ball," Viola prompted.

"Oh, the last I remember Lord Hucklestone was droning on and on about—"

"Go on. Tell her what the gossip rags are saying." It was Lady Darlingiver's turn to prod her father on.

Her father captured her gaze and refused to let her

look away. A new sadness filled his eyes. "All of London knows, Viola. All we have done to hide your activities the last several years was for naught."

A chill crept down Viola's spine. He could not mean what she thought he meant. Her activities over the last several years . . . *All of London knows . . . for naught.* The words flew through her mind. For a moment, it seemed as though *she* was in danger of fainting.

"It is true," Lady Darlingiver said. "They know your father funded Foldger's Foals and that you have been running the ranch since your exile from society."

Her mouth gaping, she turned to her father. "Is this true?"

"I am afraid so."

"But it is much worse than that. The gossipmongers have moved on to your father now."

"What negative thing can they possibly say about my father? He is a pillar of London society." Vi's outrage overtook her and she stood from her seat. "What do they say?"

"Dear, that is not impor—"

"It most certainly is important," the dowager spoke up. "They say your father should have hired you out as a governess."

"Evienne." The warning in her father's voice was something Vi hadn't heard since she was a young child caught stealing the pies cooling in the kitchen.

"It is only fair the child knows what is being said about her—and you as well," she countered. "They say you are unfit to be a governess due to the likelihood that your charges would fall in love with you. They fear an epidemic of deaths in local school rooms."

"That was unnecessary." Her father's sallow skin

turned a deep crimson.

"Well, that is what they wrote. I believe the article was even accompanied by a sketch—"

"Leave us!" Lord Liperton shouted, turning from his long-time love.

She huffed and hefted herself from her seat. "I will see to your supper."

The door closed more loudly than necessary, belying the woman's ire.

"Who have you confided in, Viola?" he asked. "Have you corresponded with anyone from London? An old friend, perhaps?"

Viola shook her head in denial. "No., I promised I would not seek out anyone from my previous life. I have not even left the property in over five years." The thought of her father being ridiculed for her bad behavior wounded her heart.

"I hired Miss Ruby as your companion and you agreed—"

"I told you I have not contacted anyone. No letters . . ." Her voice faltered at the mention of letters. She'd received correspondence from London—but it was impossible that Brock knew her true identity.

"Viola?" he asked.

"It is just . . . I had an unexpected client a few weeks ago." She agonized over how much to disclose. Surely she would not discuss their kiss . . . or the many hours she'd spent daydreaming about that kiss; the feel of his arms as Brock held her.

No, that moment she would keep private. She was resigned to the reality that she may never share a heated moment with any other man.

His gaze penetrated Vi's. "Who came here?" he

asked.

If she told him the truth, would he be able to help her?

"I cannot assist you, child, if I am unaware of the full potential for damage." Her father's encouraging words shored up her courage to speak.

"Lord Haversham—"

"The Lord Haversham? Viola!" her father's voice thundered.

The door to the room opened and Smith poked his head in. "Are you in need of something, my lord?"

"I am not! My daughter, on the other hand, is in need of some common sense."

Vi turned pleading eyes on the butler, urging him to depart and forget her father's cruel words.

With a small nod, Smith retreated from the room.

"He recognized you, and now he seeks to ruin our family more than *you* already have."

"But he did not recognize me—"

He held up his hand. "I assure you, no man can forget the woman responsible for his brothers' deaths."

CHAPTER EIGHTEEN

Viola sat to her father's right as he ate his supper of cold quail and cheese. Her father and Lady Darlingiver had refused to make eye contact with her since the meal began, opting for benign conversation regarding the weather and the dowager's son, who had recently purchased an estate not far away. The praise the current Lord Darlingiver received made him sound the epitome of London's *haut ton*.

Vi continued to push the food around on her plate and awaited the opportunity to excuse herself. Why she worried about her manners now, she could not say.

The clink of Lady Darlingiver's fork brought Vi's head up. "What are we to do now?" she asked. "Lippy, she cannot hide away here in the country any longer."

"I agree, my love." Her father also set down his fork.

Her opportunity to slip from the room disappeared. Vi couldn't help but wonder if the dowager was indeed worried about her, or of her own reputation.

"I plan to remain here and continue as I have."

"That is not possible, Viola," Lord Liperton said. "It is time you confront your past head on. If you have changed, society will see that—"

"What do you mean, '*if* I have changed'?" Did he have so little faith in her? It was as if he hadn't seen her since her debut and subsequent disgrace from society. Had he not witnessed, firsthand, her transformation?

Her father continued without even a pause. "I am selling Foldger's Foals, and you will attend me in London. I do not believe a match is out of the question, but you must be seen to garner an offer."

"But, Father—"

Her father raised his hand to silence her protests. "My mind is made up, and I fear there is little you can say or do to change my plans." He retrieved his fork and stabbed a piece of meat on his plate. "And if you fight me on this matter, I will be forced to remove Miss Ruby as your companion and you will be alone."

"Going to London is out of the question—and marriage? You know I have no plans to marry. I will stay on here with Ruby. We will find things to occupy our time." Vi was certain she would go stark raving mad within a fortnight of inactivity, but that was not something she'd share with either her father or his companion.

"Now is not the time to disagree with your father. He knows what is best for you and this family," Lady Darlingiver chastised her.

The woman always managed to make Vi feel like a child—and in this case, a spoiled child. "May I be excused?" Social graces be damned. If she didn't depart the room soon she was likely to show the woman just how childish she could act.

"Certainly. Please ready yourself and Miss Ruby for our departure to London." The finality of his word caused dread to course through her.

Her years of running from her past were at an end. Her chair glided out from beneath her as she stood and made her way to the door.

"Viola?" her father called.

"Yes," she answered without looking back, fighting tears.

"Things always appear much worse than they actually are."

The words, meant to soothe her nerves, only added to her fear of what was to come. "They also say that things tend to worsen before they improve." With her head held high and her back straight, Vi quit the room.

Vi needed fresh air—the wind against her face. And she knew exactly where to go.

# # #

Brock had ridden hard and fast, at a loss for where to go or what he was even expecting to find. The directions on the back of the business card had been a bust. The caretaker had said Mr. Cale had departed earlier the same day for whereabouts unknown.

Brock had been reeling ever since. The thought of ignoring the cad's deception, acting as if he didn't know, had appealed to him at first. It was none of his affair, anyways. But as a man, Brock could not stand back and let another person lie, manipulate, and crush the future of another—especially a woman.

Every lead he'd followed, thus far, had been a dead end. Earlier in the evening, he'd heard talk of a new foal ranch somewhere in the vicinity of Winchester. Again, he'd departed London without a word, no exact destination, but hoping to find something, anything to put his conscience at rest.

He pushed Sage mercifully through the early night rains, both soaked to the skin and the fear of sickness a great concern. He'd stopped at several taverns and inns along the way, hoping against hope that the proprietor within could help him.

Alas, there had been no information to be had.

Brock didn't know how long he could continue or if Sage would make it to the next inn.

He squinted through the downpour, forcing his sleep-heavy eyes to focus on the rutted path ahead.

Above the sound of the wind Brock heard the neighing of an animal in distress. He pulled up on Sage's reins, slowing his horse as the sound of hooves rent the night air.

A violent cry echoed across the vast fields, ever closer to him, sending a chill down his spine. Sage stiffened beneath him, as though the cold continued to pass through the animal to seek purchase in the solid earth below.

Brock searched the pitch-dark night for the cause of the disturbing sounds, fatigue falling away as his adrenaline increased.

With mud flying, a mare appeared. As fast as it came into focus it continued past him and into the darkness, its ride holding strong to the reins.

From the length of the hooded riding cloak, Brock suspected the rider female.

What was the woman, let along anyone, doing riding in this storm?

Without another thought, he pushed Sage into

action, swinging around in the direction of the fleeing horse and rider. He may not be able to help Lady Viola this night, but another damsel was in distress—and likely more fitting of his assistance.

The rain hit him squarely in the face as he chased the pair. He longed to clear the water from his eyes but feared releasing his grasp on the reins.

Brock spurned Sage faster as he gained on the runaway horse.

The woman, hood still covering her head, held her face close to her horse's neck, her feet still secure in her stirrups.

Sage finally came abreast of the other horse and Brock reached for the reins to slow the animal. "Grab the saddle," he called to the rider.

For a split second he panicked, as the rider did not release her ironclad hold and her horse turned, teeth showing in a snarl, bit at his outstretched hand. His fear subsided quickly as she released the reins and Brock pulled both horses to a skidding halt.

He vaulted from Sage to calm the still-terrified mare before turning his attention to her rider.

"Can I help you down?" Brock asked, continuing to stroke the animal's neck.

The woman lifted her head, her drenched cloak hood hiding her face.

"Come." He moved to her side and grasped the woman around the waist, lifting her from the saddle and setting her on the wet, muddy ground. "Are you hurt?"

"Thank you." Her shaking hands reached up and pushed her hood back. "No, my horse became startled is all."

And Brock stared into the crystal-blue eyes of the

very women who had him gallivanting about the countryside.

"Lord Haversham——" she stuttered.

"What are you doing out at this time of night?" he said at the same moment.

"I was returning to my home when the storm hit." She stepped back and his hands fell from her narrow waist to rest at his sides.

"Your home?" The rain continued to pound the earth as Brock looked around, taking in his surroundings. They stood not far from the lane that led to Foldger's Foals. How he'd ended up here, he hadn't a clue. He'd ridden for hours, stopping at more inns and taverns then he could remember, but he hadn't expected his search for information to lead him here…with her.

The panic in her eyes matched that of her mare, and for a brief moment Brock wondered if she knew he'd figured out her deception. If the time had come for them to face their past.

The dark and dankness, with the rain's relentless beating, was the perfect backdrop for the ending of their sordid, painful relationship. He almost laughed at the absurdity of the thought. They shared no relationship, he and this temptress. No, she'd forced herself into his life. Placed herself conveniently in his path.

"I really must be returning." Lady Viola grabbed the reins from his hand and made to re-mount her horse. "My father will be worried."

Brock couldn't be sure but her voice faltered. He looked closer.

Her eyes were red and swollen, her nose ran, and her hair hung haphazardly about her shoulders. Never had he seen her anything but completely together and in control of her person. Even during their brief kiss in the pasture, she'd kept herself at a distance, never fully leaning against him.

"Whatever is the matter?" he heard himself ask, almost against his will.

Her shoulders seemed weighed down under her cloak. She smoothed her hair with her free hand. "Truly, I must return before they send someone to look for me." Her eyes pleaded with him to let her go, not to ask any further questions, and possibly forget their meeting entirely.

In that moment, he forgot who he was…and the terrible things she'd done. Before him stood a woman in all her honesty and raw self. She wore a cloak but was not hidden from his eye.

She was broken.

She was hurt.

She was forsaken.

A shell of the girl she must have been when she'd been in London all those years ago.

And Brock wanted nothing more than to take her in his arms and make everything right for her—for them. To wash away the sins of her past as the rain washed away the dirt that clung to them both. To distance her from her sorrows and burdens. To bring the winds of change to both their lives.

"Please…" She pulled away and turned to her horse.

Brock let her go.

He watched her only long enough to see that she made her way down the lane safely before reclaiming his seat atop Sage.

And with that, the ocean between them returned.

She was not Lady Posey Hale, he reminded himself. She was no victim. She was Lady Viola Oberbrook—the girl who had caused his life to crumble around him. The girl who had taken everything.

And he was the man destined to make her pay for her sins.

CHAPTER NINETEEN

"I do apologize, my lord, but I am unfamiliar with any horse business other than Tattersalls." Lord Galles turned his nose up at Brock's mention of the working class.

"Thank you for your time."

"Certainly. Do you plan to attend the musicale and poetry reading Lady Galles and Lady Sophia are hosting this afternoon?" he asked, perched high on his horse. His boots gleamed in the late morning sun.

Matchmaking fathers were almost as tiresome as the marriage-hungry mothers. "I do believe that I responded and included a guest. An afternoon surrounded by classic music and the latest poetry sounds divine." Sage shifted under his weight. Brock wondered if Galles caught the sarcasm in his voice.

"A guest, you say?" The lord visibly squirmed in his saddle.

Brock was torn between letting the man think he intended to attend with another woman on his arm—

possibly a mistress, which would be highly inappropriate—or informing the lord that his guest happened to be his best friend, Harold. Better to let the man sweat a bit. He had probably overstepped his bounds and promised an introduction to his most-likely pale and fragile daughter. Ignoring his question, Brock continued. "I look forward to meeting Lady Galles. Her reputation as a hostess of the first water is legend in London." He bowed his head and moved Sage further down the lane into Hyde Park.

The white lie had rolled easily from him, when in truth he had never heard of Lord and Lady Galles before receiving their invitation two nights prior. Their affirmative response was solely due to the high likelihood that sherry would be served as the afternoon refreshment. Harold did not miss an opportunity to drink the vile watered-down stuff in socially acceptable place.

Brock had come to Hyde Park not to frolic with the *haut ton*, but to view the place where his brothers had lost their lives. A weakness toward Lady Viola had been worming its way inside over the last few days, particularly after their unexpected meeting in the rain two days' prior. He could not take the chance of missing the opportunity to avenge his family for the wrongs this woman had done.

He hoped that visiting this site, though painful, would renew his sense of purpose.

The milling crowd slowly began to dissipate as he moved deeper into the park. Women no longer walked on the arms of their beaus with a maid close behind; men no longer rode the finest stock money could buy in hopes of attracting the eye of a certain female; vendors could no longer be heard hocking their wares. As the area fell into silence, he could not help thinking that this was what his brothers must have heard: Utter tranquility. But no, that would not be right. They had attended in anticipation of pointing a gun at each other. Had they thought it was a lark? That someone would intervene before it was too late?

What could they have been thinking when they pointed their weapons at the mirror image of themselves? He would give Lady Viola Oberbrook one thing: The woman was captivating, resplendent with her long hair and crystal-blue eyes. She had taken command of their prior dealings, a true business woman. Had his brothers been business dealings? The thought that she might not have even remembered their names crossed his mind. The possibility that she had not even known Brock as their brother slammed into him.

Sage moved slowly as they approached the legendary open area used over the last two hundred years for duels. Heaviness settled over Brock, the weight of many lives lost. It had been the same on the battlefields, the souls of the dead attempting to seek him out. He removed his foot from the stirrup and dismounted. The urge to be closer to the earth where blood had run over the years was strong.

A part of him had thought about asking Rodney to accompany him, as he would know the exact spots his brothers had lain and taken their final breaths. In the end, Brock had wanted to be alone to contemplate his future, so influenced by the past. He dreamed of leaving all this hurt and anger behind and starting anew. That would mean not seeking retribution for the deaths of his brothers and, in turn, his father.

Brock walked across the open field and dragged his feet on the hard-packed ground. Truly, he did not want to be here; had not planned on coming. Leaning down, he plucked a few blades of grass and brought them to his nose. They smelled of freshness and promise, not of death and despair. Was a person meant to learn from the smallest things in nature? What could be taught by a blade of grass? He rubbed his fingers together. The grass fell from his hand, to be picked up by the faint breeze and carried away.

He looked forward to a day when he could plan his future rather than attend his past, but today was not that day.

Sage nuzzled his shoulder from behind, ever the faithful servant.

"Let us be away from here," he whispered. Brock swung up on the horse's back and kicked him into a full gallop, back toward the crowded part of the park. He vaguely registered people moving out of the way as he and Sage thundered through the most crowded section. Men shouted in his direction and woman hurried off the path to avoid the dirt that his horse's hooves kicked up.

With the wind beating hard against his face, he did not care about a thing; not his quest in London to find a wife, nor his past.

Sage slowed of his own accord as they reached the main street bordering the park. At a fast walk, they traversed the busy thoroughfare to Brock's townhouse and he took the lane in back to his stables. Jeffers materialized at his side when he entered.

"My lord," Jeffers said, and took hold of the reins Brock threw to him.

"Please ready the coach, Jeffers." Brock

dismounted and strode for the house. A stiff drink would help clear his head before an afternoon filled with young ladies pounding on various musical instruments and dandified men reciting sonnets. He sincerely hoped the sherry was worth it.

Brock entered his room and threw off his riding coat. As always, Parsons had his afternoon attire pressed and laid out for his approval—not that Brock ever saw the need to judge his man's choices. He dipped his hands into the large bowl of water that stood on his dresser and cleansed the dirt and grime from his face.

The door creaked, and he assumed that Parsons had arrived to dress him. "I find myself not ready. Leave me." His voice was harsh.

"I see you went against my advice and visited Hyde Park."

He turned and Harold handed him a tumbler of scotch.

"From your look, I will take that I am correct." Harold moved to sit in one of the chairs by the fireplace.

"Again, your familiarity with my room is very suspect," Brock snapped.

"Your ill nature today will not affect my mood." His friend closed his eyes and took a large swallow from his goblet. "This is truly heavenly. What are the chances you can pilfer another bottle from Lady Garnerdale's personal stock?"

"For you? There is no chance. Find your own way to indulge your personal taste for women's drinks." Brock knew he had gone too far when his friend stood and made for the door.

"I will let you deal with your demons in private."

Harold inclined his head. "Do send for me when you are ready to depart."

What in the blazes did the man know of his demons? "I will be ready shortly."

"I do hope your mood improves, or you will scare the young ladies away." The door clicked shut as his friend left him.

Brock needed to get his mind back in balance. He grabbed the towel next to his water bowl and patted his face dry. Throwing the towel down, he moved to his massive four-poster bed. The sheets and coverlet lay smooth with nary a wrinkle. The coils compressed when he sat to remove his riding boots. He needed to prepare; it was in bad form to be tardy to a recital.

After he removed his boots, Brock started on his shirt and then stood to remove his soiled breeches.

"My lord, may I assist you?" Parsons appeared from Brock's dressing room. His valet's small living quarters lay beyond.

"Please," Brock sighed.

The man began his duties, seemingly gathering courage before he finally spoke. "If it is not too forward of me, your brothers would not want you dwelling on their passing."

"You overstep your bounds," Brock said, his mood growing darker by the minute. "How do you claim to know what my brothers would want?"

"I attended both men in the year leading up to that fateful day."

"I was unaware you knew my brothers." Brock raised one brow, his interest piqued.

"They were such confident men. I dressed both the morning of their duel. It was with great sadness that I learned of their demise . . ." The man's words trailed off.

Brock knew he had more he wanted to say. "Please go on."

"It is only that they were best friends, and enjoyed every bit of their lives. Did you know they prepared in the same room?"

"I did not."

"Yes, they were hardly out of each other's sight most days. They attended the same functions, clubs... They frequently shared their female companions." A small smile lit his valet's face and Brock felt a twinge of jealousy.

He had not known his brothers on such an intimate level—had not seen them since they wore knee breeches. At the time, Brock could think of little more than escaping his childhood home and the memories that came with it. The twins were children when he fled.

When Brock failed to respond, Parsons continued. "All I mean to say is that they died doing what they wanted. Your presence in London would not have changed that. If they had not died in that duel, they most likely would have perished in a carriage accident or met an untimely death at the end of a cuckolded husband's pistol." Parsons paused and took a step back from him. "You are ready, my lord. Enjoy your evening."

Brock highly doubted the evening would be enjoyable, let alone bearable. He eyed his cane leaning against the wall closest to the door, but decided against taking it. "Indeed."

The stairs passed slowly beneath his feet as Brock descended to meet Harold in the foyer, pausing before his friend noticed him watching. Harold paced back and forth. Worry marred his face. Brock could not help but wonder what weighed heavy on his mind. Did it have to do with Brock, or with his own father?

"Buttons," Brock called, gaining Harold and Buttons' attention. "Please retrieve Mr. Jakeston's cane and we will be on our way."

"Where is your cane?" Harold asked.

"I will not need it."

"Wait a minute! If you are not carrying one of those infernal things, then neither am I."

"Oh, but you are." Brock infused his words with the authority he'd used with his men. "It lends a certain air of nobility to the gentleman using it."

"Then why do you not have one?"

"Because, you see, I am a duke by birth, therefore my nobility is unquestionable." He despised alluding to his status, but the statement was true. He did not have anything to prove to the *ton*. Harold, on the other hand, had quite a lot to prove if he intended to marry well and escape his father's clutches. "Shall we be off?"

Brock did not wait for Harold's reply. He exited the front door and entered the coach that waited at the curb, his friend close behind.

The Galles' townhouse was situated about three blocks away, and they arrived fairly quickly due to the lateness of the afternoon. Most of the working class were still at their places of employment and the nobility were in their homes preparing for their evening entertainments. There were few carriages waiting outside the Galles' residence, however, which increased Brock's unease. He did hope that the musicale had not been set up for his entertainment alone. Upon his arrival in town, Rodney had warned him of the dangers of matchmaking mothers. He was thankful to have Harold at his side.

"Do wipe the doom-and-gloom expression from your face, Brock," Harold said.

Brock shifted his gaze from the window to his friend. "I most assuredly do not have a 'doom-and-gloom' expression. I am actually excited to hear the latest sonnets composed by Byron."

A bark of laughter escaped Harold. "I do not believe a word of that. I am glad you can put your plans aside to enjoy an afternoon, however."

"I would not say I plan to enjoy my afternoon, but I will suffer through."

The door swung open and the footman set down the steps for them to depart. The front door to the Galles' home opened before they had climbed the steps.

"Do come in," the butler said. The strings of a harp could be heard from within. The melody sounded familiar, and was played with a measure of skill.

Brock and Harold handed over their coats and a servant led them down a long hallway to the rear of the house. They were greeted as they entered by their host and hostess, then escorted to seats in the front row of the sparsely filled room. Lord Galles seemed rather relieved that Brock did not come with a female in tow. They took their seats and a server delivered glasses of Madeira to both of them. Brock could almost feel the happiness radiating from his friend.

The young girl before him, really no more than a child, picked at the harp strings and created a soothing melody that even Brock could not deny was exquisite. He sat though several sets as a variety of young ladies took their place behind a mélange of instruments, each girl appearing as youthful as the first.

His gaze traveled the room, which was mostly filled with doting parents and other eligible men of the *ton*. To his left, Brock caught the eye of Rodney, who inclined his head in greeting.

"Whatever is your cousin doing here?"

Brock noted the distaste in Harold's usually positive tone. "I am sure he is here to keep an eye on me. He has a vested interest in my future." He turned back to the performance when a lady seated behind him '*shhhh*'d their conversation.

With a flourish the girl currently at the pianoforte strummed a final note and stood to curtsey to the cheering crowd.

Their hostess, Lady Galles, stood before the group to speak. "If everyone will adjourn to the gardens, we will start the poetry portion of our afternoon." The lords and ladies moved as if they were a herd of colorful cattle, through the door and onto the veranda where chairs and blankets had been arranged for relaxation in the sun.

To the right stood a refreshment table with light foodstuffs. Brock and Harold moved in that direction, Brock intent on procuring a drink with a little more substance than the wine he currently held.

"Lord Haversham?" A young gentleman met him in front of the laden table. "I had heard you were back in town."

Brock could not remember meeting the man. He appeared years younger than himself and Harold, so the possibility of them knowing each other was low.

"I am sorry. My name is Lord Darlingiver. I

attended school with your brothers."

Of course—he was an acquaintance of the twins. "May I introduce Mr. Harold Jakeston," Brock made the formal introductions.

"It is a pleasure."

"Indeed," Harold said, imitating the one-word phrase Brock had perfected since his return to society.

"I have heard you are on a quest to improve your country estate, as it has been neglected in recent years." Lord Darlingiver took a glass from the table and directed Brock and Harold toward a grouping of chairs farthest from the gathering poets.

"I am indeed." Brock raised an eyebrow at Harold. Perhaps this man would know about Connor Cale's secret dealings. "I am currently looking to further expand my stables. Have you heard of D & C's Fine Foals?" Brock ventured as they sat in the straight-back chairs set out for them.

"D & C's? I was under the impression you were working exclusively with Foldger's Foals."

Where had the man gotten his information? Brock had not set out to keep his business dealings a secret, but his social circle in London was rather small—as in nonexistent.

"I have dealt with Mr. Cale in the past, however I recently heard of another foal ranch I am interested in. Unfortunately, I have been unable to acquire the location of the establishment."

"Of course, it is completely understandable you would not want to associate yourself with Foldger's Foals." The man reclined in his seat.

"Pardon me? Whatever do you mean by that?" Brock caught Harold's questioning glance out of the corner of his eye.

"Have you not heard? I do not like to be the messenger of bad news, but I assumed you knew." The man paused to take a sip from his glass. "I cannot blame you for cutting ties with Lady Viola Oberbrook—her being responsible for your brothers' deaths. Very unfortunate incident, I must say."

Brock kept his mouth shut, debating the consequences of denying his knowledge of Lady Viola's part in Foldger's Foals. Would it be detrimental to him if he admitted ignorance of the fact?

Harold did not give him time to answer before he spoke up. "Lord Haversham's family misfortune is long in the past—water under the bridge, as they say. Oh, please excuse us. I see our host is desperately seeking our notice."

Harold stood and motioned for Brock to do the same.

As they made their way toward Lord Galles, currently conversing with his wife, he asked, "What was that all about? You know that naught water travels under that bridge." Brock tamped down his anger in order to avoid garnering the attention of Lord Darlingiver or other partygoers.

Harold motioned with his cane to encompass the notice they had received since arriving. "You understand there was no way for you to save face during that conversation. To admit that you recently found out the woman had duped you again would be foolhardy. And acknowledging that you were unaware of her owning Foldger's Foals would have insinuated a lack of intelligence on your part."

"How very fortunate I am to have a friend such as

194

yourself," Brock said honestly. If it had been Rodney, the man would have been happy to make him look the fool. "Who do you think is spreading the news about Lady Viola?"

"Not you?" Harold paused and turned to Brock in question. "I assumed it was part of your master plan to ruin her life."

"While she deserves her life to be ruined as she ruined the lives of my brothers, it was not I."

"Then whom?" Harold asked the question that Brock himself had been wondering. The two men reached their host, effectively cutting off their conversation.

"Lord Haversham, may I introduce my daughter. Lady Sophia, this is the Duke of Haversham," Lord Galles said as his daughter dropped into a low curtsey.

Brock determinedly pushed any thoughts of Lady Viola aside, focusing instead on the young lady before him. If comparisons were made in the back of his mind as to this girl's waifish figure versus Lady Viola's feminine curves, the child's bland smile compared with the wit and fire he had first encountered in Viola, he refused to acknowledge such thoughts. He bowed to the vapid girl with a forced smile.

"Indeed a pleasure, Lady Sophia."

CHAPTER TWENTY

Viola's office was spare, as it held only her desk and a few chairs. The speed with which her father had acted in readying her ranch for sale shocked her. Her decorations had been removed from the walls, and most of her files transferred to her father's estate.

"You appear as if you only now watched a puppy die. It is not as dire as you fear," Ruby said from her seat in front of Vi's desk. "All will be all right...in time."

Time? It was such a relative thing. Did time ever truly make things better? Dim the pain of a person's memories? She had heard it said that time heals everything. Vi would like to meet the fool who coined that expression, because the last eight years had healed naught. It hadn't changed what she'd done, hadn't dimmed the consequences of her petty actions, and it certainly hadn't brought her forgiveness.

She hadn't forgiven herself.

Her father hadn't forgiven her.

Society had never been a forgiving lot.

And certainly, she could never expect Brock to forgive or forget.

She wished she held an ounce of the fortitude Ruby embodied. Her friend hadn't blinked at Vi's announcement that they would depart shortly for London. While Vi was scared out of her wits, Ruby seemed to look forward to the adventure. She continually forgot her friend had never been afforded a season—let alone one in which Vi's father would provide them new wardrobes complete with parasols, gloves, and dance slippers.

Vi sighed. "Lady Darlingiver has arranged for a modiste to meet with us upon our arrival to be outfitted with the necessary garments needed for polite society. Not that I plan to attend many functions."

"Do you think I will see my mother while in town?"

Vi sensed the first note of apprehension in Ruby's voice. "I would assume so, since Lady Darlingiver and your mother are bosom friends." She eyed her friend. Was that nervousness she saw? "Your mother will be quite happy to see you, I am sure." Viola dropped her head to concentrate on the letter she'd been writing before Ruby had charged in.

"Oh, I am sure she will be. How are your letters coming along?"

Viola had set about writing her clients to inform them of the closing of Foldger's Foals. It was proving to be a more arduous task then she had anticipated. She'd completed a total of fifty-three letters with only one more to write, but she found herself stuck. Unable to finish it.

Ruby stood and peeked at the letter Vi was

struggling with. "Ah. Lord Haversham."

"Yes, Lord Haversham." Vi's cheeks heated.

"Why is his letter any more difficult to write than the rest?" Ruby asked.

"I fear the next time we meet will be under different circumstances."

"That cannot be helped. Also, there is no guarantee we will cross his path in London."

"My hope is that he is at this country seat, but I fear my luck has not run on the positive side as of late," Viola said. She dipped her quill in the ink pot. Despite everything, she did hope to see Brock again, although she could not tell Ruby that.

"Your father is quite happy with your agreement to accompany him to town," Ruby said, changing the subject. "He appears years younger, and fully recovered."

"I do not doubt his exuberance at my agreement." She set the quill down and looked up at her friend. "You do believe that I did not intend to cause my father embarrassment?" It was important to her that Ruby knew her interactions with Brock had not been a ploy to tarnish her father or their family name further. Perhaps in her youth, she would have instigated such a ruse to garner attention, but that had been long ago.

"Of course, Vi. Anyone who cannot see the changes you have made to yourself and your life is as blind as a newt."

Viola could not help but laugh. "A newt? Surely you mean a bat."

"No, I mean a newt. Which is a blind salamander. They live in the New World, do you not know?" Ruby looked at Vi as if she was an uneducated street child.

"I do so enjoy random trivia. I do not know a thing about blind salamanders." Vi again picked up her quill, determined to finish the final letter and return to the estate to organize the servants in preparation for their departure to London. "As much as I enjoy—"

Ruby held up her hand. "You have work to attend to. I will leave you now and see you at supper."

She returned her attention to the letter as her friend silently closed the door behind her.

Why was this letter so difficult to write? To answer that question, she would likely need to delve more deeply into her feelings for Brock . . . and to do that, she must admit she *had* feelings for him that extended beyond mere physical attraction.

The idea of crafting the letter she dreamed of writing passed through her mind. She dipped her quill and wrote: *Dearest Brock, I have missed you during your absence. Meet me in London in a fortnight. Lovingly yours, Viola.* Yes, she signed the letter Viola. Alas, this was all only a fantasy. He did not know her given name, and if he did he would do anything not to meet her in London.

The parchment crumbled easily in her hands. *Idiot*, she thought. No man, least of all Brock, would ever endeavor to seek out her attention. Was that what truly frightened her? The thought of being shunned to her face? She had fled London in the wake of the duel and at Lady Darlingiver's insistence, before meeting any member of the *ton*. Sarah and the housekeeper had packed her belongings, dresses and hair ribbons never worn, and she had fled before tea.

What a stupid girl she had been . . . and possibly still was.

Vi smoothed her hands across a fresh sheet of

paper, quill at the ready. It was time to put words on the paper, not those she wished to say, but something to end their interactions and not prompt him to seek further correspondence.

Dipping her quill in the ink once more, she began.

Lord Haversham,

It is regretfully that I write to inform you of the closing of Foldger's Foals. Thank you for your recent business transaction. I sincerely hope your stables are a success of the first water.

Fondly,

Lady Posey Hale

Fondly—where had that come from? She quickly sprinkled sand over the wet ink and returned her quill to its holder. It was done, and there was naught she could do but re-write the letter. She blew the excess sand from the parchment, folded the letter and inserted it into the waiting envelope.

Taking out another clean, smooth sheet, Vi again began to write. She wrote of her regrets—not only her girlhood mistakes, the tragedy of her first season, but also all she knew that would never be hers. The words flowed across the page, filled with sorrow, sadness, and sacrifice.

These words were not meant to soothe her—no, she wrote these for Brock.

For his family, who no longer lived.

For his future children, who would never know their uncles or grandfather.

She wrote of her foolishness, her pride, her vanity.

But mostly, the page held the apology she feared she'd never be able to give him. She would, if she could, go back to that day and change everything. In her heart, she wished she could go back even further, long before her first season.

Next, she wrote of Brock's brothers; how vibrantly alive they had been, how much they'd loved both Brock and their father, how earnestly they had vied for her attention. To say all that, she would also need to admit her need for attention, her lack of caring, and her selfishness. She confessed it all, her hand scribbling furiously to take hold of every sin and commit it to paper before her nerve expired.

Vi stilled her writing. Her whole being ached to write of her life now. The good she was doing, the lives she had saved, the wrongs she spent every waking hour attempting to right. But there was no room for rationalization or justification of her failings—especially to herself. She had destroyed Brock's family then, and continued her deceitful path by lying to him now.

No, she could not change the past—and neither would her words, written upon a useless piece of paper. She set her quill aside and read through her unaddressed confessions once more before ripping the paper in two, as if destroying the evidence of her past would somehow fix everything. How she wished anything in life was that simple.

She finished the original note with three simple words, 'I am sorry,' written with a heavy heart. But those words could never convey all she wanted Brock Haversham to know.

She sighed and pushed her chair back, grabbed the stack of letters, and stood. Extinguishing the candles as she went, Vi left the office for the last time. She could not bring herself to look over her shoulder as she traversed the empty stable yard and moved down the path to her father's estate. Her future, whether good or bad, was here.

CHAPTER TWENTY-ONE

"How long do you plan to make your father wait?" Ruby asked.

"I've no idea what you are referring to." Had she been that easy to read? Viola had thought she'd been extremely subtle in delaying their departure for London.

"Truly? First, you insisted your father rest for a few days before our journey." Ruby held up her fingers to check off Vi's transgressions. "Next, you insist on seeing the sale of Foldger's Foals through. And lastly, you demanded his barouche be brought from London to transport us."

Vi avoided eye contact with her friend. "I only thought the journey would be made more comfortable for him in the barouche." Maybe her actions had been a bit obvious, at least to Ruby, who had spent so many years with only Vi as a companion.

Ruby sighed.

Viola had no other choice but to meet her gaze.

"Your petty behavior may fool your father, but not

I," she scolded. "How dare you jeopardize all your hard work? Is this the impression you seek to make once we arrive in London? Still the selfish, self-absorbed debutante who caused the deaths of two young men?"

The comment stung and Vi wanted to scream that that was not what she wanted.

"You must make a decision, because once we arrive it is not only your reputation—or what is left of it—in jeopardy, but mine. If you are not going to be the person I know you to be, I will cry off and return to my own home." The conviction in Ruby's voice scared Vi. "Tell me you will take this seriously and give yourself a fair chance at a better future."

"And if I do choose to be the old Lady Viola—is it your intention to abandon me?" She knew she was being unfair. Ruby didn't deserve such an ultimatum, especially from Viola.

Ruby grimaced, her expression pained.

"Ruby, I did not—"

She waved her hand, cutting short Vi's words. "Do not apologize for a question you are not sorry for asking." Hard eyes met Vi's and she continued. "Be advised that I could have forsaken you long ago. When I learned of your misdeeds, I could have written my mother and begged off from Foldger's Hall, but I did not."

Viola brushed away the tear that streaked down her cheek.

"I recognized the kindred spirit in you, so I stayed. It turned out to be the best decision my mother ever made on my behalf." Ruby's eyes glistened with unshed tears, mirroring Vi's own.

"What shall I do now?" Vi asked. "My father must

think the worst of me."

Ruby shook her head. "No, he too has seen your transformation. It is Lady Darlingiver who has her concerns. And rightly so, I might add."

The skepticism the woman held about Vi's ability to win over the *ton* once more was no secret. "I care not what she thinks of me—or what the *ton* thinks of me, for that matter."

"While I do not believe you in the slightest, I do have—"

The door to the morning room opened and the butler bowed low, first to Vi and then to Ruby. "Lady Viola, the post has arrived." On his silver platter were several envelopes.

She took the offering and thanked him.

"Is there anything else, my lady?" he asked before he departed.

"No, thank you." Vi flipped though the letters. Several were addressed to Foldger's Foals, and were likely notes of condolence posted from former customers throughout England. The last was marked with a London address. One she remembered seeing once before.

"This one is from Brock." Her words escaped on a sigh.

Ruby sat up excitedly, their earlier conversation forgotten. "Do open it." She fairly bounced in her seat.

Vi slid her finger under the embossed wax seal. With a small tug, the H-shaped seal cracked and the envelope fell open, revealing a neatly folded letter. The parchment felt crisp and fresh in her hand as she unfolded it.

"Do get on with it." Ruby scooted to the edge of

her seat and leaned precariously close to Vi.

The letter held the usual condolences and good tidings for her future, nothing more.

"I am unsure what I expected…"

Ruby seized the letter from her hand. "Well, this states his regret that Foldger's Foals is closing, but just a moment…" She leaned past Vi and grabbed the discarded envelope on the table. "We may be in trouble."

"Whatever are you talking about?"

Ruby held up the confiscated envelope

Viola gasped.

Ruby nodded.

They certainly were in trouble.

The envelope had been addressed to none other than Lady Viola Oberbrook.

"Do you think he…?" Viola stopped. Certainly Brock would not have gone to the gossipmongers with her secret…would he? It was true, she did not know him or what he was capable of, but he should certainly hate her. He had every right to curse her name venomously to any person who would listen. Viola stood, the post slipping from her lap unnoticed. "Ruby, prepare yourself. We leave for London first thing on the morrow."

Her friend only raised an eyebrow.

"His letter is addressed from London. If we hurry, we can waylay him while he is still in town." The wheels were turning in her head. "He will definitely not expect me to travel to London."

"You cannot be thinking he is responsible."

She hadn't the faintest idea what to think. "Do you have a better explanation?" When Ruby didn't respond,

Vi continued. "There is no one else. We were very careful. Do you not see the coincidence that Brock shows up here unannounced, and then all of London is abuzz?" Viola's hands rested on her hips, her stance wide as if ready for a confrontation.

"Your father will be in high spirits with this change in plans." Ruby handed the letter back. "I will ready my things."

Vi pulled the bell cord to summon the housekeeper after Ruby closed the door.

If they hurried, Lord Haversham would not have departed town. She counted on his assumption that she would keep herself hidden away in the country, fearful of traveling to London to confront him.

While she waited, her thoughts ran to their second meeting, when he had come to collect his stock. Had he known then? Had he lured her into kissing him?

And what about that night—in the rain. Surely he knew, yet he said nothing once again. But damn him for saving her from further harm. That night had run threw her mind a thousand times since. She'd argued with her father and in her haste had fled the house in nothing more than her cloak for protection. The wind and rain had seemingly come from nowhere, taking her by surprise. Or had she been so distracted, heavy-hearted, that she'd failed to notice?

If she had stayed, engaged Brock in conversation, would he have told her all? Scolded her not only for her reckless behavior that night but also for her misconduct in her youth?

Did he seek to further embarrass her? How dare he! If she was her seventeen-year-old self, she just might have challenged *him* to a duel to defend her father's name. Fortunately for him, she *had* grown up and did not have a violent tendency.

"Lady Viola?"

Viola looked up to see Mrs. Dale standing in the open doorway. "Oh, pardon my distraction. Can you inform my father that tomorrow morning will be perfect for our journey to London?"

The housekeeper immediately dropped into a curtsey. "Of course."

If he thought she would cower in the country while society talked ill of her family, Lord Haversham had another thing coming. And if he entertained the idea that she was the same girl who'd turned coat and fled all those years ago, he would be shocked to find out the extent of her transformation.

# # #

Brock hadn't visited his family's burial plot since his return, and now he remembered why. The area had been overgrown the night he'd stopped, before he'd fled his father's home to make his way as a soldier. Times had not changed: The small fenced area was even now so overgrown by wild grass and summer flowers that he had to pull it out by the handful to see his family's final resting spots.

Resting side by side, his parents' joint headstone read simply, "Here lies the 5th Lord and Lady Haversham. May their eternal splendor be ever restful and serene."

He hadn't the faintest idea who had crafted the inscription.

And a part of him wondered what his would say.

Possibly, something as asinine and useless as his parents? *'Here lies Brock, the 6th Lord Haversham, who passed devoid of an heir.'*

Or would someone see fit to capture him as he was this day, *'Here Lies Brock, the 6th Lord Haversham, an idiot who almost fell in love with his enemy. And then treated her poorly as only a coward would do.'*

Either way, he had accomplished little of note in his time back. There would be nothing for future generations to look back proudly on. He had not respected his father as a good son would have. He had not honored the memory of his mother by carrying on the family name. Instead, he had coveted his family's adversary, still longed to hold her again. He'd also alienated his only living relative to the degree that neither could stomach the other.

Brock had returned home with grand plans to right the wrong of his past, to renew and renovate his family home, and to seek justice for his family. But all he'd done thus far was botch everything he touched.

"I thought I would find you here."

Brock turned from his parents' headstone to find Harold, who was on horseback outside the black wrought-iron fence that enclosed his family's burial plot. "My apologies, I did not hear you ride up."

"I highly doubt you would have heard a herd of wild stallions pass by." Harold tied his reins around his saddle horn and dismounted. His booted feet hit the ground solidly. "You left hours ago and I became worried."

Brock realized in that moment, he was not completely alone in his endeavors. Harold, as his friend, could always be counted on. They were closer than brothers. Much as Rodney and he should be, but it was a compatible relationship that Brock and his cousin had never attained.

"I have been overly concerned with the stables and have neglected my family," Brock confessed. "I must send someone round to repair the fencing and clear the weeds."

Harold walked through the gate and stood beside Brock. "You've had much on your mind, my friend."

Both of their gazes returned to the stones before them.

"Excuses, always excuses."

"You are too hard on yourself."

Brock looked to Harold. "There is no one else to be hard on. I have failed so many of my obligations."

Harold raised his hand and set it on Brock's shoulder, reassuringly. "There is time, Brock. You only returned recently. No one would expect you to attain your life's goals in a month's time."

"Sometimes, I wonder if ten years' time would be suitable for the task," Brock sighed. "I wonder if all the effort is even worth it. People have very high expectations."

Harold chuckled. "People? Or yourself?"

"Does it matter?"

"I guess not. But what do you think people expect of you? And why do you care so much?"

Brock turned to his brothers' graves. "I know naught what anyone expects ,but I assume it consists of more than being duped by the same woman—more than merely updating my estate and settling down with some young chit." While their bodies may be buried here, their life's blood remained in London, soaked into the field where they'd taken their last breaths.

"Will we be departing for London soon?" Harold changed the subject.

Brock nodded, still distracted. "Yes, we should be on our way back to town. I have a young woman I owe a ride through Hyde Park."

Truly, Brock wanted nothing less than to spend the afternoon listening to the senseless chatter of a young debutante.

CHAPTER TWENTY-TWO

Viola looked around the bedroom she hadn't seen in eight years, and wanted to berate the fool who'd thought the décor fashionable. Everywhere she looked was pink: pink coverlet, pink longue, and pink dressing table complete with a set of pink, pearl-handled brushes. The extravagance of her youth glared back at her from every corner—taunting her to deny the girl she'd been. She thought about the mouths she could feed and the medical treatment that could be administered with the money spent acquiring all the useless and extravagant items that cluttered just this room. The brushes alone could feed a whole orphanage for a fortnight—could have kept Foldger's Foals in business for months.

Emotions coursed through her: regret, disappointment, but mostly shame. Shame at what she'd put her father and Brock's family through. Shame at her own lack of appreciation for life, her own and that of Cody and Winston. While her world had altered greatly that day, ultimately it was Brock's brothers who had paid the price, sacrificing their lives, their chance at a future, for a foolish game and the possibility of winning her affection.

She slid onto the bench at her dressing table and looked in the mirror. It had been so long since she'd worried about her appearance. What stared back at her was a woman barely recognizable compared to the girl she had been when last she'd occupied this room. Her hair trailed long down her back in wild waves that couldn't be tamed, her skin so dark it appeared she'd lived in the sun for years. Vi pushed her mane of mocha-colored hair behind her ears and her hands came into view. They were just as worn as her hair and skin, covered in calluses from her hours caring for the horses.

It had been a form of punishment that she'd adopted early on after her exile. All the money she had spent to purchase fancy clothes, all the time she'd taken to have her hair styled in just the right fashion—what had that gotten her? Nothing but blood on her hands. The loss of two innocent lives. If she hadn't been the vain and shallow girl she had been, where would Cody and Winston be now? Happily married with families of their own, or still foolish boys seeking to entertain themselves with the next big thrill? It didn't matter what path they each chose; at least they'd be alive. Only she was responsible for robbing them of this.

There was naught she could do about her appearance except tie back her hair, apply powder, and don gloves morning, noon, and night. It all seemed hardly worth the effort.

She sighed. And what of Brock? Would he still be serving the King if his father was alive? The image of Brock smiling as he twirled a tall blond-haired beauty around a crowded ballroom filled her head. The woman laughed, joyously and without reserve, as they spun faster, moving between other couples effortlessly. Had she stolen this from him, too? The chance to live unencumbered by sadness and loneliness would be her wish for him.

A light tap sounded at the door.

"Enter," she called.

Ruby stuck her head into the room, a broad smile on her face. "The modiste is here."

Viola pasted on an answering smile and turned to her friend, determined not to damper the girl's jovial mood. "Wonderful. Have you a list ready of all you will require?" Her father, true to form, had given them unlimited funds to obtain all they needed to re-enter society in the height of fashion. Like her surroundings now, it all seemed a colossal waste. "Shall we?"

With one last look at her girlish room, Vi followed Ruby to the morning room—which turned out to contain even more pink than her bed chamber. She wished once again that it was possible to go back in time. She would have a lecture—or five—for her younger self. What she wouldn't give for the opportunity to go back and warn herself about the consequences of her actions.

"Mademoiselle Viola." A short, lithe woman with ebony hair and ample bosom dropped into a deep curtsey. "It is an honor to dress you in the latest fashions." The woman's accent disappeared with the last.

"You must be Madame Sauvage. Thank you for attending us on such short notice."

"There is no problem with short notice." The

217

petite woman snapped her fingers and four women materialized at her side, each with measuring tape in hand. "My girls will attain your measurements and those of Mademoiselle Ruby. Then, we will discuss color and material."

Viola did not have the chance to respond before Madame Sauvage again snapped her fingers and the girls set about measuring every plane on her body—and some planes she had not known existed. Ruby looked similarly uncomfortable as one girl measured her around her breasts and then her hips.

Thankfully, the girls were adept at their job and quickly motioned them over to where Madame Sauvage laid out bolt after beautiful bolt of rich silks, gauzy gossamer, and sturdy cotton. "You both will need eight evening gowns, five morning dresses, two riding habits, and a few night shifts. . . . And of course kid shoes, gloves, parasols, ribbons, and wraps to match each," the woman said without looking up from her task.

As the woman listed off the items, Viola attempted to keep track of the cost in mind. Too late, she realized she had not the faintest idea of how much a dress fit for London society cost. She had been accustomed to ordering ready-made gowns from the local seamstress in Winchester.

"I believe this would look exquisite on your Mademoiselle Viola." The woman held up a length of the most beautiful, iridescent purple silk.

Vi stepped forward and ran her hand along the material.

"It will look divine, Vi," Ruby gushed. "The men will be falling all over themselves to place their names on your dance card."

"I sincerely doubt that—"

"*Non*, you will be the talk of the town in this," Madame Sauvage assured her. "I will cut the front daringly low, you are not a debutante any longer, and I will craft you a one-of-a-kind cap." She stood back and assessed Vi's bosom.

The comment about Vi's advanced age might have bothered some women, but she was comfortable in her status as an aged, unmarried lady. "Not too daring or I fear my father will not allow me to leave the house." Vi winked at the woman, and all three broke out in laughter. Whether or not they were all laughing at the same joke, Vi could not be certain.

"I think an emerald green and deep red would also suit your . . ." the woman trailed off.

"Yes, I have always had naturally sun-kissed skin," Viola said to cover the awkward moment. She could not help wondering if the woman knew her past.

Without missing a beat, Madame turned to Ruby. "You, Mademoiselle, will do well with pastels. Your youth will be enhanced by lavender and powder blue."

Ruby and Vi glanced at each other and both broke into another fit of giggles.

"I do not understand what is so funny," Madame Sauvage said seriously.

"It is only that Ruby is five years older than myself," Viola said in between giggles.

The woman looked back and forth between them, her brow scrunched as she examined both Ruby and Vi. Finally, her gaze settled on Ruby. "You, it will be much easier to find a husband for."

Ruby blanched and her eyes popped open wide.

The woman's proclamation would prove truer than

she knew.

Whether her friend's look was due to the forwardness of the Madame's response or the idea that she might actually attract a match, Vi wanted to learn. She'd been so worried about her own future, she had not stopped to think about Ruby's. Surely her friend's goal was not to stay with Vi for the rest of her life.

"Well, I think pastels are all the rage," Vi said to cover the awkwardness that had settled on the room.

"And with Mademoiselle's coloring it will be just the—"

Raised voices and footsteps stopped the modiste mid-sentence. The door flung open before the butler could announce their visitor, and Ruby mother stormed into the room, her nostrils flaring.

"Momma!" Ruby squealed in delight. The smile that settled on her friend's face made her appear barely out of the schoolroom.

"What are you doing in London?" Mrs. St. Augustin barged past Vi and the modiste to stop directly in front of her daughter, who now cowered like a child.

Viola was about to step in to defuse the woman's agitation, but Mrs. St. Augustin took a breath and seemed to regain control of her emotions.

That is odd, Vi thought. Why would Ruby's mother be upset at her presence in London? Most mothers would be overjoyed to learn that their daughter would be afforded a season in London—even if only part of a season—at no expense to them.

The smile plastered on the woman's face threatened to crack her hard exterior. "Excuse my shock. I had not expected you." She embraced Ruby in a stiff hug. "Why did you not write to inform me you were planning a trip to town?"

A faint smile returned to Ruby's face. Vi could not help but wonder how long it had been since they'd seen each other. Vi had only met Mrs. St. Augustin once in all these years and Ruby had stopped traveling home for holidays some years ago, stating she did not want to leave Vi and her father alone.

"I fear I am to blame for Ruby not sending word that we were coming," Viola said. She rushed over to stand beside Ruby, not sure why she felt her friend needed her support, but more than willing to give it. "I decided to uproot everyone on a whim and here we are. I am so fortunate to have a dear friend such as your daughter to indulge me." Now, all three of the women had not-so-genuine smiles pasted on their faces.

"Mother, please have a seat and I will ring for tea."

"No need, I cannot stay. I only wanted to see if I had heard correctly." The woman appeared to look around the room for the first time, noticing the modiste and her staff milling about. "A fitting? Do you plan to stay long?"

"That is up to Lady Viola and her father," Ruby said.

"We will be staying on in London for the duration of the season," Viola answered, turning a reassuring look at Ruby.

"Well, that is good to know. I look forward to seeing you ladies out and about. I must be going now, for I have tea with Lady Darlingiver shortly." Mrs. St. Augustin moved to leave without a final goodbye to Ruby. Viola could swear she heard the woman mumble, "London is in trouble."

While Vi missed her mother greatly, she would

rather not have a mother than be saddled with Ruby's. The woman had not even asked her daughter to stay at their residence, or invited them to accompany her for tea.

"Shall we get back to our fun? We still have fifty shades of pastels to sort through for you." Vi squeezed Ruby's shoulder in support. "This puce would look stunning with your green eyes."

"I am sure your complexion is much more suited to the color then my own."

"I do believe the color will look exquisite with both your coloring," Madame called.

Vi and Ruby exchanged a horrified glance over the thought of wearing puce in public. With a laugh, the tension was broken and they returned to the table overflowing with materials.

"Do you not think your mother was a bit on edge?" Vi asked as they searched through ribbons after selecting their materials. She did not want to overstep their friendship, but she was curious about her friend's strange relationship with her mother.

"Oh, Mother is always on edge, fearing the world will end at any moment and such nonsense." The nonchalant reply did not fool Vi. Ruby had been guarded since her mother's departure, and in fact always stiffened a bit at the woman's mention.

One day, Vi would press her for the reason. Alas, today was not that day.

"Do you fear she does not agree with our association while in London? I will understand if she does . . ." Viola glanced up to find Ruby closely studying two green ribbons, almost identical in hue. "I mean to say, she must be concerned with you finding a worthy match."

"My mother gave up on the possibility of a match for me years ago—when my father died, to be exact. Any offer at this point would most assuredly be acceptable to her," Ruby answered as she brought the ribbons closer to her face for inspection. "Which shade of green do you prefer?"

"Verily, they appear the same to me." Yes, today was not the day to dampen her friend's spirits, but one day in the very near future Vi would pursue the topic.

CHAPTER TWENTY-THREE

Viola took in the scene around her, so familiar yet completely foreign. Did the trees appear taller? The walking path more trodden? She'd forbidden herself from returning to this place since that fateful morning, which had not proven difficult since she'd fled soon after returning to her father's townhouse that day, her slippered feet still wet with the morning dew.

At least that was different. Today, she and Ruby visited Hyde Park at a more civilized hour, long after the morning moisture had dried and in its place were members of the *ton*. So far, no one had thrown anything at her, neither rotten food nor foul words. A part of her wanted to scream in joy at the thought of her return to society going smoothly. People passed on horseback or foot with little more than a nod in their direction.

Ruby pulled at Vi's arm where their arms were linked. "I still do not understand your need to walk, especially in Hyde Park."

Vi had tried to explain her reasoning earlier that

morning, to no avail. "It is inconceivable that our paths should cross Lord Haversham's if we are not in places that he may happen to be."

"But why would Lord Haversham be in Hyde Park—the very place his brothers died?"

"I do not expect him to be here! But to gain invitations to some of the London functions, we must appear in public." She found herself talking slowly, hoping Ruby would understand.

"Why would anyone invite you of all people—I do not mean to be rude—into their home?"

That was a good question, something Vi had pondered several times since their return, before coming to a conclusion. "Because the *ton* loves scandal. You will learn quickly that if your ball or musicale is not rife with gossip, it is not a success. I believe that hostesses will be falling all over themselves to have me at their gatherings. And imagine the *coup* of a hostess securing the attendance of both Lord Haversham and myself . . . under the same roof, on the same evening."

"People would seek to incite a scene between you two?" Ruby asked skeptically.

"Do not be naive, Ruby, or you will be eaten alive here." Vi wished she'd known the dangers that lay within the *ton* before her own coming out. Alas, she'd had no female to guide and assist her. Lady Darlingiver may have sponsored her, but only as a way to increase her favor with Vi's father. It had worked, with the bonus of Lord Liperton being beholden to the lady after Viola had been shunned, effectively tarnishing the dowager's sterling reputation.

Vi smiled and nodded to a passing group of debutantes who struck out with their maids trailing after, keeping watch.

"Did you have many friends during your season?"

Ruby's unexpected question took Vi by surprise. "None that stuck by my side after I was shunned." She thought for a moment before continuing, "But I was not a good friend, either. I was much too concerned with gaining the attention of the most eligible men of the *ton* to be a tried and true friend."

"Then it is good that I met you when I did."

"Why is that?" Vi turned a questioning look on her friend.

"Because no other had claim on your friendship—which is their loss."

Vi wanted to laugh. It was quite possible that Ruby had never truly had another female friend. "I promise to not give my friendship to any other."

"Is that my mother?" Ruby stood on her tiptoes and searched the crowd in front of them. "I do believe it is! Mother! Mother!"

Vi also stood on tiptoes to see who Ruby was looking at, her short stature a disadvantage to Ruby's taller frame.

"It is her. She is headed this way. I cannot wait for her to see me in my new walking habit." Ruby bubbled with excitement.

It was beyond Vi's comprehension why her friend sought to please her mother at every turn. "How fortunate we are to have received dresses this very morning." Vi raised her hand and waved to Ruby's approaching mother. Ruby did look stunning, tall and willowy, in her new apricot-colored dress. Vi had also opted for a pastel, lavender-colored garment for their excursion. They'd agreed it lent a certain demure quality.

"I do believe that is Lady Darlingiver with her." She'd thought she had escaped the woman when she'd left the country.

"Good afternoon," both Vi and Ruby said as they curtseyed to Lady Darlingiver.

"I had not expected the pair of you out and about so soon. I trust my modiste was agreeable to the both of you?"

"Of course. Thank you, my lady, for arranging our fitting," Vi said.

"Lovely." Lady Darlingiver's eyes fixed on an object over Vi's shoulder. "Oh, I do believe I see an acquaintance I must speak with. You young ladies enjoy your walk." The women moved by Vi and Ruby in the direction of a group of older ladies. When they reached the waiting group, Lady Darlingiver maneuvered even further from Vi and Ruby, making it obvious that any association with a shunned girl was something the lady wanted to keep secret for a time longer.

# # #

Brock maneuvered his phaeton through the fashionable London *ton* currently promenading through Hyde Park, while he sought to drown out the whining voice beside him. Whatever had gotten in to him, agreeing to accompany Lord Galles' daughter for a ride in the park? He'd only collected the girl from her father a handful of minutes before, but was already tempted to stop his horses and ask her to walk back. If it were not completely and unforgivably outside social norms to abandon a young lady in Hyde Park, he expected he would have.

"You do not say?" he responded when Lady

Sophia went quiet.

"That was my response as well, my lord," she began again. "Imagine the nerve of the girl, dancing the waltz without Almack's permission."

"The shame!" he faked interest while imagining himself shoving pointed quill pens in each ear, effectively putting a stop to the girl's verbal volcano. It was a wonder she hadn't picked up on his lack of enthusiasm in the conversation.

His eyes roamed the many unfamiliar faces in the sea of people taking their daily constitution in the park. It amazed him the amount of people London held. He could attend a ball every night for years, and still manage to meet new members of the *ton* at every turn. He nodded to a group of matrons, picking Lady Darlingiver and Mrs. St. Augustin out of the crowd. Their gazes took him in in surprise before both women lowered their chins in a return salute and increased their pace in the opposite direction.

Returning his attention to the girl beside him, Brock's eyes suddenly caught a familiar face on the walking trail. His breath caught. Even with her dark hair captured under a fancy hat and gowned in a fashionable walking dress instead of the sturdy cotton he was used to seeing, Lady Viola stood out.

"My lord?" his carriage mate asked, a hint of annoyance in her voice.

"Pardon me, what was that?" Brock turned his eyes from Lady Viola and trained them on the screeching girl beside him.

"I asked if you would perhaps be willing to escort me to Gunther's for an ice one day." The irritation vanished when his attention settled on his companion once more.

"I do believe that would be an enjoyable afternoon," Brock responded, though he had no intention of calling on the girl again.

She smiled and greeted a woman in a carriage to Brock's left.

When he gazed over Lady Sophia's shoulder, Lady Viola had disappeared.

He would certainly see her again soon, he had no doubt. Together, they accounted for the worst scandal to hit London in the last decade. It was inconceivable that their paths would not cross.

He flicked the reins and his horse sped up as they exited the park. He could not wait to unburden himself of young Lady Galles' company and return to his townhouse. The post should arrive shortly, and he had invitations to accept.

"My lord," she said, and clasped onto his arm as the horses lifted their legs higher, increasing their sped. "It is time to return to my father's already?"

He wiped the utterly bored expression from his face before answering her question. "Time does pass when two like-minded individuals gain acquaintance, does it not?" He bit his tongue before he added that it could also drag on and on. Before long, Brock's fine carriage stock found their place among the swift-moving afternoon set as he headed back toward Lady Sophia's townhouse.

"I do agree, my lord." She did not release his arm. "I will be at the Viannate's ball this evening, do you plan to attend?" Her voice came out a bit needy; Brock could only imagine the lecture she'd received before leaving with him. Her father most likely instructed her to make sure she confirmed another meeting with Brock.

He could not say whether or not he would be at any ball Lady Sophia planned to attend. The young girl probably didn't know who Lady Viola was, and no doubt wouldn't understand his need to see her. Attaining a list of functions she planned to attend, however, would prove difficult.

As his brothers before him, he was determined to get what he wanted. Except that instead of Lady Viola's attention, Brock only wanted retribution.

CHAPTER TWENTY-FOUR

Viola laughed as she and Ruby descended the last
stair into the foyer. She truly did not know what had
come over her. Since their return from the stroll in
Hyde Park, Vi had enjoyed a most jovial mood, and
quite looked forward to their next outing. Maybe ices at
Gunther's. There was something about this town, her
fancy new dresses and her friend at her side, which
instilled hope. Not only hope that the remaining part of
the season would pass without further embarrassment
to her father, but a genuine optimism for her own
future.

Could it be possible, despite the continued gossip,
that society could forgive and forget her transgressions?
She was not naive enough to expect this, but she
couldn't help but dream of the possibility.

"Tell me, which outfit will you wear first?" Ruby
asked, but did not wait for an answer before she
continued. "I for one plan to wear the puce dress. You
and the modiste were quite right, it does indeed suit my

233

coloring."

They continued toward the dining room, arm in arm, much as they had walked while in the park. "You must trust my guidance more," Vi said. "Do not forget that I have done this before."

"And you did it smashingly well, from what I have heard." Ruby barely made it through her reply before she giggled.

Viola smiled, taking the joke for what it was. "Point taken."

They entered the open door to the dining room, where Vi's father and Lady Darlingiver sat, awaiting their meal.

"Ah, good evening, you two!" Her father's tone suggested a new zest for life, one that had assuredly been missing when he was rushed to the country not long ago. "I see you are both enjoying your time in London."

Vi was hard pressed to agree, for she'd resisted accompanying her father to town for so long. "I find the change in scenery refreshing, Father."

"And you, my dear? This is your first time in town, if I am not mistaken." He turned his dashing smile on Ruby, and Vi breathed a bit easier.

"It is, my lord. Thank you so much for the beautiful gowns."

"Nonsense, my child. You are as another daughter of my own."

Vi took the seat next to her father, Ruby on the other side. As the footman pushed in her chair, Vi swore she saw tears glisten in her friend's eyes.

"Lady Darlingiver was just going over all the invitations she has accepted on your behalf, Viola," he said, giving the woman a warm smile. "Do tell what you have planned, dear."

All eyes turned to the older woman. Ironic that she had not wanted anything to do with them in the park earlier, but now—in the presence of her father—Lady Darlingiver was the epitome of polite hostess.

"After visiting with you both in the park this afternoon, I went directly to Madame Sauvage's shop to verify that gowns would be ready soon."

"Go ahead, tell them, my dear." Her father practically bounced in his seat, excitement radiating from him.

Lady Darlingiver looked from Vi to Ruby and then back to Lord Liperton before she set her utensil down and spoke. "I had hoped to keep it a secret a bit longer, but I agree with your father." She turned back to Vi. "You will need time to prepare."

The woman's smile grew. Unease filled Vi, sending a shiver down her spine. "The word is spreading quickly about your return to town. I thought a celebration should be in order. So, I—"

"What do you mean, 'celebration'?" The question came from Ruby before Vi could utter a word. Her mouth was still open, gathering wool.

"Well, Lady Viola—and you, as well—need a proper introduction to society. Have either of you noticed that not one person has arrived to visit or leave their calling card?" She raised her eyebrows in question and folded her hands in her lap.

Vi had been dreading the day she would be forced to attend a soiree, actually secretly holding out hope the modiste might misplace their gown order.

"I see you have not." A smug smile replaced the

dowager's serene one. "It is highly improper—as you should know, Viola—to call on a person without a proper introduction. So, I am hosting an intimate dinner party in your honor."

"Intimate?" Vi recalled the 'intimate' group Lady Darlingiver had invited to her coming-out ball during her season. It was a laughable term to use. Invites had been sent to every lord, lady, sir, and miss in all of England—and possibly a few close to the Scottish border. "Father, tell me you—" She turned an angry look on him.

"Now, Viola, calm down. Are you not serious about finding a husband?"

Of course she was not serious about finding a husband, but she could not tell her father that.

Her father continued. "And I am not a young man. What will happen to you after I leave this earth?"

Viola reached over and set her hand on his. "Do not speak like that. I did agree to come to London." She sounded evasive, even to her own ears.

"There will only be fifty of our nearest and dearest friends invited," Lady Darlingiver continued. "This, by London standards, is quite intimate. Do you not agree, Lippy?"

"I concur," her father said and picked up his fork, signaling his involvement in the conversation was at an end.

But Vi was not done with the conversation—not even close. "And when will this 'intimate dinner party' occur?" It was like pulling teeth.

"Why, tomorrow evening, of course."

And just like that, Vi's control over her return to society was taken from her—if she'd ever had the control in the first place.

She turned a pleading look at Ruby, begging for her help.

"I do hope our gowns are ready in time."

Vi kicked her foot out, catching her so-called bosom friend squarely in the knee.

"Ouch," Ruby said and reached her hand under the table to squeeze Vi's leg, barely above her knee.

Vi latched on to her only thread of hope to avoid the upcoming disaster that would be Lady Darlingiver's dinner party. "Madame Sauvage could not possibly have evening gowns ready in time."

The smug smile returned to Lady Darlingiver's face. "On the contrary, dear. As I said earlier, I went round to her shop, and she will have two ball gowns ready for fittings on the morrow."

"Ball gowns?" Both Ruby and Vi asked at the same time.

"There cannot be a dinner party without a bit of dancing afterwards," her father said as he lifted a forkful of quail to his mouth.

"That is very true."

At that moment, Vi longed for the serenity of Foldger's Foals. When the household was up in arms at her father's unannounced arrival there, she could slip away and tend her horses, go for a long ride about the estate, or simply work in her office. In London, she would not be afforded this luxury.

Servants cleared the plates in preparation for their dessert. As a footman set individual bowls filled to the brim with cook's plum-sauce pudding in front of them, her father joined the conversation once again.

"It is very fortunate for us that Lady Darlingiver's

son is in town. You remember the Duke of Darlingiver, do you not?"

"How can I forget Hampton?" It was all Vi could do not to roll her eyes at the thought of the insufferable boy who had followed her around during her first season. Viola was seven years his junior, but still he had seemed fresh from Oxford. Part of her wondered if that had been his way of impressing his feelings upon her.

"Vi, you have never mentioned Hampton before." Ruby looked between Vi and Lady Darlingiver.

"*Lord Darl*ingiver," the woman said, emphasizing his formal name, "is an old friend of Lady Viola's. They were practically inseparable during her season. He is most eager to renew your acquaintance."

That was ironic, she wanted to say. He'd had all those years to visit when his mother traveled to Foldger's Hall; his estate sat less than an afternoon's ride by carriage from her father's country estate. Yet, she'd seen neither hide nor hair of Hampton Darlingiver until her return to proper society. Instead of voicing her thoughts, Viola turned a smiling face to her father and his companion. "I do look forward to visiting with him after all this time."

"Now that all that is settled, I would like to enjoy my dessert." Vi's father took a large spoonful of pudding and placed it in his mouth, sighing when the sweetness touched his tongue.

Viola ate her last course in silence and contemplated her coming time in London. Her search for Brock would have to be put on hold, at least for the next twenty-hours, while she dangled on strings and was led around by the old woman seated across from her. A marionette upon a stage.

She sighed. There was not much she could do until after the dinner party and ball the following evening.

Ruby leaned close and whispered, "Whatever is the matter with you? It is only a ball . . . One night."

Ruby had never experienced a season. The thought of attending a real ball would excite her friend, and rightly so. Hadn't Vi spent countless nights by candlelight explaining all the wonders of London: the grand balls, elegant evening dresses, and dashing gentlemen? "I had hoped to reenter society on my own terms," Vi whispered back.

"What does it matter if your first outing is a dinner party thrown by Lady Darlingiver and her son, or the opera? At least at Lady Darlingiver's affair, you will be surrounded by a handpicked few."

Ruby—always the voice of reason—had a point.

"One night . . ." Vi whispered.

CHAPTER TWENTY-FIVE

"You do realize that we are expected at our dress fitting in fewer than two hours?" Ruby asked.

"Of course I do. That is why we must hurry. Now, get into the carriage." Vi pushed her friend toward the waiting carriage, complete with a footman awaiting a lady to help into the conveyance.

"Do not wrinkle my lovely morning gown, I am moving as fast as possible." Ruby grasped the footman's outstretched hand and entered the carriage.

Vi followed hastily behind and settled on the forward-facing seat. "We will have plenty of time to make a quick detour before arriving at the dress shop."

The look Ruby turned her way told Vi her friend did not believe for a second that they would arrive on time for their appointment, if at all.

"Ruby, I promise you will not miss your first ball— or the fitting to look beautiful at said first ball, trust me."

Her friend relaxed against the cloth seat as the

carriage pulled away from her father's townhouse, headed toward East End.

"Does your father know where we are going?"

"Do you really think I would tell my father that we are headed to one of the worst parts of London, unchaperoned, with no other protection but our two lively servants?"

"I suppose not—"

"If I had, do you imagine that we would *still* be on our way there and not locked in my room?"

Ruby didn't bother answering Vi's question as a sullen look overtook her face.

Vi immediately felt badly for being so harsh. "I am sorry, I am only nervous about tonight."

"Your sour mood has nothing to do with where we are headed at the moment?"

Her mood had everything to do with where they were headed. How could she tell them that this would be all the money she could give them? That no more would ever come? They would suffer, and she would be the cause of it. She could not live with that on her shoulders, but she had no idea how to continue as she had for the last seven years. Being at the mercy of her father was not easy—although having to depend on a husband for everything she needed in life would be much worse.

"Sometimes I wonder if you even hear me when I talk." Ruby stared at her and Vi realized she had not answered her last question.

"I think I am a bit overwhelmed with everything at the moment. It is very likely that I will be shunned at the ball tonight . . . and in turn, you will also have a mark above your head." It was true, Vi did worry about society accepting Ruby into their fold if she was scorned.

"They would not accept the invitation if they did not plan to give you a chance." Ruby gave Vi a comforting smile.

Again, she wondered how her friend had gained such exemplary insight after being hidden away in the country for so many years. Vi hoped that what she said was true; she was unsure her father could handle more shame heaped upon his only daughter. "Your words are comforting."

"It is you and me against the world!"

"Thankfully, I am not concerned with the world—only our small place in it."

"Is society truly all that bad? My mother seems to enjoy her time in London immensely."

"When you are in the upper echelon of the *ton*, it is wonderful. But when you fall from grace, it is a cruel and unforgiving place." Vi tried not to let the sorrow she felt inside color her words. She was ashamed to admit that there had been a day when she had been among the chosen few in that upper echelon—and that she had taken such pleasure watching others' heartrending fall.

But no more.

Her status in society now depended on others. She could only pray they were more kind then she'd been in her youth, although she did not believe she deserved their kindness or forgiveness.

"What is that awful smell?" Ruby grimaced and covered her nose. "This is worse than that time you convinced me a bit of manual labor would improve my constitution." She fanned her rose-scented handkerchief in front of her face to ward off the offensive smells of the East End.

Vi peered out the window as they rolled through the impoverished neighborhood. She let the curtain fall back into place before addressing Ruby. "That is the smell of desperation, sorrow, and hopelessness—and exactly what I had hoped to change, at least for a small few." A weak smile crossed her face.

The carriage rolled to a stop just north of the River Thames, where the smells of filth were the strongest. Ruby pulled her curtain back and gazed out at the building before them. "Oh, my."

The curtain covering Vi's window stayed in place. She could not bring herself to look out at the deplorable condition so many were forced to live in—while the likes of Lady Darlingiver spent small fortunes throwing extravagant parties. But she owed them an explanation, in person, about the promise she would be forced to forsake.

With a gust of cold morning air the door swung open, steps were placed outside, and a hand reached in to help Vi and Ruby alight. When she stepped out, Vi could no longer deny herself a glimpse of the place where she'd been sending every coin she could spare.

The tall, three-story building blocked the midday sun, casting a shadow over both Vi and her carriage. The paint peeled so severely it would likely need massive repairs to hold the walls together. Thankfully, all the windows and doors were intact.

"Shall we knock?"

Vi shook herself out of her haze and addressed the footman. "We will only be a few minutes."

"Shall I announce your arrival?" he asked.

"That will not be necessary."

"Yes, my lady." He closed the door and took his place at the back of the carriage.

Both women stood facing the intimidating building, afraid to make the first move.

"Why would you not have the footman announce us?" Ruby whispered.

"Because it would do no good. They have no idea who Lady Viola Oberbrook is, or that I am the person funding their operation." Vi chastened herself for not having the forethought to send word of her visit.

"And to think I was under the impression that an hour with the dressmaker would be more entertaining than this," Ruby uttered as she took the first step toward the door.

Before Viola could follow, the door was thrown wide by a short, rotund woman clad in a stained blue dress, an apron of white tied securely around her waist. "An who ye be?" she asked, her hands coming to rest on her hips.

Vi wanted to laugh, but tamped the urge down. The woman looked just as Ruby did when she sought to scold Vi for something or other.

"Well? A pussycat got ye tongue? I be expect'n a delivery from the butcher soon and he be need'n to pull up right here, seeing as we don't be have'n any alley in back."

"I apologize—"

"No apologizing be need'n, jus move this here hack out of the way," the woman said aggressively, cutting off Vi's words.

The old Vi would have been affronted at the nerve of this woman calling her father's barouche a hack, and would have promptly put her in her place. Instead, Viola took a calming breath and smiled. She turned to her driver and signaled him to drive around the block.

He nodded his head, and the carriage pulled into the stream of other passing conveyances.

"That be better—now, off with ye." The woman made a swishing action with her hands as if to sweep Vi and Ruby down the block. "I don't be need'n any uppity types hangin' around or he's likely not ta stop." She turned and headed back toward the open doorway.

Viola forced a smile. "Are you Mrs. Hutton, by chance?"

The woman turned a quizzical eye on Vi and Ruby. Her back straightened and she smoothed her hands down her apron, as if to make herself more presentable to ladies of the upper class. "That be me."

Vi stepped forward and outstretched her hand in greeting. "I am Lady Viola Oberbrook."

Mrs. Hutton eyed her hand, but did not grasp it or respond.

"I am from Hampshire," Vi continued.

"Oh, heavens and damnation," the woman cried. "Please ye come in and I do be gett'n ye some tea." She hurried up the stairs and into the dreary building, leaving Vi and Ruby on the stoop.

"Yes, much better than a dress fitting," Ruby laughed. The few curls hanging around her face bounced with mirth, and she followed Mrs. Hutton.

Vi looked around her. The carriage was gone, and she feared they would be stranded in the East End. There was nothing for it but to break the news to this woman and hand over the rest of her money. She mimicked the woman's actions, straightening her back and smoothing her skirt.

Once she entered, she heard Ruby further down the hall conversing with someone. She could not make out the words. The dim lighting showed off a well-cleaned, recently scrubbed passageway with several closed doors off each side, leading deeper into the building. Somewhere within, Viola heard more voices and footsteps. She'd pictured the house teeming with activity—an activity that had always been lacking at her country home.

A light flared further up ahead and she was able to see Ruby, perched on her haunches next to a small child who sat in an even smaller chair.

"Well, Samuel, I think you are very handsome, and I would not worry about what Abby says," Ruby said to the child.

"That is very nice, miss." Even with its soft tone, the boy's high voice rang off the walls.

As Vi came closer, she studied the cherubic boy. His hair sat in short ringlets around his head, mirroring those that framed Ruby's own. His blue eyes sparkled in the candlelight that Ruby held close. It was only when she was within a few feet that Vi realized the child was missing part of his right arm.

"Shot by his own papa." Mrs. Hutton *tsk-tsk*ed at her side. The woman had appeared out of nowhere, startling Vi.

When she only looked on, the woman continued quietly. "Don't be let'n him catch ye stare'n, and don't be underestimating the youngster. He be right smart and will make a fine man someday."

The optimism in the woman's voice was hardly contagious given their surroundings. Vi could not help but wonder what would truly happen to poor Samuel in the years to come—after the last of her money ran dry. Would he be thrown into the street? Forced to labor in a work house? She doubted the boy would be able to keep up with others who were in possession of all their limbs.

"Don't be look'n so glum, Lady Viola." Mrs. Hutton laid a comforting hand on Vi's shoulder. "Samuel here be one of the least affected here."

Tears threatened to spill down her face as emotion welled inside her. She had not believed she would be affected as such—that she *could* be affected as such. The depth of her change—not outwardly, but deep within— was suddenly made real to her. She wanted to sink to the floor and cry for the unfairness of Samuel's situation; to protest the dreariness of his life, and to rage for vengeance against the person responsible—his own father. The wall in the narrow hallway stood mere inches from her. Would she be so weak as to lean against it for strength?

But she knew she did not deserve the assistance of the wall or any person. Vi had caused this devastating feeling in others—in Cody and Winston's father, and again in Brock when he had heard of the tragedy.

Vi may not have held the gun that took their lives, but she was responsible, just as Samuel's father had been. She was no different than Samuel's father. As she wanted vengeance against the man who had injured his own child, so should Brock want vengeance against her.

Could she blame Brock if he was the source of the rumor about her? It would not be fair to hold anger against him—he was the one entitled to anger and vengeance.

"M'lady, would ye like to meet the others?" Mrs. Hutton drew Vi from her dark thoughts.

A part of her did not think she could handle being face to face with any more devastation. But she answered, "Of course. I want to meet them all." She knew she was punishing herself for her past transgressions, would continue to punish herself until the day she herself went to her grave.

Ruby stood. "It was lovely meeting you, Samuel. I would be honored if you would accompany me for ices one day soon."

"Ye wouldn't be try'n ta make Abby jealous, would ye?" he asked.

"I most certainly hope to."

Vi wished she had the untainted heart her friend possessed.

"If'n I take ye to get ices we be courting, right?" The boy dropped his head and peeked out from under his brown curls.

"I would not let a man take me to Gunther's if he was not officially courting me," Ruby winked and continued. "I am a proper miss, after all."

The boy's unadulterated smile was all that Vi saw as she and Mrs. Hutton continued past the pair and moved further into the house. Even though the paint had peeled in places, the walls appeared freshly scrubbed. Vi could only hope the children were as well cared for as the property.

"We moved ta this spot nigh on three years ago." The woman spoke with pride. "We be have'n ten bedrooms now and a nice kitchen, and even a garden in back."

Based on her first glimpse of the place, Vi had

feared the inside would be as ramshackle as its exterior, but that fear had been for naught. "Tell me about your last house," Vi asked, to keep the woman talking and give herself time to look around.

"Oh, we were in a most dreadful place, m'lady. We be put'n seven, sumtimes eight, children to a room." She *tsk-tsk*ed again. "That be no way to raise a horde of children, even ones as damaged as these."

How long would it be before Mrs. Hutton and the children were forced to move into a smaller house again—or even worse, to the streets? "How many share rooms now?"

"Never over four to a room. Now we be have'n a school room and fine eating area. Right this way to me entertaining room." She pushed a door open to reveal a sparsely furnished sitting room. The couch and chairs didn't match, but they were clean. The rug covering the hardwood floor was worn through, and the drapes held more holes than the cheese Vi ordered from the dairy adjoining Foldgers Hall. "Do have a seat, and I be fetching ye some tea. The cook only comes in to prepare supper." She sounded contrite, as if embarrassed that she could not offer Vi a proper tea setting with sugar, cream, and sandwiches.

"I would love a spot of plain tea. I enjoy the natural flavor of the leaves," Vi said to soothe the woman's unease.

"I be right back." She moved out of the room and pulled the room shut until only a sliver of light filtered in through the crack.

This gave Viola a few minutes to take in her surroundings further. A thought struck her. The furniture from her sitting room at her father's townhouse would suit the room perfectly. Yes, she could do one last thing for Mrs. Hutton and the children—and when money ran out, they could sell the pieces to pay the rent. It made Vi sick every time she walked into that sitting room, but here... Here, it would lighten the atmosphere and make this a home—for however long it lasted.

"Your dress is very pretty, miss."

Vi turned slowly toward the door, not wanting to frighten whomever had spoken. A set of brown eyes stared through the crack in the door, a wisp of blonde hair swung through the opening. "Thank you. Would you like to come in and sit?"

"Mrs. Hutton says this room is for guests only. Not us children—but we never have any guests."

The girl's voice was cultured, as if she'd been born into a family of means.

"I am sure Mrs. Hutton will not mind if you keep me entertained while she makes the tea."

"Are you sure?" The question in the girl's voice did not hold fear or anxiety at being discovered in the sitting room, merely curiosity.

"I am very sure. Please join me and we can talk."

The door was hesitantly pushed open and the girl moved into the room at an angle. Viola caught her breath at the angelic look of her: long blonde hair with startling brown, almost greenish, eyes, and her skin was so fair.

Vi padded the seat next to her on the sofa. "You can sit here."

A smile lit her face and she turned to fully face Vi. When she did, Vi steadied her breathing and forced herself to remain impassive at the sight.

The left side of the girl's face was horribly caved in, her eye sewn shut.

"What is your name?" Vi asked, pleased to note that her voice remained calm.

"My name was Lady Cynthia, but everyone here calls me Abby." She perched on the seat next to Vi and arranged her skirt, crossing her ankles as a lady of the *ton* would do.

"Samuel's Abby?"

The girl blushed. "I most certainly am not *Samuel's* Abby. Did he tell you that? I should box his ears. He has not even asked my father if he might court me."

Vi wanted to laugh, to pull the wounded girl to her and hug her tight. To promise her the world and beyond, but none of that would be appropriate. It was important—to Vi, at least—that the girl not think she was being judged because of her injury. "My apologies, Abby. That is a situation Samuel should rectify if he wishes to continue his association. How old are you?"

"Eleven. My birthday is next week and I will be twelve."

"Almost a true lady of the *ton*. How long have you lived with Mrs. Hutton?"

The girl fidgeted uncomfortably. "Almost four years. My birthday will make it four years."

Abby had come to live here on her birthday.

"Mrs. Hutton is going to make a cake—just for me." The excitement in the girl's voice was hard to miss. "Will you come to my party?"

"I would love to."

"We do not have the money to send out fancy invitations . . ."

"That is okay. Do you mind if I bring a friend?"

"A man friend?" Abby giggled.

"No, my nearest and dearest friend, Ruby." Why did thoughts of Brock pass through her mind? "She is here with me today."

"Only if she brings a present."

Viola did laugh then, a deep laugh. It felt good, something she had not known she needed. "Of course we will bring gifts. It would not be a birthday celebration without gifts."

"Last year, Mrs. Hutton gave me the prettiest purple ribbon for my hair."

"Purple is my favorite color, too." Vi instinctually reached out and smoothed the girl's hair, pushing it behind her one good ear. "What would you like this year?"

"To go live with my family again." The request was so simply stated.

For the third time that morning, Vi wanted to fall to the floor and weep. The *ton* had not only shunned her, they had sheltered her from the unfairness of the real world.

At that moment, they both heard footsteps headed their way. Abby popped up off the couch. "I must be going. I have chores to do above stairs."

"It was lovely meeting you."

"Say you will come to my party." The girl's one good eye pleaded for Vi's affirmative response.

"I would be delighted to."

"Do not forget my gift. I have to go." Abby slid through the door and under Mrs. Hutton's arms, laden with the tea tray. "Good day, Mrs. Hutton. I am almost done with my chores." She hurried down the hall without waiting for a response.

"That child will be the death of me, ye just wait and see." Mrs. Hutton shook her head back and forth, but there was a gleam in her eye. She was clearly fond of Abby.

Vi realized that Mrs. Hutton was all she'd hoped for when she'd heard of the house taking care of children injured by firearms. She was caring and compassionate, much as Vi envisioned her own mother to be.

"She is a lovely child. What happened to her?" It was the question that Vi feared to ask but needed to know.

Mrs. Hutton set the tray down on the table, sat in a chair opposite Vi, and proceeded to pour the tea. "Our resident member of the *ton*. She and her nursemaid were walk'n to Abby's papa's fine house when a bloke tried to rob a coach, right there in broad daylight! Can ye imagine? His gun went off and the bullet hit poor Abby square in the side of her face." Sadness filled her eyes. "Her papa wanted ta jus let the poor child die—right there in the dirty street. But not my sister, her nursemaid. She rushed Abby to the ol' house and I called a doc. A whole year of yer money went to her be'n treated." The woman could not meet Vi's eyes.

Did she fear she'd misspent money? To save the girl?

"You did the right thing, Mrs. Hutton."

"We ate no meat for nigh on two years ta make up for it. Part of me wished I coulda been strong enough ta let the child go to the Lord. What kinda life will she lead now? Never one where'n she belongs." She paused and looked down at the chipped cup of tea she clung to. "Would ye be like'n some sugar?"

"No, thank you." She had another question to ask, uncertain of how the woman would react to it. "Why do you call her Abby, and not Lady Cynthia?"

"Simple. When they come ta me most have been abandoned. Shunned by their families. Here, they be free to choose who they be want'n to be. They're na longer street children— or members of the *ton,* in Abby's case. They be belong'n ta me. There was a day that I was given the chance ta be anyone I wanted ta be. It be the least I can give 'em—and some days it be the most I can afford."

Oh, how Vi wished she could be someone else, anyone else. Who would she be if she had the choice?

Mrs. Hutton continued. "She had a doll at her home. A right pretty and expensive doll. Her name was Abby, and she had to leave the doll there. Her father would na allow her back to his home."

Vi marveled at the woman's ability to talk about the sadness of Abby's situation without shedding a single tear, when she felt her insides being ripped out at the depravity of the girl's father.

"Don't be look'n all sorrowful for the girl. I be have'n plenty others here with far worse stories. Abby be one of the lucky ones—she be knowing the good life."

"But does that not just make the pain all the more great, knowing what she lost?"

"Ye can look at it that way," Mrs. Hutton said thoughtfully. "I prefer ta think she be knowin' who she can be once agin."

"But how?"

"Lady Viola—"

"Please call me Vi," she interrupted.

"All right, Vi," Mrs. Hutton said uncomfortably, "Abby is educated, far beyond that of most of my children. She'll have options. I be hope'n she one day will take over the house."

In that moment Vi resolved she would not—could not—crush this woman's dreams and the future of all the children under her charge. Vi had to find another way to take care of these children . . . even if she had to sell everything she owned. Though even then, she knew the proceeds would not be nearly enough.

"Why are ye here, anyways?" Mrs. Hutton changed the subject, and Vi was grateful. "Did ye come to see that I not be misusing ye money?"

Vi had not come for that reason, although she'd been curious. It would have been easier to send a servant round with her money. "No, that is not why. I happened to be in town and wanted to drop off my donation personally." She did not add that it might very well be her last.

"I be start'n to worry about ye. It had been a long time since ye last sent any. I feared ye had found another place for yer money."

A long time since she had last sent money? But Connor had been in town less than a fortnight ago. He had said he dropped off the envelope. There would be a good explanation, she was sure.

"I do apologize for worrying you so." Vi opened the small receptacle that dangled from her wrist and pulled out an envelope. "This should make up for that."

The woman's eyes were round and her hand shook as she took the thick bundled envelope she was handed. "M'lady? This is too much."

"No, it is exactly right and sounds like I came just

in time. Please make Abby an extra-special birthday cake. Something that will impress her father."

Mrs. Hutton looked up. A new sorrow filled her eyes.

"Did I say something wrong?" Vi spoke without thinking.

"Why would ye seek to impress her papa?"

Vi set down her cup, unsure how to answer. "It is only that when I asked her what she wanted for her special day, Abby said to live with her family again."

"She is still going on about that . . .? Poor child."

"Is everything all right with her family?"

"Oh, I am sure they be do'n quite fine, but I would not know. Ye see, I haven't seen hide nor hair of them since Abby come to live here."

CHAPTER TWENTY-SIX

Brock entered the Darlingiver ballroom as the strings of a country reel started. He and Harold had deposited their coats at the door long after the host and hostess had quit their receiving line; they had arrived too late for dinner. Now, pairs moved around the dance floor in the same manner he had seen at countless soirees since his return to polite society.

They had planned to visit White's that evening for a round of cards, but had changed their plans when the invitation had arrived with a personal note from Lord Darlingiver, requesting their attendance.

"Are you sure you are unacquainted with the Duke?" Harold leaned close to ask over the swell of the music.

"Most positive. All I know about the man is that his mother is linked to Lord Liperton. Hence our acceptance of this fashionably late invitation." Brock spotted the Unker twins on the fringes of the dance floor, each swaying to the music. "Why do we not adjourn to the card room?"

Harold followed behind Brock, his cane thumping the floor as he went. "Do you see him?"

"I have not a clue what he looks like, so no, I have not seen him." The man had requested a reply to his invitation and they had complied; Lord Darlingiver would be expecting them. Why he had extended entrance to his home, Brock was not sure.

"I will obtain drinks for us and meet you in the card room." Harold did not wait for Brock to warn him about the consequences of returning with sherry.

Brock moved further into the room, toward the smell of cigar smoke and congregating men. Knowing of the link between Lady Viola and the Darlingiver family had convinced him to accept the invitation. After the glimpse of her in the park two days before, he had not seen her again. He and Harold had attended a ball, a musicale, and the opera since then, but she had not been at any of the gatherings, his spirits dashed as each evening drew to an end.

Time was running out. Brock had neglected his estate in his quest for vengeance, and could do so no longer.

The crowd in the room moved to the music, even those not dancing. Extravagant hats and colorful dresses swirled, much the same as any other ball he had attended. Every evening proceeded the same way, although he hoped the outcome of tonight would be more favorable.

As he reached the double doors leading into the card room, a rush of men sought to exit. "What is going on?" he asked a passing gentleman he recognized from White's.

"She is here."

"She?"

"As if I need to tell you of all people who *she* is," the man huffed, and hurried past Brock into the suddenly quiet ballroom.

Brock turned to survey the room behind him. Everywhere he looked, people faced the door through which he had entered only moments earlier. Skimming the hat-clad heads of women and the balding and sometimes wigged heads of men, his gaze alighted on a few figures congregated at the top of the stairs leading into the room.

Her back was to him as a footman removed her cloak. Brock was unsure what made the woman the center of attention—until she turned to face the crowd that stood in stunned silence.

Light from the candles far above glistened off her iridescent purple evening gown, cut low off her shoulders and barely concealing her breasts from view. The tightly gathered middle showed off her lean waist. Her chestnut brown hair had been swept up into a loose knot high on her head, unlike the severe knot she'd worn when working with her foals. No ridiculous hat hid its magnificence from view.

Brock dragged his eyes from her and realized he was not the only one affected by her presence. Every man and woman stood with their mouths open in awe. Dance pairs separated. Servants froze where they stood, the bubbles in their wine glasses slowly rising to the top.

And the small group did not seem to notice any of this.

A part of him wanted to scream, to protest the adoration the crowd turned on her. The other part of

CHRISTINA MCKNIGHT

him only thirsted for more time to watch her, take in all her glory, before his extreme need for revenge overtook him.

Their hostess, Lady Darlingiver, and a younger man—their host, Brock presumed—met the group as they finished removing their cloaks. Curtsies and bows ensued, followed by hugs of acknowledgement.

Finally, the group turned to the waiting crowd. Lady Viola smiled.

Not the smile of a confident woman of the *ton*, or even the shy smile of a newly introduced debutante. This smile was one of outright terror. It pulled unnaturally across her face.

How did he know this? Because he had been privy to her smiles before. If he looked closely, he could see her hands shake when she lifted the skirts of her gown to descend the few steps into the ballroom.

And then, everything returned to normal. The music filled his ears again and the members of the *ton* broke into their ceaseless chatter once more. Had it ever actually stopped?

Brock gave his head a slight shake to clear the image of Lady Viola from his head.

As if on cue, the crowd separated and an empty path was created for him. Directly to her.

It seemed his moment had come, although he had not anticipated giving her the upbraiding of her life in an overly crowded ballroom. Possibly on a sparsely attended veranda, but here?

Unfortunately, he did not have any further time to ponder his options.

Her head lifted and their eyes met, her sapphire blue to his brown. What he saw reflected back was much the same as what he knew his own held: anger, cold and raw.

What in heavens could she be so mad about? Brock and his family had been the injured party, not her. While his father had suffered, she had retired to the country to take up a new hobby, although he knew she had not completely left her old ways behind. He had seen the love letter on her desk. Had she traveled to London in hopes of rekindling that romance?

Could he allow her to ruin the lives of another family? Every fiber of his being screamed no. He could not allow it. But how could he stop it? He had been unsuccessful thus far in locating D & C Fine Foals, and he feared he would also fail in this.

Lady Viola reached her hands down and lifted her many layers of skirts, her slippered feet carrying her across the now-vacant ballroom floor, in his direction.

Her purposefulness sparked something inside him and Brock began in her direction, his footfalls echoing in the again-silent room. Is this why he had been invited tonight? Had they been forced into this meeting? He did not care; all he cared about was putting this whip of a girl in her place. She'd destroyed many lives and it was his responsibility—no, his *duty*—to see that she also suffered.

He glanced over her shoulder as their paths drew closer. Miss Ruby followed hesitantly behind her, and her father, Lord Liperton, stood stunned and useless.

Their fate had been decided. Brock prepared himself for battle as he had all those years serving the King, his shoulders back, his chin tilted ever so slightly upward, his steps long and sure.

Too late, he saw his own determination mirrored in

her stride. He couldn't help but wonder if this would be a fight to the death. At least one of them would leave this ball a victor, unlike the duel that took the lives of both his brothers—and ultimately his father, as well.

Her progress across the expanse of the room seemed to last days, possibly years.

He halted. Let her come to him. He did not seek to be known as the gentleman who accosted a lady of the *ton* in the middle of a ballroom.

Placing his hands on his hips and widening his stance, Brock looked around. Just as he had suspected, all eyes were on the collision about to take place—including the young man at Lady Darlingiver's side. A smile lifted the corner of the dullard's mouth, and Brock had no doubt this meeting had been orchestrated. A part of him wanted to avert exactly what the man hoped for, but at that moment Lady Viola stopped in front of him.

As her stride had matched his so did her stance, feet spread wide and hands on hips.

"Lord Haversham. How nice of you to attend the ball thrown in my honor."

In her honor? She had his attention now. "Do you believe I would ever seek to honor you?"

"Is your presence here not confirmation enough?" she shot back.

"So, we are doing this? In the middle of a crowded ballroom?"

She dared to laugh, a cold cackle as she threw her arms wide. "I know it is not your preferred style. You are the type to sneak around and spread gossip about others. Being out in the open in this way must be uncomfortable for you."

"You dare to confront me about 'being out in the open'? I have never lied about who I am, or my motives."

A hand grasped his elbow and tugged lightly. "Brock, I think—"

"Harold, if you do not seek a broken nose I would stand down and release me," Brock said, never taking his eyes off the woman in front of him.

"I did not peg you for a violent man, Lord Haversham." Lady Viola's voice dripped with venom.

"Mr. Jakeston is correct. I believe we should—"

"Ruby, do see to my father, or Lord Haversham is likely to lash out violently at you as well."

"You cannot believe that Brock would—" Harold started.

"Oh, I most certainly do, Mr. Jakeston," she said, not breaking eye contact with Brock.

"May I interest you in a sherry, Miss St. Augustin?" Harold asked nervously.

"I think a cool drink is just the thing," Brock heard Lady Viola's friend reply, and the weight lifted from his arm. He rotated his shoulder, attempting to ease the tension there.

"May I say, you look positively ravishing this evening, my lady?" He tried a change of tone. While every fiber down to his core sought this confrontation, thought it was too long in the making, he did not wish to air his family's soiled laundry in such a public place. "I suspect you looked similarly . . ." he took in her appearance from head to toe before continuing, ". . . scandalous when you manipulated my brothers."

"And I am sure that when I was luring your brothers to their certain death, you were gallivanting around the continent."

Her response brought him up short; he could hardly believe his ears. She'd admitted her responsibility in Cody and Winston's deaths—more than that, she had practically thrown it in his face. The woman was every bit as evil as he had presumed. "Do not make light of my service to my country—your country."

"I would not dare belittle the man who sabotaged my business to appease his own guilt for being absent for so much of his brothers' lives."

"Do not misunderstand the situation we both see ourselves in. It was you who ruined my life. You took my family from me with your petty, selfish games. You admitted as much only moments ago!"

"Enough!" shouted Lord Liperton.

Brock blinked, breaking eye contact with his target. Lady Viola's father stood at her elbow, his face red with rage.

"This is quite enough! Viola, we are leaving . . . now."

The tension broken, they both looked around them, seeing for the first time the scene they had caused.

The eyes staring back at Brock held contempt, although he was not certain if it was aimed at him or the loathsome woman before him. He swiveled to his left when a burst of laughter rang through the room. His cousin, Rodney, leaned in the doorway to the card room. From his broad smile he was enjoying the night's entertainment greatly.

When Brock returned his gaze to his target, all he saw was her retreating form, hauled by her father toward a waiting footman holding out their coats.

Again he looked around him. Members of the *ton* continued to look upon him with disdain. Yes, the feelings of scorn were indeed directed at him.

Blast it! He'd botched the situation royally.

# # #

"What in the bloody hell were you thinking?"

"I do not know," Vi answered her father. The truth was, she'd been thinking so many things as she'd come face to face with Brock: Her morning, which had turned into afternoon, at the orphanage; her loss of Foldger's Foals; and, ultimately, the forfeiture of herself all those years ago.

Before the carriage departed, both St. Augustin women entered. Ruby sat next to Vi, her mother next to Lord Liperton. Vi had been so consumed by Lord Haversham's presence she hadn't noticed Ruby's mother in the crowded ballroom—not that she'd noticed anything once her gaze alighted on Brock.

"That truly was uncalled for, Vi," Ruby chided her.

Lady Darlingiver's parting words passed through her mind at that moment. *I knew this was a mistake! My lord, I've put up with a lot from your daughter . . . but this? Her first social engagement back?* Her use of his formal title told Vi the woman her father appeared to love was already distancing herself from her family—for a second time.

It hurt, but not nearly as much as it wounded her father, she was sure. Who would he choose this time? How many times would Vi make him select his daughter over everyone else?

He huffed on the seat across from her. "Do not think your sullen attitude and silence will make this go away, Viola," her father warned.

She knew this would not go away—could not go away. The thought of repeating the actions she'd taken eight years ago repulsed her. She'd no intention of running again or letting the *ton* shun her a second time.

An arm came around her shoulders and rested comfortably on Vi's shaking form. She had not realized she was crying, her body racked with silent sobs. She had attained what she'd traveled to London for. Although the confrontation had occurred at an unexpected time and place, it was done. The hurtful words that had spilled from her mouth were also unexpected.

Would he know her words to be untrue? She knew she could not leave town without him knowing she had not—even in her youth naiveté—planned the demise of either of his brothers. It was true she had not cared for either one of them; no tenderness passed through her at the thought of either twin. Alternatively, at the mere image of their elder brother, her body hummed with . . . she did not know what.

"We will leave town posthaste. Ruby, you are free to stay with your mother through the end of the season, if you would like," her father continued.

"Father, I do not—" Her head shot up to meet his gaze.

"I do not want to hear another word from you."

Ruby recoiled beside her at Vi's father's angry words. "If you do not mind, my lord, I prefer to travel with Vi back to the country."

Viola nearly broke down in a fresh stream of tears at her friend's loyalty—and after she'd ruined any chance of Ruby being a success in London. "That is unnec—"

"I agree with your father, Vi," Ruby said. "I do not want to hear a word from you. I am coming and there is naught you can say about it."

"Yes, perhaps you are both better suited to country life," Mrs. St. Augustin muttered.

Vi did not bother following the conversation from there. The three discussed her future, her options, without even bothering to ask what she wanted. But truly, they were past being able to give her what she desired. *She* was past being able to verbalize what she wanted. She only hoped to gain back her father's love and her friend's trust—anything beyond that, she knew she didn't deserve.

"You did not return to London to find a husband, did you?"

Those words, uttered from the defeated shell of her father, solidified her knowledge that she was about to embark on a long and hard road.

CHAPTER TWENTY-SEVEN

Dawn had yet to break as their carriage crested the last ridge before arriving at Foldger's Hall. How Viola longed to tell the driver to keep going, past her father's estate and on to Foldger's Foals—her safe haven. The place she'd grown from a petty, naive girl whose only dream had been to uphold the standards of a society that took pleasure in forsaking their own, to a woman who had learned to support not only herself, but others who had survived fates so much worse than her own.

It would not be a safe haven for long, she knew; they'd only returned to liquidate the remaining property. Soon, they would return to London and, her father had explained as they sat out late the night before, Vi would have to make amends—to Lady Darlingiver, Lord Haversham, and society as a whole.

She sighed.

While she did owe Lady Darlingiver an apology for ruining her party, she didn't understand why she'd be made to make amends with Brock or the insufferable people who made up the ruling class in London. Had they apologized to the girl who'd been ridiculed relentlessly over the years for mistakes made in her youth? Mistakes that were caused by the entitlement bred into her since her birth? In her estimation, they owed her, and every other debutante, an apology. Atonement was owed for the pressures they'd put on young girls to dress a certain way, act a certain way, show deference to their betters, but mostly for robbing them of their youth—a time better spent educating themselves in the languages of the world, the art of poetry, and the fulfillment of hard work, not the quest to marry above their station without the benefit of love or respect.

Now, where had that come from?

Vi knew she would never know the true, undying love of a man, except that given by her father. And respect…in her experience, men rarely respected females. Whether it be their wife, mother, or a passing acquaintance, it mattered naught.

Ruby leaned lightly against her, having fallen into a deep slumber the second they left her father's townhouse. Vi envied her friend's relaxed state. Several times on the four-hour journey she'd sought oblivion in sleep, but that comfort eluded her. With nothing else to do, she'd stared out at the inky night as it passed, listening to her father's light snoring from his seat while she pondered her mistakes, trying to reconcile her future.

Occasionally, Ruby sighed in her sleep and Vi wondered what she dreamt about. Part of her was glad sleep didn't find her, because she was certain it would be wrought with nightmares. Yes, while awake she could guide her thoughts, but in sleep she'd be helpless to stop her mind from wandering to subjects better left alone.

"Father," she called quietly as they rolled to a stop, not wanting to startle him out of his slumber. When his eyelids fluttered, Vi continued. "We have arrived."

The next few hours passed in a haze as Vi inventoried all her belongings at Foldger's Foals and also at her father's estate. She hadn't known his intent was to be rid of all her worldly possessions. Did he see it as a sort of punishment for her actions and behavior the previous evening? He should see that she'd punished herself relentlessly over the last eight years... Discarding her possessions would have no effect on her.

Her sitting room had been emptied and her bedroom likewise, except for her bed and dressing closet. If she'd hoped to return to her father's country estate in the near future, that hope was dashed as she packed every item, from her many dresses to the hair ribbons nearly forgotten since her youth.

Vi had instructed a coach be filled, and knew it was already en route to Mrs. Hutton and the children. *Her* children. A note tucked safely into a box of old dresses instructed Mrs. Hutton to cut down her sturdy stables dresses to make durable clothes for the children. Simple frocks for the girls, and pants for the boys.

Now, Vi was preparing to meet with a man who sought to purchase the excess tack from the ranch when she realized she still wore her purple gown—the gown she'd thought would start her life anew, wipe away all the sins of her past. That hadn't been the case, and for a moment she feared she had not changed or grown as much as she'd tried to convince herself. Truthfully, she'd been successful in deluding every person she knew—with the possible except of Lady Darlingiver.

No matter how much she'd disappointed her father, Vi had disappointed herself far more.

She returned to her sparsely furnished room and changed into a more suitable gown, this one of sturdy cotton, and made her way back downstairs and out the front door. The need no longer existed for Connor to act as liaison, as Vi's affiliation was known by one and all. She dreaded meeting with him before she departed for London; he was an intelligent man, and no doubt knew his employment at Foldger's Foals could not last longer than the property belonged to the Oberbrook family.

The walk to the hidden gate and her office was a short one. She found herself unhurried as she made her way—possibly for the final time—to the place where she'd found solace for so long. Where would she find that contentment now? Years ago she hadn't been mature enough, concerned enough, to feel the unease she did at this moment.

The grass, wet with late morning dew, clung to her slippers much like that early morning years ago. The smell of the oak and silver birch trees; the sight of all the men huddled in small groups… the sound of pistols firing. The shots had echoed loudly as both men dropped to the ground. Why had she not registered the ear-splitting sound then?

"Lady Viola?" a vaguely familiar voice called.

She took her gaze off her feet and looked ahead to the man who had spoken her name. "Hamp—Lord Darlingiver? What a pleasant surprise. Were you not just in London last eve?" He had been there, she was positive of that.

"Yes. I rode to my estate, only an hour's ride from here, early this morning." He smiled. "I am scheduled to meet with you today…" He looked up at the sun, as if judging the hour before he continued. "Right now, actually."

"I am afraid I do not know what you are talking about." The only meeting she knew about was with a man seeking to purchase her used horse tack. "Foldger's Foals is no longer in business. I am sure your mother informed you thusly." He had most likely been one of the first to know, or should have been. The image of faceless masses laughing at her expense clouded her vision.

His smile faded. "Yes, I am aware. I am the one you're here to meet."

"Oh." She couldn't think of a better reply and wasn't sure the effort of thinking of one was worth her time.

She continued to walk toward the barn with Lord Darlingiver strolling beside her. His stride slowed to match her much shorter one, his hands clasped behind his back. She peeked at him from the corner of her eye. He hadn't changed much since their time in London when she was still a girl; he still dressed to the height of fashion, or what she presumed was fashion. He was a good looking man, cultured with a hint of arrogance.

One thing that was different about him was his confidence. He no longer walked with light steps, but with the sure, solid stride of a man comfortable with his place in the world.

"Why do you have need of my tack?" she ventured.

They entered the barn before he answered. "I have my own ranch not far from here. A stable can never have too many bridles and bale hooks—at least that is what my stable master says." He chuckled, but Vi had no urge to join him in banter.

Why would he not send his stable master to negotiate and retrieve the supplies, she wanted to ask? Unfortunately, that would invite the question of why she was conducting her own business. They moved further into the stable, toward the tack room located halfway down the long corridor of stalls. As they approached, she heard the sound of jangling metal.

Who would be in the tack room? All her employees had either been let go, or moved to her father's stable or their London townhouse. She did not halt or hesitate as she entered the room.

A tall form with dark hair leaned over a box, laden with bridles, lead ropes, and whips.

"Connor?" What would he be doing here? His presence reinforced her need to be done with things and tell him it was time he moved on.

His head shot up as he turned in her direction. "Lady Viola. I thought I would pack the last of this room."

He'd always sought to make things easier for her, and she felt a flicker of gratitude for the man who had stood by her side all these years. "Thank you. I would like to introduce you . . ." Vi looked to her side, expecting Hampton to be there. The spot was empty. "Lord Darlingiver?" She poked her head out the door, looking up and down the stable corridor. The man had vanished.

"Lord Darlingiver, did you say?" Connor tensed as he asked the question.

"Yes. He met me to have a look at the remaining

items for sale. Are you acquainted with him?"

Connor turned back to his task, and the ensuing clatter of bridles almost drowned out his reply. "No. I mean, yes. . . . He has property not far from here, correct?"

Vi shouldn't have been surprised: Connor had been in charge of acquiring new clients for many years. He was a good business man. "That is correct." Why should this particular name make him uneasy?

"Well, I must get—" The bridles he's been hanging on their pegs laid at his feet in disarray.

He was in a hurry to depart. But why, Vi wondered.

"Connor, thank you for all your hard work over the years."

He straightened and faced her, as though sensing what was coming.

"You have always applied yourself to my business and—"

"Vi! Are you in here?" Ruby's voice drifted down the empty stable house, echoing off the walls. "Do not think I am going to wander through this dark stable in search of you. Do come out."

Vi laughed, glad for the reprieve. "Connor, could we talk later?"

"Of course, my lady." He bowed.

"I am coming," Viola shouted in Ruby's direction. "I will come see you before I leave."

"Good day." He seemed to want to put off the inevitable, as well.

"Good day, Connor."

She turned on her heel and ran from the room and down the long corridor of stalls, glancing in each as she passed in hopes of locating Hampton. She skidded to a halt before exiting the stables to take a long look behind her. Memories from the last eight years flooded her: her first time with a foal... the first time she'd been thrown from a horse... her many afternoon picnics in the hay with Ruby. How she would miss this place—the place where she'd discovered who she was, and who she would continue to strive to be. It wasn't easy, and the journey ahead wouldn't prove any less grueling, but it was something she had to do, if only to prove to herself that life was worth living and living well. Even if it meant going against society's protocols.

"Do not dally," Ruby said.

Startled, Vi turned to her friend with a smile. "You should not sneak up on people. You might see something you wish not to."

"I hardly think so."

Viola laced her arm to Ruby's and turned them toward the door. "Shall we?"

"I believe that would be wise. Your father is preparing to leave, and he says we must be in the carriage within the hour."

Within the hour? She'd thought they would spend a few days before journeying back to London. "We cannot argue with him, can we?"

Ruby shook her head. "I would not suggest it."

As they made their way back to the estate, Vi remembered that she hadn't been able to properly dismiss Connor, or push him to find another employer.

She stopped in her tracks before they alighted the steps into the grand house, and Ruby came to a halt beside her. She had not asked Connor about her last donation, she remembered suddenly—the one he'd said he delivered when he traveled to meet with Brock in town. The money had never reached Mrs. Hutton. Where had it gone?

It had slipped her mind with all the uproar of the past night. Now, however, the puzzle struck her full force. Vi rebelled against the possibility that a person, a friend she trusted unequivocally, might betray her. But she was certain Mrs. Hutton would not lie; she had never received the money Vi had trusted Connor to deliver. And based on the words the woman had said, this was not the only time Connor had held back funds meant for Mrs. Hutton and her children.

If he had taken the money, how was he any different than men like Brock, who had used her as his own hammering block? His verbal assault the other night had at least been aimed at her face and not behind her back.

Would she be able to handle the possibility that he'd secretly been working against her? It was not human nature to devote your life, your time, and all your energy to the dream of another. She'd often wondered why Connor was so loyal to her, and why he had given up his place in society to help her. At first she'd thought he fancied her, but as the years passed, they settled into a relationship akin to family. So much more than master and servant. Was it possible that his motivations were not as she'd thought? That he had secrets she was unaware of?

"Hurry, Vi, the household is up in arms preparing for your father to leave. There will be no one left to help us finish packing our belongings."

Vi had been forced to leave Sarah, her maid, in town in her father's haste the night before. "You go up and pack. I must return to the stables and have a word with Connor." Before she could change her mind or Ruby could voice her objection, Vi turned and ran back to the gate separating the properties.

Safely out of view, she slowed her pace and squared her shoulders, hoping to gain an air of confidence.

The stable looked just as she'd left it only moments ago: empty. Devoid of the stable hands she'd gotten accustomed to running about, bare of the bales of hay that normally lined the outside of the building on one side. She knew the stalls within would seem hollow without the foals she had treasured. If she called out, her voice would bounce off the walls, barren of bridles, ropes, hay hooks, and pitch forks.

Blank, void, empty, hollow, barren. These words—the feelings invoked by them—also represented her life. There was naught left. Her ranch was gone. Her father slipped further away with each mention of the scandal she'd caused, both in her youth and the previous evening. Now, she'd also be forced to abandon Mrs. Hutton and the children. If she couldn't give them funds, did she have anything else to give? She feared not. She was a worthless shell of a person, like so many vapid debutantes were happy to be.

"Connor?" She called into the stables quietly, not wanting to hear her voice echo. When no reply came, she moved further into the dim interior to the room where he'd last been.

As she'd expected, it sat empty.

Maybe he'd finished his task and set off for home. Maybe he knew she'd inquired with Mrs. Hutton, and found he hadn't dropped off the donation.

There was nothing for it. When she arrived in London, she would send word to him and never have to learn the truth. It was said that what a person didn't know could never hurt them. Vi hoped this was the case.

As she turned to go, voices raised in anger floated her way from the rear of the stable. One belonged to Connor. She'd heard it raised in volume many times as he called across a field to a stable boy or when directing a group of foals. The other voice, however, she didn't recognize.

". . . come here? She is done, her business failed."

They spoke of her?

The rear stable door stood open as she approached. Her view showed no one in sight. Who could Connor possibly by arguing with? All the stables hands had been let go before she left for London.

"I wanted to ascertain that you were proceeding according to our plans."

"You need to go. If Lady Viola sees us conversing, she will put things together. Regardless of what you think, the woman is sharp." Connor's voice grew louder.

"Do you think I am concerned with her and what she knows?" The unseen man chuckled. "It is too late for her to change anything. Besides, I have other reasons for being here."

"What, then? You are in need of more funds?"

Vi pictured Connor throwing up his hands in exasperation.

"Running a ranch takes money, as you well know."

"I have no more money. As soon as the carriage departs carrying Lady Viola, her father, and Miss Ruby, I will travel to your estate. I will take over the financials and figure everything out."

Dread, cold and thick, ran through her body. She did know that voice—it belonged to Lord Darlingiver. But why? Had they schemed against her, stolen money that should have gone to disabled children, merely to see her fail? To what end?

She took a step back and knocked into a partially open stall gate. It let out an unoiled groan as it swung closed an inch.

Vi froze.

When the men continued to argue she moved into the stall, hoping to hide in the shadows, effectively stopping their angry words from reaching her. Soon, her slow steps brought her to the back wall of the stall, and she laid her hand against the rough wood. Her other hand shielded her eyes. Some irrational part of her brain told her that if she couldn't see them pass by the stall, then this moment hadn't happened. She had not heard what was now seared into her memory: Betrayal. As if her world hadn't tilted on its axis enough, this might just push it off entirely.

Her breath left in a rush of nausea and her head came to rest next to her hand on the cool wooden wall. The thought that someone had been working against her—not just someone, but one of the only people she'd trusted without reserve—was unimaginable. Unforgivable.

A sob wrenched from her chest, loud to her own ears. Tears streamed down her face and her breath quickened once again. Her chest felt as if something was trying to claw its way out and she gave up the effort of staying on her feet as she slid to the straw-covered ground.

In the distance the yelling stopped and footsteps echoed not far from her. She concentrated on determining if they belonged to one man or both, trying to stop the spinning in her head.

"Bloody hell," Connor yelled.

A loud crash sounded as something solid hit the stall door she hid behind.

Thankfully, Connor continued through the stables and out the door.

CHAPTER TWENTY-EIGHT

"Bastard!" Connor slammed his mug of ale onto the wood-planked bar in front of him. The warm liquid sloshed over the rim, coating his hand. "Christ's sake."

He'd been in a foul mood since he had left Foldger's Foals. Instead of traveling to Hamp's estate as he'd promised, he had ridden hell bent toward London. Besides the small inn they'd visited on occasion to discuss business, there wasn't a local place that could afford him a spot of privacy. He sought a place—and the time—to clear his head and figure out his next move. In London, it would be easy to disappear for a day or a week, no one the wiser.

The Fox and the Hound is where he'd settled. Eight ales later, he had yet to resolve even one of his problems. He'd had a hand in ending the business that had afforded him financial security for the last seven years, he'd gone into business with a no-good ne'er do well who consistently spent money without adding to the coffers, and there was little chance that all of

London wouldn't find out the truth of it all by the end of the season.

Connor had set his course of action years ago and was given many chances to alter his path, but he'd hedged his lot and levied all his bets—on the wrong side.

"Can I get ye another pint, sir?" The barkeep dried a recently rinsed mug with the grimy towel that hung from his waistband.

Connor's pocket was quite a few coins lighter since he'd entered the bar. If he was to continue his time in London, he had to watch where he spent the last of his money. He'd funneled not only pilfered cash from Vi's money box but also his own wages to keep Hamp afloat. It was his foolishness that had him believing his friend's word that the man had been working, making connections for D & C's Fine Foals. In reality, Hamp had spent most of the coin to set his mistress up in a flat on the most fashionable part of town. "The cod!"

The barkeep stopped his rhythmic wiping and stared hard at Connor. "Look, I jus be ask'n ye if you be need'n another drink."

Connor reached into his pocket and pulled enough coin out to settle his tab. "My apologies. I was talking to myself." He set half of his remaining money on the bar. "This should be enough. Have a pleasant evening." Connor surveyed the crowded room as he slipped his overcoat on.

The bar had filled since he'd arrived hours before, but Connor hadn't heard the laughter of men deep in their cups or the shuffling of cards from the table in the corner. He moved through the crowd and out the door. When had the sun set, and how long until it again rose?

He rubbed his smoke-heavy eyes, happy for the fresh air the outdoors provided. Looking left and then right, he turned in the direction where a great amount of foot traffic and light lit the way toward a more populated area of town. The last thing he wanted was to find himself on a deserted stretch of road frequented by robbers and pickpockets.

As he traversed the street, the quality of attire the men and woman wore changed from sturdy cottons to tailored pants and fine dresses. He pulled his coat tight around his worn-work attire to hide the dirt from view.

During his moping at The Fox and The Hound he'd lost sight of the large picture—the start of his problems.

Lady Viola Oberbrook.

She was not a friend.

She could not be trusted.

She'd deserved everything she'd gotten—and deserved even more than all that had been taken from her recently.

Yes, she had manipulated him. His fists clenched. She'd lead him on. She should have come around with time—even her father hinted at a possible match between the pair. He'd sunk years of his life into her. Truly, she was the only person to blame for where he stood, what he'd missed out on, and the further decay his life would no doubt face.

She'd chosen her path in life. She'd treated people such as himself unjustly all those years ago. It was not his concern that she was only paying for her sins now.

But pay for her sins she must. People could only outrun their misdeeds for so long—something he was only beginning to understand now.

He was unsure how long he'd walked, how much distance he'd covered, or what time of night it might be. The chilly London air had seeped through his overcoat and chills spread through his body. He needed to find an affordable inn, or at least a bar to escape the cold. Looking around, he tried to determine his exact location.

Unfortunately, he'd made his way to a very high end part of town.

"Mr. Cale?" a voice called to him in the semi-darkness.

Connor looked around to see who had called him when a man stepped out of a well-lit doorway several feet behind him. The dark street, combined with the bright lights from the establishment he'd just left, cast a shadow across the man's face.

"It is I, Rodney Swiftenberg." The voice paused as the man moved toward Connor.

Of all his bad luck, he'd been spotted by Lord Haversham's cousin. "Yes, good evening, Sir." Connor kept his voice level and bowed—placing his hand firmly against the wall to stop from swaying. "How nice to see you again."

"Very good, indeed. Can I interest you in a drink?"

Pedestrians made their way around the men on the walkway. It would not do to loiter where someone else could spot him. "That would be agreeable. The weather has turned cold quite quickly." Too late, he realized they stood outside of White's. The interior of the club was teeming with men seeking refuge and drink after a night spent toiling at a ball or the opera house. Every man worth a grain of salt was either in the club or on their way there. Connor's luck was not on point this evening.

Moments later, Rodney sat in an empty chair inside White's and gestured for Connor to do the same. "Scotch or brandy?" he asked, and motioned for a server to attend them.

"Brandy, please." Connor scanned the room as Rodney spoke to the server. There didn't appear to be anyone he knew in attendance at the moment. Possibly his luck was returning.

"Now that everything is out in the open, may we speak candidly?"

And as quickly as he'd thought his night was improving, it was cast back into the gutter. "Of course." How else could he respond?

"I understand that we both have a certain young lady," Rodney paused to accept his drink from the servant, "whose disappearance would benefit us greatly. Am I correct?"

Connor eyed him, uncertain how to answer. The man could very well be tricking him into revealing himself. "I am unsure what you mean."

"Oh, come now." Rodney brought his glass to his lips patiently, as if waiting for his meaning to sink in. When Connor remained quiet, he continued. "Lady Viola and her presence here in London could seriously jeopardize both our futures."

Connor had a viable reason for wanting Lady Viola far from London, but what could Rodney's reasoning be? He decided to wait the man out, forcing him to reveal his motivation first.

"You see, I have a vested interest, as you may well know, in the Haversham estate. It would not behoove my cause if my dear cousin was to go off and get

289

himself wed now."

Puzzled, Connor asked, "How does that involve either myself or Lady Viola?"

The man chuckled. "Do not pretend that you do not see the way your mistress captivates my cousin. The man looks fairly awestruck every time her name is mentioned."

It was Connor's turn to take a long sip of his drink. "And you think after the other evening, that either Lady Viola or Lord Haversham will ever wish to seek each other out again?"

"The past has shown that the Haversham men are not the best judge in women." Rodney sat forward in his seat and set his empty glass on the table between them. "And it would be very bad for you if Lady Viola were to expose your disloyalty."

Connor cringed. He would have no reprieve if all of London knew he'd sabotaged Lady Viola; his chances of gaining employment would be lost.

Curse Hampton and his foolhardiness.

Curse Lady Viola and her selfish youth.

Curse Lord Haversham for his horrible timing.

But mostly, he cursed himself!

"What shall we do about this dilemma?" Connor asked. It couldn't be anything more revolting than what Viola had done to him.

The man smirked. "To be honest, I do not care about solving your problem. Only mine."

"Then why are we speaking?"

"Because you will help me solve my problem, lest I spread word of your transgressions amongst society. See how we can help each other now?"

It was perfectly clear to him. If Connor helped

keep the pair apart, then Rodney would not help to spread his secret faster than it would spread eventually. He must resign himself to the fact that'd he'd aligned himself with a shady character—namely Hampton—who had taken advantage of him. Now, that cycle would continue. Lying begets liars. "And if I refuse to help you, what then?"

"It is very simple. I will—" Rodney paused to look over Connor's shoulder in the direction of the door. "Cousin, how lovely to see you. Do join us for a drink."

Connor turned in his chair as Lord Haversham sauntered toward them, a dark look on his face.

"I haven't the time, Rodney," Lord Haversham said as he moved past the seat Connor occupied. But before he entered the card room, he turned. "Mr. Cale?"

A cloud, darker than what had already been there, settled on Lord Haversham's face.

Connor immediately stood, bowing low in greeting. "Good evening, my lord. I trust you are well?" Too late, Connor saw his mistake. Of course the man was not well. He'd entered into an epic battle of wits with Lady Viola in front of the entire *ton*. It made what Lady Viola had done to Connor seem minuscule in comparison. "I mean to say—"

Lord Haversham turned fully to address Connor. "I do not particularly care what you mean to say...or to hear you say naught at all."

The venomous words pushed Connor back into his chair as if he'd been struck a physical blow. "My lord?" Connor looked to Rodney for help but the man was gone, leaving Connor to endure Lord Haversham's wrath alone.

"You are a poor excuse for a gentleman. It is the

height of immorality to abuse a woman's trust thusly!" Lord Haversham spit out.

"But—" Connor shuddered. "How is what I've done any different than what you've done?" He knew the question was unwise to ask, and regretted his loose tongue immediately.

Lord Haversham's nostrils flared and his eyes shot daggers. "And what precisely have I done that in any form resembles the atrocities you have committed?"

Connor knew he needed to select his words wisely if he meant to make it out of White's alive. Men from every corner of the room moved a bit closer to hear their heated conversation. No doubt the betting book would be full within minutes with speculation as to what they argued about, who would challenge whom to a duel, and whether it was more likely that Lord Haversham or Connor currently slept with Lady Viola. Connor had seriously miscalculated Lord Haversham and his rage.

"It is just...ummm...she lied to you, used you, and hurt your family. Just as she did to me all those years ago. I know exactly how much you must loathe the woman." He was babbling and he knew it, but he could not turn back now. He needed Lord Haversham to understand. "She is a charlatan of the first water. A conniving bit—"

#

"Son of a bitch!" Brock massaged his clenched fist. He'd never been a violent man, but Connor had begged for it. No man insulted a woman in his presence, not matter what Brock felt for the woman himself.

The club's butler rushed toward him, and the men who'd gathered closer to watch now took a step back.

"My lord." The butler took Brock by the elbow and guided him to a small meeting room next to the card room. "This way, please."

Brock was aware that White's frowned upon violence within its walls, and it was common for men to step outside the door when driven to fisticuffs. He glanced over his shoulder one last time before the door to the room closed tightly against the prying eyes of the *ton*. Men lined up eagerly to place wagers at the famous betting book within the club. He didn't doubt that speculation would run rampant and only add fuel to the fire for the gossipmongers about town. He only hoped the flames didn't take both him and Lady Viola down.

The room seemed to shrink as he paced the length waiting for his temper to recede. His long stride ate up the floor underfoot and before he knew it he was turning once again to return to the other end of the room. The walls closed in on him and he struggled to pull the warm air into his lungs. Before he knew what he was doing, he'd ripped off his perfectly knotted cravat and it lay discarded with his jacket.

"Fuck!" He dropped into an overstuffed arm chair positioned in front of a roaring fire and rolled up his shirtsleeves. "Bloody hell and damnation."

The cursing relieved a bit of his anger. What had he been thinking? Yet again, he'd caused a scene—a needless scene, at that. Connor wasn't worth his time or the possibility of being disbarred from a club his family had been members of for over a hundred years.

Violence wasn't him. Even during his many years as a soldier he'd sought to resolve conflict in a non-violent way. Why now?

The door to the room slammed open on its well-oiled hinges, knocking into the wall behind it.

Brock jumped to his feet, ready for he knew not what.

"What in the hell happened out there?"

He heard Harold before he saw him.

"Hello? Answer me!" Harold yelled. "What has gotten into you?"

"Close the door, will you?" Brock sighed. "And keep your voice down."

Harold nudged the door shut with his foot and continued toward Brock. "Keep my voice down? Keep my voice down?" Harold repeated in disbelief. "That is rich. You punch a man in the face—unprovoked, as the story goes at the moment—and you are worried about me raising *my* voice?" He grabbed Brock by his unbuttoned lapels and shook him.

"Get your blasted hands off me or you will meet a similar fate."

Harold's grasp on Brock's shirt tightened. "Is that your new solution to your problems? To go around striking any person who dares insult you? That is pathetic."

"No one would dare insult me," Brock yelled back. "I am Lord Haversham, and I will be respected."

Harold laughed, but did not release his grip. "You talk about respect, but who have you shown respect to recently? Definitely not your mother's memory—"

"Do not bring my family into this." Brock pushed into his friend's grip, but Harold held his ground.

"That is fine. I can leave your family out of it." Harold continued to stare hard at Brock. "How about

Lady Viola and her family? Was that respect you showed her when you embarrassed her in front of all of society?"

Brock only returned his friend's hard stare.

"If you are going to hit me, then do it," Harold whispered. "If that will make you feel better, more of a man, then by all means take your anger and frustration out on me."

With that comment, the tightness left Brock's body. He averted his gaze.

"No? Pity." Harold released Brock's shirt and moved toward the door.

"Harold," Brock called as he sank to the chair behind him.

His friend halted but did not turn. "I will see you at home."

With that, Brock was once again left alone. Utterly, completely, hauntingly alone.

CHAPTER TWENTY-NINE

How long had he sat there?

Brock had no clue, but he was damn tired. At some point, a servant had quietly entered the room, leaving him a bottle of scotch and a light meal, securely closing the door behind him.

Harold's words rang in his head.

Brock knew the answer to his problems did not lie in violence.

Then why had he hit Connor, besides the obvious reason that the man was a cod?

Connor had harmed Lady Viola's reputation, which any upstanding gentleman would not let another man get away with. Then, he'd had the gall to accuse Brock of doing the same thing. Had he hit Connor because he resented the insinuation that they were in any shape or form similar?

The notion was absurd. And absolutely—beyond a doubt—true. The realization shook him, brutally altering his personal paradigm. He was exactly the man Connor—and Harold, to a lesser degree—had accused him of being.

Since he had returned from the continent, Brock had been self-absorbed, self-indulgent, combative, and an all-around jerk. He'd matched wits with Lady Vi instead of deferring to her and handling their disagreement in a more private setting.

If he was being honest with himself, which he knew he hadn't been recently, he had sought to lure the woman to London, force a confrontation, and give her what for. He could hardly be upset with the consequences, considering the fact that he'd been the one to set the entire catastrophe in motion.

A knock sounded at the door. Brock rubbed his sleep-heavy eyes and stood.

"Enter."

The man who passed through the door had a large bruise that extended from his jaw all the way to the corner of his eye. A cut at the corner of Connor's mouth, recently cleaned, still seeped blood.

No wander his hand hurt like the devil.

"My lord—"

"Do you think it safe to be in a room alone with me at this juncture?" Brock asked.

Connor kept his eyes firmly aimed at the rug under Brock's feet. "I only seek to explain my actions."

"What explanation could you possibly give to justify your horrid treatment of Lady Viola, and your complete lack of loyalty?" He continued to rub at the soreness in his knuckles. "Do you not have any honor?" Brock asked the question even as he wondered where he had lost his own honor. The last place he could remember seeing it was when he'd left his men behind in France, on his way to assume his new title as lord.

Connor's chin lifted, but his eyes didn't quite meet Brock's. "Which question should I answer first?"

The man tried Brock's patience. "I truly doubt you have a satisfactory answer to either."

"But I do, my lord. You see, when I said you and I were alike—"

"Do not utter those words." Brock's voice thundered off the walls in the small, empty room.

Connor held up his hands, palms toward Brock. "Wait, wait," he stuttered. "Lady Viola did not only ravage your family, taking the lives of your brothers—"

"She did not take their lives," Brock interrupted. "They chose their path in life. They were foolhardy and reckless." His need to defend her seemed to come from nowhere.

"I only seek for you to understand my hurt, the suffering she has caused me."

"Go on, but be quick about it. I haven't all night."

"My tale is much the same as your brothers'. I too courted the young, lively, energetic Lady Viola during her first season. I took her for carriage rides, for ices, to the opera…we even danced on many occasions."

Every part of Brock wanted to rebel at the man's words. Scream that they could not be true. Had Connor been Lady Viola's love interest all these years? Had she lowered herself to taking a lover outside of wedlock?

"I, and my family, spent great amounts of money to impress her. Money we did not have," Connor said.

Brock felt his temper simmer just below the surface, aching for a release. "And you tell me this why? Are you here to rub it in my face that she chose you over my brothers?"

He shook his head. "How I wish things would

have progressed thus. Alas, she fled London after that fateful day without a word to me. No note explaining her coming absence or reasons for her part in the duel. Nothing."

"Should I feel sorry for you?"

Tears glistened in Connor's eyes. "Yesterday, I would have answered yes to that question. Now, I am uncertain. You see, it took me months to find Lady Viola. I was prepared to be her knight in shining armor. I planned to gallop in on my steed and sweep her off her feet. I'd return her honor as a lady of the realm."

Brock regained his seat. "How noble of you," he drawled.

"Yes, well, I was a different person then. A trusting person." Connor sighed. "And to answer your question, I believe that is the day I gave up my honor."

When Brock only stared back, unmoved, Connor continued.

"I tracked Lady Viola to her father's estate, Foldgers Hall. Wearing my finest suit, I knocked on her father's door and was immediately shown into their morning parlor. My first thought was that she had been waiting for me and I chastised myself for not coming sooner."

"Get to the point, Cale."

Connor began to pace the room. "Of course. Well, when Lady Viola walked into the room, she had no idea who I was. Thought I was there to interview for the position as her man of business. All those months I'd longed for her, dreamed of her and our future, she had not given me a passing thought. By that time, my family was destitute and I had no other option but to take the position she offered me."

Brock laughed at the absurdity of Connor's claim. "That must be the most pathetic story I have ever heard. You think just because a woman scorned your advances, she deserves her life ruined?" Unthinkable!

But how was that any different than what Brock had sought to do to her? His brothers had both died in a vain attempt to gain her attention, and Brock had been on his course of vengeance since his return to society. "Damn it."

"I will let myself out, my lord." Connor turned to retrace his steps to the door, and his freedom.

"Stop," Brock commanded. Regardless of his recent insights, he couldn't let the man get away with his misdeed. Just as Brock would seek to punish himself, rectify his wrongs, so must Connor. "You will make things right with Lady Viola."

"The damage is done. Her business is closed and her clients have all forsaken her. How could I possibly change that?" Connor asked.

"It is quite simple, actually. I assume you have a partner in your current venture, D & C's Fine Foals?"

Shock crossed Connor's face. "Ye-s-s-s," he stumbled over his reply.

Brock was toying with the man, but he didn't care. Connor deserved every bit of trouble Brock chose to send his way. "And that person would be?"

"Hampton. Lord Darlingiver."

A sudden coldness rocked Brock to his core. Lord Darlingiver? "As in *the* Lord Darlingiver, whose mother is currently romantically involved with Lord Liperton— Viola's father?" Brock sat up straight in his chair. What he wanted to do was throw the chair across the room. Punch a hole in the perfectly wallpapered wall. Both options were better than his fist connecting with Connor's face once again.

Connor cleared his throat, clearly uncomfortable, and nodded.

"And what, exactly, has he brought to the table for this business venture?" From what Brock knew of Lord Darlingiver, he lived off a small stipend, his estate essentially bankrupt. Much like Rodney, he moved day to day keeping up appearances of grandeur and wealth, when in reality he was lucky not to be in debtor's prison.

"Very little. He was supposed to lend his good name and family standing, but he's done little more than spend every cent I have given him on women and gambling." Connor sighed. "I was to meet him upon leaving Lady Viola's country estate today—or was that yesterday? No matter really."

Brock felt as if he was herding sheep, trying to keep the conversation on topic. "For?"

"Does not matter now. I do not plan to meet the fool."

"But it matters to me," Brock said.

Connor shrugged. "To give him Lady Viola's client list."

His ears perked. "Do you have the list with you now?"

"Of course! Do you think me stupid?" Connor searched through his pockets. First, he turned his pants pockets inside out, then he moved on to his coat, but still found nothing. "I am sure it is here somewhere."

Brock sat back, content with watching the man scramble.

Next Connor moved to his shirt pocket. "Ah! Here it is," he said when he pulled a folded sheet of paper, dirty and worn, from his pocket.

"Give it to me." Brock held out his hand.

"And why would I do that?"

"Because you seek to make amends for your wrongs."

"If that were so, why would I give the list to you?" Connor asked. "You have more cause to despise the woman than I. How do I not know you will use the list against her, as well?"

"Do you question my integrity?" Brock stood. His rage returned. "It would be wise to stop equating you and me. We are nothing alike." Even saying the words was begging the lord to strike him down for his lies. "You will give me the list, and then you will leave London."

Brock plucked the paper from Connor's hand when the man only stood in stunned silence before him.

"Is that clear?"

"But where will I go?"

"I care not as long as you stay far from London, Lady Viola, and myself."

"What about Hampton?"

"He will likely put himself in debtor's prison before the end of the season." Brock brushed past the man and out the door before he could give much thought to his own reasons for wanting the list.

CHAPTER THIRTY

Brock did not know why he was here, what he would say, or, most importantly, what he sought to accomplish. What he did know was that he was tired. He hadn't slept the remaining hours of the night after he'd left White's. Instead, he had chosen to think.

About the man he was.

About the man he wanted to be.

About the sons he hoped to raise in the future, and what type of men they would be.

His carriage had been parked down the street from Lord Liperton's townhouse for going on twenty minutes, and he still couldn't bring himself to get out and knock on her door. He only knew he had to make peace with her. Regardless of what she was guilty of, he knew he carried his own sins upon his shoulders.

Could he blame her for acting the way she had? No more than she could blame him for what he had said. The fact was—as Harold was happy to remind him—he had embarrassed a lady of the *ton* in public, before all

305

her peers.

He reclined against the velvet squabs and let the curtain fall into place, obscuring his view. It did not matter who he was, or what she had done in the past. Members of the *ton* would not forgive any man who defamed a woman, no matter that they had shunned her long ago. The night before been dreadful. Men had hurried to remove themselves from his and Harold's path, matrons had turned their noses up as he passed, and every young, available female's dance card had been mysterious full even though dancing had yet to begin.

Honesty was something he had prided himself on his whole life. And now was the time for him to be honest: He was here to soothe the feelings of the *ton*, nothing more. It had nothing to do with him regretting what he'd shouted in his anger, or repairing Lady Viola's wounded self-worth.

No. This was about redeeming himself in the eyes of the *ton* long enough to find a wife.

If only he could forget his need to avenge the wrongs done to his family.

For only ten minutes, twenty if she kept him waiting to be seen, he told himself. He could do this— he had to.

Brock wished he had insisted on Harold accompanying him, acting as a buffer of sorts. Harold had a way of calming people. But his friend insisted Brock go alone, and part of him was grudgingly thankful. It was a very good possibility that he would not be allowed in Lord Liperton's townhouse. Or that he would be admitted only to be thrown out again just as quickly. Then again, Lady Viola may request a long, drawn out apology, and he doubted he could keep up his charade for very long.

He thought of calling to his coach men to return to his townhouse, say to hell with apologies, and retire to the country—permanently. The irony of the situation was not lost on him. Lady Viola had done just that all those years ago. She had expected to stay in the country, but he had drawn her to town.

"My lord?" his coachman called from his post outside, awaiting his command to open the door and lower the steps.

"Yes, Jeffers. I am ready to depart."

"It is not that, my lord. She is leaving."

"Who is leaving?" Brock asked.

"Lady Viola. She is hailing a hack now."

Brock pulled his curtain aside. Sure enough, he spotted her not far from her townhouse, a bundle tucked under her arm. No more had she put her hand out to signal a passing hack than had it stopped and she clambered up and onto the seat next to the driver, settling the package between them.

Something about the way she carried herself, or perhaps it was the mysterious bundle in her arms, made Brock pause. Lady Viola glanced about surreptitiously, as though doing something illicit, before she clambered into the waiting carriage.

What was the dread woman up to now? Who else's life was she out to ruin?

In an instant, Brock made his decision.

"Quick! Follow that hack!"

Jeffers pulled away and maneuvered around a group of men astride horses.

Brock poked his head out the window and shouted, "Keep them in sight. Do not let them know we follow."

The curtain fell back into place, and Brock settled in to wait for her carriage to stop. Why would she take a hired hack?

Visions moved through his head: him following her to a lover's tryst. Maybe she'd snuck away to meet the man who had sent her the love letter he had found on her desk. His anger resurfaced. The nerve of the woman, running off to meet a man when he had tamped down his pride enough to make amends for an incident he honestly did not regret, nor one he was sure would not be repeated if they both chose to continue attending the same society functions.

An odd smell invaded his nose, and Brock again leaned over to pull the curtain aside. Peering out, he watched as they crossed the River Thames into the End East. What an unsavory choice for a tryst location. Surely they could find a more reputable locale in which to meet—she was obviously not short on funds.

His coach slowed as his driver navigated through the congested streets, deeper into the impoverished neighborhood.

"They are stopping, my lord," Jeffers called over the sound of the wheels on the rough street.

"Stop here."

Brock watched as Lady Viola handed the man some coin, picked up her bundle, and clambered down from the hack. With a quick look around, she made her way up to the door of a building that looked ready to collapse, if it were not for the buildings on each side holding it up. She lifted her clenched fist and rapped on the door. It swung open and a woman who looked much like a maid ushered her in. The door closed solidly, leaving Brock staring at the empty stoop.

From her use of a hack, she was obviously somewhere she should not be. If her father agreed with her activities, she would have traveled in the family carriage, trailed by her maid.

His curiosity was indeed piqued. To his knowledge, Lady Viola had not been to town in many years. Who could she possibly know in this area?

What plot had the woman gotten to now? If she indeed had taken a lover in this loathsome part of London, he would see it for himself. He told himself all of these things, refusing to acknowledge the truth: Despite everything, he was concerned. Worried for Lady Viola's safety. Difficult as it might be to admit, he did not wish the woman harm. In fact, the thought chilled him to his core.

Before Brock could change his mind, he pushed the door open and jumped down. "I will return shortly," he called as he crossed the street. The stoop was clean of debris, which was odd for this part of town, where the population was so great that garbage lined the streets and walkway, with no other place to dump it but the river.

He knocked and awaited the maid who had opened the door for Lady Viola. He heard voices, raised in song from within and then footsteps heading in his direction.

The door swung open to reveal the portly woman, a smile on her face. "Can I help ye . . ." She looked him up and down, "M'lord?"

Bloody hell. He had no idea if the woman could help him. "Ah, yes. I was driving through the neighborhood—"

"That is a bit odd for a gent such as ye self," she

cut him off.

"Well," he cleared his throat and started again. "As I was saying, I was driving by and I believe I saw a dear, dear friend enter your home." His friend? He already doubted his impulsiveness.

Her hands went to her hips and her brow furrowed. "An' who would that be?" she asked.

"I do apologize." He would issue many apologies today, it seemed. "I am Lord Haversham. Perhaps your master is in?"

"I be the master in this house." She made to swing the door shut in his face.

Brock stuck his foot out to stop her as a voice rang out behind the woman.

"Mrs. Hutton, Mrs. Hutton," came the squeal of a child. "Look what the lady brought me. Is it not the finest thing ever?"

The woman, Mrs. Hutton, held the door tight against his boot and turned to address the child. "Do be wait'n a minute, Abby. Can ye not see I be tending the door?"

"But look at this. I have never seen—"

"Please go back to the celebration," she scolded.

With the woman's attention diverted, Brock gave a solid push on the door. It burst from the woman's grasp and slammed against the wall.

"M'lord!" Mrs. Hutton tried to regain her hold on the door, but was unable. He stepped around her and into a dimly lit hall.

In front of him, a young girl twirled. Twirled so fast he could see nothing but her pale hair fanning out around her face. A candle, mounted to the wall above, gave off a small amount of light that reflected off the iridescent purple gown the girl was marveling at as she spun. A gown he had seen not long ago—but that was impossible. That gown had been crafted to the height of fashion and made to fit the curves of a mature woman. He remembered it had plunged low in front to show off its owner's assets. Now, the gown had more of a modest neckline.

He stood staring as the child came to a halt, noticing his presence.

The child—Abby, he dimly reminded himself— pushed the long golden locks from her face, and Brock did everything he could not to gasp. Part of the girl's face was missing, her eye sewn shut over a gaping hole he knew lie beneath. He had seen injuries such as this many times while at war. Why did the wound seem so much worse, so much more heartbreaking, on a child? He had no doubt her injuries were due to a gunshot.

"You do not need to stare." The child's hands went to her hips, much like the woman who stood beside him, and her one eye glared at him.

It looked as though he owed yet another apology. "I beg your pardon, my lady." Brock bowed low to the child.

She giggled and her head dipped to hide her deformed face. "You are forgiven."

The child was certainly born a member of the *ton*, her poise, speech, and manners bred into her from birth. Was she the child of whomever owned the home? The person Lady Viola was obviously here to meet?

"Perhaps you know whom I seek," he addressed the child.

Mrs. Hutton huffed beside him and pushed the door shut, blocking the light that poured in from the street.

"Do you mean Lady Vi? She came just for my party, and brought me this splendid dress." The child's enthusiasm was infectious.

"Child, go back ta the party--"

Brock smiled his most charming smile. "Why yes, it is Lady Viola I seek." He had no idea what he had walked into, and part of him wanted to walk out the door just as fast as he had entered and not look back. But it was too late for that. A peek down the hall and he saw little heads poking out of a room at the end. The singing and chatter had stopped.

There was no turning back now.

CHAPTER THIRTY-ONE

Vi got up from the blue and gold brocade sofa that had once occupied her office at Foldger's Foals. "Children, come back. Mrs. Hutton said she would return momentarily." She moved to the doorway to stop them from spying on their adoptive mother as she attended to the person at the door.

"Lady Vi, it is a man. We don't be seeing many of them here," Daisy, a dark haired child missing her hand, said.

"I am certain it could not be that exciting. Surely the butcher visits, and do you not have a male tutor?"

"Yes'm, but this be a right fine gent," Samuel chimed in as he pushed his way past the younger children to get a better look. "He has a fine coat, too, no holes or nutt'n."

Now it was her turn to wade through the group and have a look. "Please step back and allow me to see."

"Lady Vi, he is so handsome," another girl—Lily, she thought—declared. The girl raised her hand to her forehead, feigning to swoon.

Vi laughed.

"Oh, he is ever so tall, and his hair looks as soft as a pillow."

She could not be certain which child spoke; they all clambered around the door to get a look at their newest guest.

"Do you be think'n it be Abby's pa?" Samuel asked, a bit of nervousness in his voice.

"Couldn't be him. Abby has yellow hair and he has dark hair."

"Well, she sure be stare'n at him like he's her pa," Daisy said.

"Then I better be ask'n to court his daughter," Samuel said seriously.

Vi looked to the boy as he tucked in his shirt and smoothed the front of his pants.

"No, we will wait here until Mrs. Hutton returns. If she wanted all you bombarding the man she would call for you," Vi said as she guided the children away from the door and back into the room decorated for Abby's birthday. "Now, back to your game."

As the children hid in various yet obvious places around the room, Vi moved back toward the door with the intent to push it shut.

But a voice traveled down the hall—a very familiar voice. ". . . Lady Viola I seek."

How dare the man! Did he plan to storm the room and belittle her in front of the children? *Her* children.

Instead, she peeked out the door, trying not to draw the children's attention. Oh, but Brock did look dashing, and Abby did look quite smitten with him.

Odd how he had that effect on people.

314

What was she thinking? She squared her shoulders and prepared to march down the hall and throw him out. This was hers, and he would not ruin her newfound sanctuary as he had done with Foldger's Foals.

She paused as she started to leave the room. Suddenly, she realized that given recent developments, she no longer knew for certain that it had been Brock who spread the horrid gossip around London. It was much more likely the culprits had been Connor and Hampton Darlingiver.

This did not change the fact that he had completely humiliated her when all she'd wanted was a fresh start, a new beginning. Yes, he still needed to go.

With new resolve, she pulled the door open and started down the hall—and immediately came face to face with Brock, holding Abby's hand as she led him in Vi's direction.

"Lady Viola—"

"What are you doing here?" Her voice dripped with venom.

"I was at your house—"

"You followed me here?" she asked cutting him off again.

"Well, yes, but—"

This was too much. "You need to leave. Mrs. Hutton, can you show Lord Haversham to the door, please?" Vi turned a smile on Mrs. Hutton who stood, eyes wide, behind Abby.

"Of course. This way, m'lord."

"But, Lady Vi, he said he is here for my party." Abby's face looked crestfallen, her small lips pursed in a pout.

As quickly as it had come, Vi's anger fled. She was

315

being selfish again, she chastised herself—it seemed she was unable to be anything but, at times. How could she disappoint the girl on her special day? With Vi's source of income gone, Abby might not have another celebration. Mrs. Hutton would rightfully be concerned with feeding all the children; there would be no money for gifts or cake.

Maybe it was better that she leave, so they could continue to enjoy the party. Vi had delivered her altered dress to Abby, her gift given—she could depart.

"M'lady," Mrs. Hutton's voice drew Vi from her thoughts. "Do you want me to show him out?"

"No, actually, I was just saying my goodbyes to the children. I am afraid I must be off." Vi's voice did not waver.

"But, you only just arrived," Abby pleaded. She let go Brock's large hand and stepped forward to take Vi's. "Can you not stay a bit longer?"

"I fear I have many engagements to prepare for now that I am back in town." Vi squeezed the girl's hand. "But I will return. Enjoy your new dress, and have a very happy birthday." She disentangled her hand from Abby's and took a step toward the front door.

"Lady Viola, I do hope ta see ye again soon." Mrs. Hutton hurried to open the door.

"I will see you out, Lady Viola. My carriage waits just outside."

"Oh, no. That will not be necessary." But she knew she was fighting a losing battle, for he had already moved to her side and slipped her arm into the crook of his own.

He smiled at Abby, Mrs. Hutton, and then the children, who had gathered only a few steps down the hall. Images of everyone in attendance raising their hands to their foreheads as Lily had entered her mind.

Vi wanted to scream.

Next, he turned his toothy smile on her. "Shall we be off?"

No, she did not want to 'be off' with him. But there was nothing else she could say with everyone looking on. "Of course." It seemed the entire group let out a collective sigh, as if they had been expecting a fight.

"They make a dashing couple," Vi heard Abby whisper to Samuel, who had moved to her side.

"We could be dash'n, too," he huffed back.

Belatedly, Vi realized their sighs were not because of the disaster averted, but because they all thought Brock was here to court her!

Brock shook with mirth beside her.

Of all the absurdity.

# # #

The door closed behind them and Vi ripped her arm from his. "How dare you," she seethed.

"Please allow me to escort you home." It was the least she could do after forcing him to chase her all over the streets of London, finally coming to a stop in the East End.

Brock would be lucky if his driver had not been assaulted and his carriage stolen. Did she not realize the jeopardy she faced by coming here unescorted—and in a hack, no less? The woman was careless and reckless, but now was not the time to point out all her flaws. First, he needed to get her into his carriage, which thankfully sat across the street whole and unharmed.

317

"Are you delusional enough to believe I would enter a carriage with you after you practically shouted to all of London that I would be better off dead?"

Bloody hell, she had a very valid point. "I do apologize for my behavior." Now was as good a time as any, although he never dreamed this would be happening on the streets in front of anyone passing by, in the worst part of town. "Now, would you—"

"Just stop."

Brock shut his mouth to stop himself from making an utter fool of himself, more then he already had.

She glared at him and he glared back at her—much as he imagined his brothers glaring at each other as they looked down the barrels of two matching pearl-handled pistols. There was nothing separating Brock from her now, with the exception of every person on the crowded street and the children who no doubt had their noses pressed to the window panes of the house behind them.

Obviously, forcing her into the carriage was not an option, and their glaring was also getting them nowhere. "The children are staring." He tried a new tactic.

From the stiffening in her back, he knew he had chosen the right one.

She glanced over her shoulder and when she turned back to face him, she was smiling. It was a frightful, wooden smile, but it was a smile nonetheless.

He held out his arm and she slipped her hand in to rest lightly at his elbow.

"Blast," she muttered.

"I promise I will not do away with you on the ride to your father's house. I only wanted a moment of your time to make amends properly." Brock looked both ways and stepped from the walk in the direction of his carriage. "See, this is not so horrible."

"You are correct, my lord," she looked up at him. "It is far worse than that."

Ignoring her remark, Brock handed her up into his carriage and turned to Jeffers. "The Liperton townhouse."

"Of course, my lord."

Brock entered the carriage to find Lady Viola perched as if ready to flee on the front-facing seat. Her hands looked ready to launch herself toward the closing door. When it clicked shut, she sagged against the seat, her arms across her chest.

The carriage pulled into traffic and jolted down the uneven street. He only had a limited time to talk with her; there was no doubt in his mind that as soon as they pulled to a stop, she would either bolt out the door or jump through the narrow window she was currently eyeing. And that might look even worse than the scene they had made before.

But how to get her talking?

"What was that house?" he asked, hoping to break her icy exterior.

"That is none of your concern. You will not be going back."

"I am not so sure I will not be returning. Little Abby was quite affronted that I arrived at her party without a gift. I promised that sometime in the near future I would rectify my *faux pas*."

The carriage hit a large hole, and Viola put her hand against the carriage wall to steady herself before she spoke. "Why would you care about a little girl?"

"I am not a heartless man, Vio—"

"Lady Viola."

"Fine. *Lady* Viola, I am not a heartless man. And now it seems I know you are not the heartless, cold woman I have pictured all these years." He spoke the truth. "It is odd. I never thought you to be a woman who would like children."

She crossed her arms once more. "You do not know me in the slightest."

"That is true… But I find myself wanting to know you." Images flashed through his mind unbidden—thoughts he had kept at bay from the time he first learned that the tantalizing Lady Posey was, in fact, the very woman he had blamed for his family's misfortune for the past eight years. For a moment, he let those thoughts wash over him once more. He wanted to know the way she would feel close against his body; the way her lips would melt against his own. He wanted to see her hair cascading loose down her back . . . and possibly over her unclothed body, his hands running through its silken waves.

"Why are you looking at me such?" Her lips pressed together in a firm line.

He knew where to find something else that was currently a bit firm. At least her comment drew his attention from thoughts of her naked body . . . to her lips pressed against his.

Bloody hell! This was the woman responsible for Cody and Winston's deaths, how could he be looking at her with any sort of lust? What she had been and who she was today were completely at odds.

"You are still staring," she said. "Why did you truly follow me?"

All right, she wanted to talk. He also wanted to

talk . . . among other things. "As I said, I felt it was only honorable that I apologize for my behavior the other evening." That was not as truthful as his other admissions. "And to return something that had been taken from you."

"Could you not have waited for me to return home?"

"You left in a hired hack, without a maid, and ended up in the East End. My actions were very justified."

"Be that as it may, I am a grown woman."

The stiffness in his breeches dissipated at her icy tone. He took her in from head to toe, then back to her face. "I am extremely aware that you are a grown woman."

She straightened, as if just now seeing the folly of entering his carriage without contesting more. "Well, I do accept your apology and I hope that we can ignore each other in the future."

They would be arriving at her father's townhouse at any moment. The street had leveled out, and he felt the rhythmic passing of the cobblestones under the wheels. "I have yet to apologize—I have only expressed my desire to do so."

She eyed him suspiciously. "And I suppose you expect an apology in return?"

"Not at all. There is not enough time in one day for you to apologize for all you should." His words were overly harsh.

She scowled as she pulled the curtain aside. "We have almost arrived, and I am quite busy, so thank you for your 'wish to apologize.' I believe it would behoove both of us to act as if we are unacquainted from now on."

"Oh, I think we are far beyond that."

"And why is that?"

"I will find it hard in the future to not let others know you are not the cold and selfish girl they all think you to be."

"I should have run the second I heard your name at Foldger's Foals," she muttered, her arms still firmly crossed.

"Ah, but then we would not know the chemistry between us."

"There is no chemistry between us, unless you count hatred."

"Come now, Viola, you cannot deny that you felt something that day."

"I do not know what day you refer to."

"No? What about our kiss? Or that night in the rain? Do you also deny our connection then?"

She couldn't possibly deny she had felt something. He knew he could do so no longer. Truth be told, if Brock had not found out her true identity, he knew he would have sought out her company again—under very different circumstances.

"Luckily, I know the exact day, the time, and the weather overhead. You were striding in from the pasture—"

"I do not stride, that is very unladylike."

"I do beg your pardon, my lady. You floated across the low grass in the pasture toward me, your hips swaying with a barely restrained sensuality, and . . ."

Her cheeks flushed pink and her head dipped, breaking eye contact.

"Your foal followed you, completely caught in a

hypnotic trance in which I too found myself."

Now, her face flamed red, spreading down her neck and below her modestly cut neckline.

"As you walked toward me, all I could think about were my hands resting on your narrow hips. . . . My lips against yours."

Her eyes met his again.

"And then, our lips were touching—dancing—and it was everything I had dreamed of it being." At the thought, heat flooded his body. Without thinking, he moved to sit next to her, his body drawn to hers.

To his surprise, she didn't withdraw, but leaned toward him.

"Your lips were soft, so accommodating." His hand rose to stroke her jaw. Again, she didn't pull away. "I would have wrapped my arms around you and never let go, if it had not been for—"

His hand dropped from her chin. What was he doing? Had he gone mad? She was the one responsible for all he had lost—all that he missed. Family.

But no, he'd held a glimpse of the woman she'd become that night when he'd found her, soaked to the skin on her runaway horse. She had been raw with grief, beaten down emotionally—beyond anything a woman should ever have to experience, and quite possibly lower than Brock's lowest moment.

Despite all she'd lived through, she'd found the courage to start anew, rebuild her life and give back to others. What had he done but focus on ruining what little she'd accomplished?

Viola had paid her penance tenfold.

Brock lost himself in her eyes in that moment, and he wasn't sure any of their past mattered anymore.

CHAPTER THIRTY-TWO

A sense of loss overcame her when Brock's warm hand dropped from her chin. She wanted to tell him everything: about Connor's deception, her work with the children, and most of all, her regret and pain over all she'd put him and his family through. She couldn't change anything about her past, though. But she wanted to do something, anything, to again bring him close to her.

Could it be possible her father was correct? Did she crave the love and companionship only a man—a husband—could provide?

Her body told her yes.

Her heart screamed it.

But her mind was not so sure.

His brown eyes, so dark she was lost in their depths, drew her in. She wanted to trust him, believe they could put their past behind them. How, she did not know, but she longed to try.

Vi sighed. It was now or never. "I have spent these

last seven years making amends for the grief I caused your family," she uttered, so low she was unsure he heard her.

His brow drew together and closed off the view to his soul. "Is that what you were doing with those injured children?"

"Yes—"

"Have you been coming to London all these years?"

She was uncertain what she expected him to say or how he would react, but this was not it. "No, I entrusted Connor—"

He leaned away. For a moment, she feared he would move back to his own seat. "You do not trust that scoundrel, do you?"

At his question, she felt the betrayal of the past few days return. "Only a short time ago, I would have said I trusted him with my life . . . but no more." She averted her eyes. She'd been a fool, and now it was time to admit it to him. "I am sorry for blaming you for feeding gossip to the *ton*. I know it was not you."

He lifted her chin. For a moment, their eyes held. She found it hard to breathe, her heart taking wing in her chest. And then, at last, he touched his lips to hers. It wasn't the eager kiss they'd shared all those weeks ago. No, this was a kiss of forgiveness—of mending wounds left too long untended.

The soft insistence of his lips captivated her own, tempting them into parting, allowing his tongue entrance. She knew she had unwittingly allowed him into her heart, as well. The secrets, the lies, and the hurt... None of it mattered when she was in his arms. Dare she dream that none of it would matter to him, either?

Her hands lifted to pull him closer, moving of their own accord, more insistent, her lips now urging him on.

Not to be outdone, his own hands moved up the side of her corseted dress until they grazed her bodice. A moan escaped her parted lips. Suddenly it didn't matter who she was, who he was, or what society thought of either of them.

His thumb stroked her nipple through the fabric of her dress and his tongue matched its rhythm, pushing in and retreating. Her back arched and he took the movement as encouragement. His fingers pulled the bodice of her dress down and exposed her breast. The cool air in the carriage swept across her bare beast and her nipple hardened into a tight bud.

A deep chuckle escaped his mouth as he trailed kisses down her neck, over her collarbone, and finally to her exposed breast. This was what she had been missing—

"What in the bloody hell are you doing?! Unhand my daughter at once."

Her father's voice was miles away. She didn't want him to intrude, to end her time in Brock's arms. Her grasp tightened around him, moving up his back and locking in his hair.

"Viola, unhand this young man!"

Oh—Now her father realized Brock could not possibly be taking advantage of her, so it must be his daughter in the wrong, instigating the compromising situation. Thankfully, her back faced the door and her father would not see her exposed breast. She grasped Brock's hand in her own and deepened the kiss, knowing it would not last much longer—and then it was not guaranteed she would ever be in his arms again.

He moved between them to shift her bodice back into place. Just as quickly, he disentangled her hands from his hair and returned them to her lap with a quick squeeze before letting them go.

"That is better. Now, Viola, you come out of this carriage at once. What will the servants think? See you out here like a common hussy in Cheapside." The carriage groaned as her father stepped down.

She couldn't turn to face him, to see the disappointment in his eyes once again, although she feared raising her face to meet Brock's, either. What would she see there? Disgust, disdain, repulsion.

"Are you listening to me, young lady?"

Suddenly, she was a child again caught pilfering her father's favorite sweets. Vi shored her courage and prepared to face her father's wrath. She straightened her shoulders and Brock laughed.

A loud, deep chuckle that echoed in the small carriage.

Slowly, her eyes met his. There was no aversion, trepidation, or distaste. What she did see looking back at her made tears spring to her own eyes.

Joy, acceptance, and admiration stared back at her.

"Here, take this," Brock said, and pressed a folded piece of paper into her hand.

She closed her fingers around the worn paper. "What—?"

"Viola, do come out at once!" her father's angry tone drifted into the carriage.

Brock laughed again. "Open it later. You will understand, I promise. Now go. I will see you soon, I am sure."

She turned then, taking her father's outstretched hand as she departed the carriage.

"Young man, I expect to see *you* on the morrow."

"Of course, my lord," Brock called as his carriage pulled away from her father's home.

Vi tucked the paper into the pocket hidden in her skirt and marched up the front stairs, her father only a few steps behind. She didn't wait for the scolding she knew was coming, but rushed to her room. As soon as she slammed the door, she withdrew the paper from her pocket.

As she unfolded it, she realized it was two pieces of paper. One was written in Brock's bold handwriting; the second was a list of some sort. She set Brock's note aside.

She unfolded the second piece of paper and studied the words. Every one of her clients, past and present, including purchase details and estate locations, were listed in Connor's hurried hand.

Next, she retrieved the note accompanying the list.

It simply read, *"This was taken from you. Allow me to extend my deepest apologies for the wrong done to you and your livelihood by the scoundrel who called himself a man. You will not have cause to fear this type of treachery in the future. I have handled the situation in a manner best fitting the misdeed."*

The note was signed with only a B.

Vi smirked. "I guess he was able to give his apology after all," she whispered.

EPILOGUE

The reflection staring back at Vi was one of contentment—and unbelievable happiness. The last month had passed in a haze of euphoria and disbelief. The euphoria was thanks to the love she saw in Brock's eyes every time he looked at her; the happiness in her father's demeanor at these recent developments. The disbelief stemmed from the very notion that Brock could feel affection for her after all they had been through. He loved her despite the pain she had inflicted on his family.

She smiled and turned from the looking glass and makeshift dressing room that had once been her office. The room was different now. *She* was different.

A crown of fresh flowers encircled her head and laced through the rich mane of hair that flowed down her back. Her dress had arrived only hours before from Madame Sauvage, in London. The shimmering, pearl-white dress flowed down her body, much as her hair did down her back, hugging her in all the right places.

All the right places—one of them being here at the one place she felt at home. Although, after today Haversham House would be her home. She only dreamed it would be the sanctuary that Foldger's Foals had always been.

A light tap sounded and the door opened. It was time.

Time for her new beginning.

Time for her to take her place where she belonged.

Beside Brock: That was where she belonged.

"Come in," Vi called.

The door opened on well-oiled hinges and Ruby stepped in, her smile matching Vi's. "You look beautiful." Her friend looked her up and down.

"Is everyone ready?"

"Yes. My mother and Lady Darlingiver finally arrived, and everyone is seated."

"Is *he* ready?"

"By 'he,' I presume you are speaking of Lord Haversham. He is in attendance and looking quite dashing."

"I remember you using just that phrase not long ago. How things have changed." Butterflies fluttered in her stomach and her face heated.

Today, he would be hers and she his.

"I am so very happy you found Lord Haversham," Ruby said as she embraced Vi.

"I, too." Vi drew back and looked, truly looked, at her friend. "You look stunning, as well."

Ruby was dressed in a deep plum-colored dress, the neckline high and the back cut low to expose her trim shoulders and long neck. Her hair was piled atop her head with nary an ornament to distract a person from her natural beauty.

Color blossomed and her friend dipped her head. "Thank you. This is one of the dresses I hadn't a chance to wear while in London."

"I am sorry." Vi pulled her friend in tight for another hug. "I truly wanted you to have the season you were not afforded when you were younger." It was Vi's only regret since her departure from London the month before, to prepare for her wedding. It hadn't started out that way. Her father had once again shipped her to the country, fearing another scandal. But Brock had quickly made his intentions known, and had come to Vi with a proper proposal.

Ruby pulled back and turned a bright-eyed smile on Vi. "Do not fret over me. I will travel to my family's estate until next season. Which means you and I will not be far apart."

"That is wonderful news," Vi gushed.

The door burst open and Abby came to a halt, a glowing smile on her face. "Look, Lady Viola!" the child screamed. She pushed a hand full of silky material in Vi's face.

"Whatever do you have here?"

"Oh, only the loveliest gloves ever!" Abby continued, pulling the gloves back and waving them around. "And just look at this."

Vi grabbed the gloves that matched Abby's pale pink dress perfectly.

"All the other girls got them, too, and the nice handkerchiefs."

"They are lovely." Ruby stood behind Vi, admiring them over her shoulder.

The material moved between Vi's hands as she too

admired the finely tailored accessory. In a lower corner were the monogrammed initials *LAH*. "What does this stand for?" she asked Abby.

"Why, Lady Abby Haversham, of course."

Stunned, Vi looked from Abby to Ruby and back again. Both smiled, as if they knew a secret that Vi wasn't privy too.

"Lord Haversham said since you will be married to him—and your name will be Lady Haversham—all your children will also have the title. I did not tell him I'm completely aware of the correct way to address an earl." The child winked at Vi. "So, as of today, I am Lady Abby Haversham."

Both women burst into laughter.

In that moment, she fell in love with Brock all over again. How she'd ever thought him cold and arrogant, she would not know.

"Shall we, ladies?" Ruby asked, sweeping her arm toward the open door.

"There is nothing I want more," Viola answered. And there wasn't.

The trio stepped out the door and were greeted by a crowd of Vi's nearest and dearest friends and family. They all stood, their smiles beaming, mirroring her own.

And just past them all stood the most dashing, forgiving, compassionate man she had ever met. The man who had been brave enough to cast off the past and embrace the future, with Vi at his side. He held his hand out to her. It took everything in her power not to run to him.

He was a part of her tragic past.

He was the reason for her present joy.

And he would be her salvation in the future.

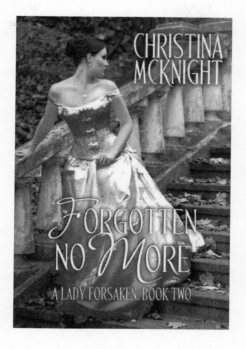

New from La Loma Elite Publishing in 2014!
Forgotten No More, A Lady Forsaken (Book Two)
Release Date: December 15, 2014

About the Author:

Christina McKnight is a book lover turned writer. From a young age, her mother encouraged her to tell her own stories. She's been writing ever since. Currently, she focuses on historical romance, urban fantasy, and paranormal romance.

Christina enjoys a quiet life in Northern California with her family, her wine, and lots of coffee. Oh, and her books . . . don't forget her books! Most days, she can be found writing, reading, or traveling the great state of California.

Follow her on Twitter: @CMcKnightWriter
Keep up to date on her releases:
www.christinamcknight.com
Like Christina's FB Author page:
ChristinaMcKnightWriter

Author's Notes

Thank you for reading *Shunned No More, A Lady Forsaken Book 1*.

If you enjoyed Shunned No More, be sure to write a brief review at Amazon, Barnes and Noble, or Goodreads.

I'd love to hear from you!
You can contact me at:

ChristinaMcKnight.author@yahoo.com

Or write me at:
P O Box 1017
Patterson, CA 95363

www.ChristinaMcKnight.com
Check out my website for giveaways, book reviews, and information on my other projects,
or connect with me through social media at:

Twitter: @CMcKnightWriter
Facebook: www.facebook.com/christinamcknightwriter
Goodreads: www.goodreads.com/ChristinaMcKnight

Don't forget to watch for the second book in my *Lady Forsaken* historical romance series,
Forgotten No More, to be released December 2014.

On a personal note, I wrote this novel during a huge time of change in my life. I'd like to thank all the people who believed in me and my writing journey. You never gave up on me, even when I lost sight of my own dreams! Especially Marc McGuire, Lauren Stewart, Jennifer Vella, Brandi Johnson, Chenoa Pearce, Rachelle Ayala, Lucie Ulrich, and Mary Merrell. You have all been very patient and wonderfully supportive of my eccentric ways.

A very special thank you to my editor, Jen Blood. You took on *Shunned No More* without a second thought. I look forward to many future endeavors with you. Jen Blood can be contacted by email at jen@jenblood.com.

Cover art credit to LFD Designs for Author.

Wraparound cover design and website design credit to Sweet 'N Spicy Designs.

Finally, thank you for supporting indie authors.

Made in the USA
San Bernardino, CA
06 August 2014